FOR YOU AND YOU ALONE

(Pine Grove, #9)

Jean C. Joachim`

Moonlight Books

I0627828

FOR YOU AND YOU ALONE

PUBLISHER

Moonlight Books

Dedication

To my children and their spouses, who keep the love of family alive.

FOR YOU AND YOU ALONE
Jean C. Joachim
Chapter One

T*wo days before Thanksgiving.*
Deke Walsh stood on the set of his latest movie, an action-adventure flick. His co-star, nine-year-old Luke Keller, stood next to him. The director called out, "Cut. That's a wrap. Happy Thanksgiving. See you in a week."

Six-foot-three, Deke crouched down to talk to Luke.

"Well, buddy, this is it. You having a big turkey on Thanksgiving?" Deke asked, angling for an invitation. He'd called his current girlfriend, but she had family plans that didn't include him. Then he'd tried his acting buddies, gym buddies, and past girlfriends. Everyone had some place to go, and they didn't invite him to tag along. Luke was his last hope.

"Luke!" Joe Keller called. The boy turned. His father and mother stood at the edge of the set near the door. "Come on, son!" He gestured.

"Bye, Deke," Luke said over his shoulder as he ran to his dad. He flew at his father, who embraced the boy and pulled him into a big bear hug.

Lorna Keller faced Deke. "Sorry. Family time. Have a nice holiday."

Crushed, he watched the man, his wife, and son stride away arm-in-arm. Jealousy shot through Deke like a bolt of lightning. Didn't he and Luke have a special relationship? He'd expected the boy to prevail on his parents to invite Deke to join them. No such luck.

Here it was, one of the biggest holidays of the year, and thirty-six-year-old Deke Walsh, movie star and hottest guy in Hollywood, would be celebrating with a turkey sandwich from the deli. As he stood there, reality hit him. His twenty million bucks didn't mean shit if he didn't have a family, a place to go to, or people waiting for him. Alone. He shivered with the chill of the truth.

"Yoohoo! Bobby!" A female voice rose over the din of conversations of the cast and crew buzzing about him as they packed up.

Bobby? Couldn't be him.

"Bobby! Bobby Walsh!"

Christ, it was him. Nobody had called him that in years. He turned toward the voice. A petite, dark-haired young woman waved to him.

"Yes. You. You, that's right. Bobby Walsh."

He took a few steps in her direction. "It's Rob now. To my friends. And Deke to everyone else. Who are you?"

"I see your memory has gone the way of your first name. I'm Rachel. Rachel Cohen. From Pine Grove?"

Crap! Pine Grove? That was light years ago. His gaze took in her cute figure from head to toe. He did not remember anyone who looked like this from where he grew up.

"Do I know you?"

She clicked her tongue. "Shame on you. Forgetting your childhood playmate."

"Sorry. Don't recall."

"I'm Eli Cohen's little sister."

"Eli? Holy shit. Oops. Sorry. Damn. Yeah. I remember him. He did have a little sister."

But he thought to himself, *she sure didn't look like you.* Where was the skinny, frizzy-haired little pest who used to hang around with Eli and his friends? How many times did they try to ditch her? A thousand? Maybe more.

"Still does. Now that that's settled, get your coat. We have a plane to catch." She checked her watch.

"Plane?"

"Yep. Your grandfather is failing. He wanted to have one last Thanksgiving with you. Since you have not answered my texts, emails, or voicemails, I'm here to haul you back to Pine Grove in person. Let's get going."

"Gramps?"

"That's right. If you'd kept up on any of the information I sent you, you'd know that. And you might even have made plans to see him yourself. But I doubt it."

A hostile stare bored through him.

"I thought you were some crazed fan."

A mirthless laugh slapped him back. "Me? Oh no, no, no. A fan? Absolutely not!"

Her sharp tone cut him to the quick. "My bad. Sorry."

"Don't tell me you're sorry. Tell your grandfather. Let's go. We don't have time for you to pack. You can pick up some stuff at the store. Plane leaves in two hours."

"Gramps still running the general store?"

"No, he's not well enough."

"But it's still there?"

"Yep. I'm running it now. Let's go." She whipped out her phone. "I think I have an Uber coming. Let me check."

"No need. The studio makes a limo available for me. It's right outside." He gestured toward the door. "Ladies first."

She sniffed but didn't soften her gaze. He flipped his backpack onto his shoulders and followed her out the door. He got a good view of her perfect butt. Nice!

"If you're staring at my butt, you can forget it. This is one chick who won't be warming your bed. Now or *ever*!"

He shook his head, chuckled to himself, and pushed through the heavy studio door. Once outside, he waved, and a black limo pulled up. He opened the back door and allowed Rachel to get in first.

"Where to, Mr. Walsh?"

"The airport, Stan."

"Which airline?"

"American," Rachel said.

"Okay."

Deke sat back against the leather seat. Looks like he got his wish after all—a family Thanksgiving, sort of. Raised by his grandfather after his parents died in a plane crash, he'd always been close to the old man. How could he have let this go by? Deke quietly berated himself but sighed when he realized he'd have a chance to make it up to the old guy.

RELIEVED WHEN DEKE fell into a sound sleep on the plane, Rachel ordered a vodka and tonic.

"Heavy on the vodka," she said.

It had been a long time since she'd seen Bobby—no, Rob now—Walsh. Eons. She'd followed his career in the tabloids, sucking up every juicy story about his rich life soaked in luxury and his "revolving door" relationships—if she could call them that. More like his bedroom with a revolving door. A turnstile on the bed? She snickered to herself.

Had his lightspeed lifestyle affected his health? She'd fantasized about him being in makeup for four hours to remove the ravages of his dissolute existence from his face. She'd laughed to herself about how much he must spend on plastic surgery. Then she saw him in person.

Damn. Up close and personal, he looked better than ever without a single sign of any surgeon messing with the perfection that was Deke Walsh. He only drank apple juice on the plane, so she crossed off possible alcoholic from her imaginary list of his faults. But the women? Uh, no. That was real. They hardly made it through the airport without being accosted a dozen times at least. How many strange women stopped him? She'd lost count.

"Oh, Mr. Walsh! I love your movies. Can I have your autograph?"

"Would you sign my bra?"

"Hey, Deke, here's my number. Call me. We'd be great together."

It was sickening. No, no, it wasn't jealousy drumming a loud beat in her breast, but disgust, righteous indignation. Deke Walsh, an over-grown spoiled brat, had ignored his ailing grandfather, and Rachel Cohen was going to bring him to task.

But first, she'd have to quell the butterflies in her stomach. She took a gulp of her drink, then dared to cast her gaze on his sleeping face. With an angelic expression, a cross between total innocence and bad boy, he was gorgeous. Hell, even at ten years old, the boy had had the looks and charm of an adult—well, almost.

Not accustomed to drinking, she sensed sleepiness creeping up on her. Rachel sat back and closed her eyes. Vivid images of her childhood flashed through her mind. She remembered when she'd first fallen in love with Bobby Walsh.

She'd been five. He'd chased away a couple of bullies, wiped her tears, brushed the dirt they threw at her off her dress, then picked her up and carried her home. Yeah, he was big for his age, and she was little.

"No one's ever gonna call you that again when I'm around," he'd said.

She'd rested her head against his shoulder and made a mental note to ask her father what "kike" meant. In that moment, Bobby Walsh had made her feel safe. She couldn't help but love him. Her brother, Eli, who had been at home doing his schoolwork, rushed out to take over. Bobby had explained everything to him and her father, who thanked him for looking out for his little girl. She sighed. He'd been her real-life hero.

But ten became twelve and five became seven and Rachel followed Bobby everywhere. She'd eavesdrop on his conversations with Eli, then shadow her brother at a distance. All through his middle school years, Rachel had tagged along, totally unwanted. Eli had tried everything to shake her, but she'd been stubborn, the way only a girl in love can be. Bobby hadn't minded. Being an only child, he soaked up every drop of adoration she had poured over him.

Once Eli and Bobby entered high school, everything changed. Bobby got his driver's license. He and Eli pursued girls, speeding away in Bobby's car, leaving twelve-year-old Rachel, lovesick and choking on their dust. Crawling with older, female attention, he'd ignored Rachel.

After he graduated, she rarely saw him. When he finished his freshman year at UCLA, Bobby dropped out and returned home to take odd jobs and work in the store. After an act of kindness brought him a lucky break, he went to Hollywood. Starting as an extra, it wasn't long before he got a supporting role in a movie. Another stroke of good luck got him the lead in an adventure movie and launched his career. From then on, he never appeared to have the time or money to return for holidays. His grandfather would fly out to Los Angeles to see his grandson. Within two years, he got a contract for a second leading role in a movie. The film hit big with women and his career took off.

Rachel has followed Bobby's, now Deke's, career in the newspaper and online, even collecting articles about his meteoric rise to stardom.

She recalled the last day she'd seen him. He'd returned to Pine Grove just long enough to pack up his belongings and jump into his old car, heading back to California. A crowd had gathered outside his grandfather's general store. Rachel had arrived home, as it was the end of her sophomore year in college.

"Bobby's moving to Hollywood," her father had said. "Permanently."

"What?"

"Yep. He's up for a leading role in a movie. He's leaving now. Better hustle if you want to say goodbye."

With her heart in her mouth, she ran full out. She got there just as he put the car in gear. The vehicle lurched forward and took off. He sped down the empty country road, his arm out the window, waving to the townsfolk gathered to send him off. As he approached her, he slowed. She jumped up and down, raising her arms. He gave her a long look, his eyebrows drawn down.

Her heart sank. He didn't recognize her! Rachel Cohen was no longer the skinny, frizzy-haired nerdy little pest he'd rescued so long ago. Now she was a beautiful young woman with dark, luxuriously long hair, and a slender but well-constructed body.

She felt his brief stare land on her chest. When his gaze finally connected with hers, there was no recognition in his eyes. The last thing Rachel wanted was Bobby lusting after her like he did every pretty girl. She wanted him to remember the smart, funny girl who hung around, trying to be his friend. She wanted his heart, his love. With a sigh, she leaned back against a large oak tree and frowned. There was only one Bobby Walsh, and he was gone forever.

On the plane, Rachel fell asleep.

She opened her eyes and jerked forward when the flight attendant tapped her shoulder. "Sorry to wake you. Do you and your husband want a snack?" Crap! She'd realized she had her head snuggled up against Deke's shoulder. He yawned.

"My husband? Oh, lady, no, no, he's not my husband."

She watched as Deke unwrapped his sandwich and took a bite.

"Why do you hate me so much?" he asked.

"I don't hate you." *Not much. Maybe extremely dislike? Okay, maybe hate.*

"Yes, you do. Look, just because I'm an actor doesn't mean I'm stupid. I know when people don't like me."

"Don't imagine you have to deal with that often," she said.

"You'd be surprised. The jealousy in this business is huge."

"Yeah?"

"Trust me. You're not an actor, are you?"

She shook her head.

"So why don't you like me?"

Frustration swirled inside her. She'd rehearsed her "spoiled brat" speech to him a hundred times in her head and in her room late at night. Mostly after a glass or two of wine.

"Maybe you're not on my top ten list because you've ignored your grandfather—for years. While you're flitting all around the world, sleeping with every unmarried woman, and a few married ones, he's been struggling to keep the general store going—alone."

"Alone? I thought he had a partner?"

"He did. My father. But he died three years ago."

"Oh. I'm sorry."

"Yeah right. Like you actually care."

"But I do."

She raised her palm. "Please. Don't insult me. So, I've pitched in."

"You work in the general store?"

"I gave up my job teaching at Pine Grove Elementary to become a retail slave, trying to keep your grandfather's business from going bankrupt."

"You did that for Gramps?"

"Let's say for him, for my Pop too."

"That's pretty nice."

"Yeah, it is, isn't it? So maybe I got a little ticked off that you couldn't make it back for Christmas and stuff."

"I went skiing in Switzerland with my co-star last Christmas. Her father owned a chalet. Who could turn that down?"

"I could."

"So, you're a fucking saint. Well, pardon me. I'm not." He tore off an angry bite of his sandwich.

"I'm no saint. But I had to deal with the fallout of you living your own sweet life and ignoring Gramps."

He narrowed his eyes. "You played up to him every holiday? Bet he paid you a bundle too."

She burst out laughing. "Paid me a bundle? Are you kidding? We barely scraped by."

"Don't give me that shit. I sent Gramps money every month."

She raised her eyebrows. "You did? Really? He never said."

"Damn right I did. I wouldn't let him starve."

"That's news to me."

"And I paid off his loan from Cassie too. He owns the place free and clear."

The captain came on the loudspeaker, announcing they were landing at LaGuardia Airport, and the seatbelt sign went on.

The flight attendant stopped at their seats. "Please finish. I have to clean up before we touch down. Thanks."

Deke and Rachel ate in silence.

SCHLEPPING THROUGH the airport, they encountered a brand-new batch of drooling, adoring fans. Like slogging through a swamp, Rachel and Deke picked their way through the crowds. Deke took her elbow.

"This way," he said, pointing to the baggage claim sign.

"But we don't have baggage."

"Just be quiet and follow me."

When they got off the escalator, there was a man in a chauffeur's uniform holding a sign with Deke's name on it.

"Oh," Rachel said.

"I texted from the plane. Come on." He approached the driver who asked, "No luggage?" Deke shook his head, then stepped back to let Rachel go first.

The chauffeur opened the door of a pristine black limo, and she slid across the luxury leather seat. Deke followed.

"Where to?" the driver asked.

Rachel gave him the address, and he put it in his GPS.

Deke stared out the window, though it was too dark to see much except the lights of New York City. Knowing he'd be trapped for another two hours in the car with the 'hound from hell,' he set his mouth in a frown, compressing his juicy lips. He could take it. Besides, he'd put up with diva co-stars, bitchy girlfriends, and controlling directors. Two hours with Rachel Cohen? A piece of cake.

"So do you live above the store like Gramps?"

"No. I'm not his girlfriend. I don't live with him. And I'm not his nursemaid either."

Deke took a breath and ignored her nasty tone. "Does he need one?"

"Actually yeah. He does. He has a home health aide three days a week."

"And the rest of the time?"

"He can take care of himself reasonably well. I fill in. Cook, tidy up. That sort of thing."

"You're like a paid companion?"

"Yeah. Sort of. I'm a paid employee of the store."

"So where do you live?"

"Remember that little guest house in the back by the paddock?"

"The one behind the store?"

"Yeah. I live there."

"Really? I remember that being a real shithole. Pardon my French."

"It was. I fixed it up."

Deke nodded. No amount of sentiment or money could ever get him to live in that shack. Shanty was too good a word for it. "Must have cost a bundle to get that thing livable."

"I had help."

"Money from Gramps?"

"No, if it's any of your business. Combination of Pop's life insurance money, money from the sale of his house, and volunteers from town. They wanted the general store to stay open and realized your grandfather couldn't run it alone."

"What about the house he lived in? Didn't you live there with him?"

"No. He only rented. They raised the rent, and he had to move. We made-over the store's second floor. He lives there now. Does any of this concern you? I mean, do you care or are you just making small talk?"

"Small talk." He smiled. Finally, he zinged one past her. Immediately after, he regretted it. She had been caring for his grandfather and keeping the ramshackle store together. The least he could do was lend a sympathetic ear to her story.

"I figured." She faced the window.

Now he'd done it. Not only did he hurt her feelings but showed her she was right about him. He was a selfish, insensitive idiot. Shame heated his face. He wrapped his fingers around her forearm.

"I'm sorry. That's not true. I am listening. I'm surprised anyone in Pine Grove had the moxie to tackle that old rundown excuse for a house."

"It's not completely finished. I want to loft it."

"Maybe I can help?"

"During the few days you're here?" She laughed. "I doubt it. Thanks for the offer. Spend the time with your grandfather. It may be your last chance."

He nodded and removed his hand. Her arm was surprisingly strong, the muscle firm. She must have done a lot of work on that old place herself. Mentally, he shrugged. After all, what else was there to do in Pine Grove?

"Gramps lives upstairs?"

"Yep."

"Can he get up and down the stairs by himself?"

"We had one of those elevator chair thingies installed on the stairs. He can manage that."

"Tough old bird." Deke smiled and shook his head.

"He is. Determined."

When she turned to look out the window, Deke studied her. For an odd bird, she dressed well. She wore what looked to be a black wool blazer with a white turtleneck underneath and black jeans. A red wool scarf draped around her neck and tucked into her jacket completed a simple but elegant outfit.

Even attired in such plain clothing, she appealed. Though not his usual turn-on—blonde, busty, wearing tight clothing—he was surprised to find himself drawn to her. His gaze slid down her body, noticing every inch.

Slightly olive-skinned, she had lustrous, dark mahogany-color hair he itched to touch. A small, straight, non-descript nose and a determined jaw added up to a pretty but not beautiful face. Narrow shoulders, smaller breasts than he was used to, a normal waist, a little wider in the hips than most movie stars, and short, quite short, maybe five foot two or three? She would never star in a movie or win a beauty contest.

Her bad attitude would do her in every time. No director or producer would ever want to work with her. When she turned back to face forward, he removed his gaze and stared at his hands.

"What?" He shot her a quizzical look.

"Never mind. I'm just going to close my eyes for a moment," she said.

Within minutes, she was fast asleep and leaning against his shoulder. As the warmth from her body penetrated his, he remembered the frizzy-haired, charming little girl who buzzed around him endlessly, hanging on his every word and adoring him shamelessly. He lifted his arm and drew her close. At least someone wanted him around for the holiday, no matter how much she pretended otherwise.

Chapter Two

"That you, Rachel?" a wheezy, old voice called down the stairs. "Yes, Gramps. Guess who's with me?" She motioned for Deke to be quiet and follow her. "In here," she whispered, indicating a tiny room in the back of the store. There was a twin bed, a reclining chair, and a small chest with a lamp on it. She flicked on the switch, and a soft glow filled the small space.

"I can't sleep in here. I'm too big for the bed."

"For a few days, it'll have to do."

A mechanical whirr drew their attention.

"Is that the...?"

"Yes." Rachel held her finger to her lips. She walked toward Gramps', with Deke following but still keeping his distance.

"You here alone?"

"Nope. I told you I'd have a surprise," she said, stepping back, and nudged Deke forward. "And here it is."

"Bobby?" The old man sat in the chair, motionless. "Is that really you?"

"Sure is, Gramps. But they call me Rob now. Here, let me give you a hand."

George, known as "Gramps" by everyone in town, slid his arm out from Rob's grip. "Never you mind. I manage just fine. Not in my grave yet." He staggered into the store.

But he stumbled and almost fell. Rob caught him. He steadied the old man, who hitched up his pants and cleared phlegm from his throat.

"It's about time you got your butt home." The old man straightened up and trained his keen stare on his grandson. "You look mighty fine. Glad you could make it. We got a big turkey this year and need you to hoist the damn thing into the oven."

"A big turkey for three?"

"Nope. We got ten. Some of Rachel's charity cases are comin'."

"Gramps! I asked you not to call them that." Rachel put her hands on her waist.

"Okay, okay. Sorry. Kids she tutors. They're comin'."

"And they'll be helping too. They promised to come early to clean and cook," Rachel said.

"Settle in, boy. Let's have a drink to your homecoming."

"Don't get too excited, Gramps. He's only here for four days."

"A week, actually. We have a week off from the shoot," he said.

"Can I still call you Bobby?" Gramps asked, taking baby steps to a credenza that housed the liquor. After opening the door, he fumbled with the glasses, knocking one to the floor. Fortunately, it didn't break.

"Dag nab it. Rachel?"

"Coming." She scurried to his side, picked up the glass, and deftly brought out one more shot glass and a bottle of Glenlivet.

"I'll do the honors," Rob said, taking the bottle from her hands. "Don't you want one?"

"Nope. I've got stuff to do."

Rob glanced at the bottle. "The good stuff, eh, Gramps?"

"Nothing but the best for you, boy. Man with money like you got doesn't drink rotgut."

"You got that right." Rob poured the liquid. The old man took the glass in a shaky hand and downed the whiskey quickly, not spilling a drop.

Rob raised his to his lips, took a sip, then downed the rest. "Whoa! Mighty fine."

"Yeah."

"So how you been, Gramps?" Rob raised his leg and plopped his butt on the corner of a small dresser.

"I'm still here."

Rob poured another round. "Let's drink to you."

"Don't mind if I do. Too stubborn to die." The old man laughed, then wheezed until his face turned red. Rob reached over, took the glass from his hand, and stared.

"Oh, I'm all right." He coughed up phlegm and wiped it away with an old handkerchief.

"I can see that," Rob said, shooting a look at Rachel.

Gramps downed the whiskey. "Don't want to keep you from preparing a fine meal, Rachel." The old man eased himself into the stair elevator. "Time for a nap," he said and pushed the button. The device moved slowly up the stairs. Within minutes, they heard snoring from Gramps' bedroom.

"Does he take naps like that often?"

She nodded. "He's losing ground."

Rob's chest constricted. He hadn't considered what losing his grandfather would mean for his plans and the new life he wanted. He'd dreamt of a gorgeous wife, two perfect children, and his grandfather in the background, enjoying the simple country life. A sting at the back of his eyes told him the truth. Gramps wouldn't be there for Rob's grand plan. When Gramps passed, Rob would have no family at all. The truth gripped his gut, shooting pain across his stomach. He grimaced. Rachel's voice broke into his thoughts.

"Your grandfather is almost ninety years old. What did you think? He'd last forever?"

Rob cast his gaze to the floor. "I just didn't think. He was always so healthy. Never got sick. Always there, like a redwood tree. I had no idea things had deteriorated so much."

"Maybe if you'd read your email you'd know." She folded her arms across her chest.

Rob raised his hand. "Stop!" His gaze sought hers. "I get it. I've been selfish, self-absorbed. I've ignored my grandfather. I'm a careless brute. I get it."

"I didn't say that."

"You didn't have to. Your face says it all."

At his comments, she blushed.

"Guilty as charged," he said, moving to the front of the store.

"But it's not too late. You're here now. And we can have a great Thanksgiving," Rachel said, following him.

Rob picked up his backpack he'd left at the front door, went into the small bedroom, and tossed it onto the dresser.

"Later," he said, his voice rough. He closed the door.

AT SEVEN THE NEXT MORNING, Rob slipped on his jeans and opened his door. The smell of brewing coffee lingered in the air. He padded barefoot from his room and went up the stairs to the spacious kitchen. His grandfather sat at the small table sipping from a mug and gazing out the window.

"Damn squirrels! They don't leave nothin' for the birds," the old man muttered.

"Morning," Rob said. "Where's Attila the Hun?"

Gramps turned and gave him a warm smile. "Rachel? She'll be around in a minute. She's usually up at six. Feeds me at seven and the chickens at eight."

Sure enough, Rob heard soft steps coming up the creaky stairs. "Morning," she said, heading for the refrigerator. "Swiss omelets okay?"

"Sure as shootin', missy," Gramps said.

"Sounds great."

With a pointed glance at Rob, she said, "Why don't you get the dishes down and set the table?" She took eggs and cheese from the fridge.

After opening a couple of cabinets, he found the one with plates. It didn't take him long to notice that none of the plates matched. Sure, there were ten plates, all with different designs. Not that he usually noticed stuff like that, but it embarrassed him to realize through a mismatched bunch of dishes that their deprivation had filtered down to a basic level.

He tried to cover his surprise by looking away from Rachel and Gramps.

"I know. We're not exactly Betty Crocker here. I like to get unusual dishes from garage sales. Then if one breaks, it's not like a set is ruined."

He nodded, but her lie didn't cover up the truth. His chest tightened. Blinking rapidly, he turned away. She reached out and squeezed his forearm.

"It's okay. We're gonna have a great Thanksgiving. We will. Really. You'll see." She glanced at her watch. "Let's do breakfast quick. The kids will be here in an hour. We've got a lot to do."

When his gaze met hers, he raised his eyebrows. "Really?"

"Yeah, really. Let's go. No time to waste." She threw butter in a pan, turned on the heat, and cracked the eggs. In ten minutes, she had loaded three omelets on plates, and they sat down to eat.

"Thanksgiving," Rob said, shaking his head. "I'm no cook."

"But I am. There's plenty for you to do, especially the heavy lifting," Rachel said. She opened the fridge. "Like right now. Can you please pull out that bird?"

Rob reached in and grabbed the turkey, lifting it out with ease. "Where do you want it?"

"Here. Right in here." Rachel patted the sink.

"Who put it in the fridge? You?"

Rachel chuckled. "Lord no. Kiwanis has a Thanksgiving thing they do by giving away turkeys to seniors. They delivered it. I talked the delivery guy into carrying it upstairs."

Rob read the label. "Geez. Twenty-five pounds? Is that necessary?"

"Last year, the kids picked the bird dry. Of course, it was only twenty pounds. Had to buy a bigger one this year since you're here." She eyed him up and down.

"I don't eat that much. Have to stay trim." He noticed a sly smile on her lips as she checked him out.

"I just bet you do." She snickered.

Gramps folded a newspaper and slipped it under his arm. "I'm going to read."

Rachel kissed the old man's cheek. He grinned and shuffled off to his room.

"I made a list. One for me and one for you."

"When are these helpers showing up?"

Rachel checked her watch. "Soon. I have lists for them too."

"Not surprised," he muttered. "Gimme." He snatched the list from her hand.

After looking it over, he commented, "I got all the heavy stuff."

"You're a man. Superior upper body strength and all that."

He grinned. "Yeah. Superior. Remember that."

"Oh please. Get over yourself. I used to help you with algebra, or don't you remember?" She wore an evil smirk and rested one hand on her hip.

Suddenly that memory flooded back. He'd been in ninth grade, and she was just a kid, maybe eleven? He'd been stumped, and she taught him how to do it. He'd made her swear to secrecy.

"Nice of you to bring that up." He didn't give up without a fight.

"Wasn't it?" She raised her eyebrows once, then turned her gaze to the list remaining in her hand. "Let's get started."

"What do you want me to do first?"

"I'll dress the turkey. While I'm doing that, get the boards out of the closet there and put them in the table. Then spread the table-cloth. It's on a chair by the table. Then get down dishes," she said.

"How many?"

She counted on her fingers. "Ten."

"Counting on your fingers? Guess your math never progressed."

"Oh shut up. Get the plates." He moved toward the cabinet.

"Not those. We do have good dishes. They are in the corner cab-inet in the dining room. The good silver is in the corner cabinet too. Set the table. By the time you're done, the turkey will be ready to be lifted into the pan and put in the oven." She started the oven and then turned on the water in the sink.

Rob searched the closet until he found three boards. "Do we need all three?" he hollered from the other room.

"Yes!"

He pulled out the table gently and placed the boards and shoved it closed. After he spread the tablecloth, he went to the cabinet to gather the dishes. When he opened it, he saw pink and green flow-ered plates and stopped. Those were his mother's plates. Her best china. Emotion constricted his chest and his eyes filled. Ma and Dad. His parents. How many years had it been since he'd had Thanksgiv-ing with them? Too many.

Memories of past Thanksgivings flooded his brain. All his aunts, uncles, and cousins would come to their house. His parents and grandparents had the biggest house and the most money. Everybody brought a dish. He remembered the feeling of excitement to see his relatives. His mouth watered with the visions of the delectable home-made dishes that crowded the sideboard. Creamed onions, Brussels sprouts, buttery mashed potatoes, and sweet potato casseroles with tons of marshmallows on top. His mother's secret recipe stuffing, and the juicy, tender turkey. His stomach growled.

It had been so many years since he'd thought about the happy days of his childhood. Mostly he remembered his troubled teen years, how he fought with his grandfather all the time, and how he couldn't wait to get out on his own.

He pulled a handkerchief out of his back pocket, wiped his face, and blew his nose. What good did it do to wallow in memories of things past that would never be again? None. He'd made that decision shortly after hitching to California and seeking his fortune in the movies.

Yet now, as he prepared for a different kind of family Thanksgiving, he couldn't quell those memories, couldn't stop the longing in his chest to be part of a family again. Maybe this time he'd be the dad, do the carving, and be revered by a passel of little ones. He shook his head. Nah. That was just a vision from a movie he'd seen once. He'd never have a life like that. It wasn't meant to be.

He put the stack of dishes on the table, stopping to run his palm over the top plate. How his mother had coveted those dishes. He remembered the Christmas his father had lugged the huge box into the living room and shoved it under the tree. His mother had gone batshit over them. And ever since, she'd treated them with tender care. Rob stepped back and counted. What did you know? There were still twelve plates intact.

He found the silver, which was his grandmother's sterling silver flatware. Each piece was wrapped in a soft fabric and bundled together. They were a little tarnished but mostly still gleamed in the light. He carefully unwrapped them and, with respect, placed them at each place setting.

"Napkins?" he called into the kitchen.

"Oh. Yeah. In here," she said.

He opened the drawer she pointed to and found ten white cloth napkins and returned to the dining room. Folding each one with care, he placed them under the fork at each place setting. When he finished, he stood back and stared.

Rachel moseyed into the room. "Wow. Nice job."

He jumped at the sound of her voice.

"Sorry. Didn't mean to scare you."

"You didn't."

"Whatever. Looks really nice."

"Just like it was when I was a kid." Rob continued to peruse his work.

"Oh?" She raised her eyebrows and faced him.

"We used to have a big Thanksgiving dinner with my aunts, uncles, and a couple of cousins. Gramps and Gran too."

"You actually miss it?"

"I'm not made of stone. Yes, I miss it."

"Your parents have been gone a long time."

"Thanks for reminding me." He turned his gaze to the list.

"I'm sorry. I didn't mean to." She reached out and squeezed his forearm. He shook her off and stalked out of the dining room.

RACHEL MUTTERED TO herself. "I keep doing it. Putting my foot squarely in my mouth. I need to learn to shut up." She shook her head as she returned to the kitchen.

She'd give him a moment to compose himself and maybe forget her insensitive comment. Memories of the Bobby Walsh she knew as a kid flooded back. Ah, yes, she remembered gathering in the big house with her brother and huddling by the fire in the living room of the Walsh's home. Quiet as a mouse, she'd sneak off to sit cross-legged behind her brother and watch the Thanksgiving Day parade on the Walsh's television.

The TV in her house was much smaller. Besides, if she stayed home, she'd be roped into cleaning and doing chores. Inevitably after the parade, the phone would ring. It would be her mother asking Mrs. Walsh to send Rachel and Eli home.

She'd follow Eli on the long route home. Thanksgiving in their house was smaller. They didn't have any relatives nearby. Dinner would be just the four of them and any stragglers her parents managed to pick up from work who had no place to go. Mrs. Cohen taught at the elementary school and Mr. Cohen worked at the post office. While they were not rich, they were comfortable and set a nice table.

Rob leaned against the door jamb in the kitchen.

Just as Rachel opened her mouth to speak, the doorbell rang.

"I guess the little monsters have arrived," he said.

"Don't call them that. They'll hear you." She pushed to her feet.

"Don't get up. I'll get it."

Before she could get to the door downstairs, he was there.

"Well, well. The little helpers. Come on in," he said, opening the door and making a grand gesture with his arm.

Rachel cringed. The young teens stared at him, wide-eyed.

"Who's this?" Mikey said.

"OMG! I know who this is! It's Ironman!" Sophie squealed.

Rachel stifled a chuckle. *They don't recognize him!*

"No, no. I'm just Rob Walsh. George is my grandfather. Come in, come in."

Mikey brushed by Rob, ignoring him.

After all the kids were inside, the group walked upstairs to the kitchen.

"You have my list?" he asked Rachel.

She dug a folded piece of paper out of the back pocket of her jeans.

"Yeah. Here." She handed it over. He nodded and unfolded the paper.

One by one, the kids took their lists and gathered supplies. Rachel gave two small buckets to two students.

"You guys are on bathroom duty."

"Bathroom duty." The boy laughed.

"Very funny. Not. Let's not waste time. The turkey is cooking." She motioned to two girls. "You two are on pick up duty. Straighten up, vacuum, and fluff pillows."

One by one, the students headed to complete their jobs. The last four joined Rachel in the kitchen.

Rob looked at his list. "Hmm. Build a fire," he said to himself.

"You're Bobby?" a boy asked.

"No, no. Used to be Bobby. Rob now. And you are?"

"Simon. I'm assigned to help you."

"Okay. Come with me. We have to build a fire and that means chopping wood and gathering kindling. This way." Rob led the boy out of the store and toward the woods.

Rob chopped wood and Simon gathered kindling. They made several trips and stacked some logs by the fireplace upstairs in the living quarters. Since he lived in Southern California, Rob hadn't made a fire in a fireplace in years. But the method came back to him as if it had been yesterday. It was one of the things his father had taught him.

Simon placed his haul next to the fireplace.

"So, what are you studying in school, Simon?" Rob broke up the kindling into smaller pieces.

"Stuff." Simon sat on the floor.

"What's your favorite subject?" Rob laid logs on top of the sticks.

"Lunch."

Simon had a few extra pounds, so Rob believed him. The boy did not cozy up to Rob and get chatty. Hell, he didn't even recognize the movie star. Rob's ego deflated like a week-old balloon. To Simon, Rob was simply some guy helping Rachel.

"This is how you build a fire. Kindling first. Then put on the logs. Make sure they are steady and won't roll off or anything."

Simon's eyes never left Rob.

"Once that's done, you crumple up newspaper and shove it under everything like this," he said, demonstrating.

Simon nodded.

"Then you roll up a bunch of newspaper, light it, and stick it up the chimney."

"Why?"

"It heats up the cold air sitting in the chimney to create a draft."

"Why do you need a draft?" Simon asked.

"The fire needs oxygen. If you don't do this, the smoke from the fire will sit in the chimney and back up into the room. By heating the air, you get circulation. The warm air will rise, move, and draw the smoke from the fire up into the chimney and out."

Simon nodded.

Rob lit the newspaper and held it up in the chimney for a few moments and then shoved it under the wood. Next, he ignited the rest of the bunched-up paper. It worked like a finely oiled machine. Rob sat back, away from the blaze, and watched their hard work.

"And that's how you make a fire in a fireplace," Rob said, grinning.

Simon nodded. "Thanks."

Rob slapped Simon on the back.

"Tuna fish," Samantha called from the kitchen.

"You hungry?" Rob asked.

Simon nodded.

"Me too. Let's go." They got up and joined the others in the kitchen.

"Samantha is just about finished making tuna sandwiches," Rachel said.

"Simon and I made the fire," Rob said.

"Way to go, Simon," Rachel said.

The aroma of roasting turkey permeated the air in every room, tantalizing Rob's taste buds and making his mouth water. "Hard to settle for tuna with the smell of that turkey in the air."

"Yeah, well, get over it. We'll eat the turkey when it's done. In the meantime, the kids are hungry and I'm guessing you are too."

"Worked up an appetite chopping wood."

"You chopped wood?" She raised her eyebrows.

"You should have enough to last you a week or two."

"Really?"

"Yeah. I found a dead tree in the woods. Simon gave me a hand. Piled it up nice and neat."

"Thanks."

"You're welcome." He nodded. Jammed around the small table, they quietly tucked into their sandwiches. Rachel poured glasses of milk for everyone, including Rob. The kids talked while they ate, starting with who had to do what next.

"When is dinner?" Simon asked.

Rachel glanced at her watch. "At four. Finish up. We've got a lot more to do to be ready."

When the kids finished, each one took their plate to the sink and washed it. Rob stood aside to let the crew clean up and move on to their next task. The helpers left the kitchen to finish up their chores, leaving Rachel and Rob alone.

"What do you want me to do?" Rob asked Rachel.

Eyeing his arms, she smiled. "You can mash the potatoes. But gotta cook 'em first. Here. Wash and peel them."

"Aye, aye, captain," Rob said, saluting.

Rachel flashed him a look and placed the peeler on the counter. "That's right. And don't you forget it."

"They don't seem to know who I am," he said as he filled a pot with water.

"Nope. They don't."

"Don't they go to the movies?" He put the pot on the stove and then picked up the peeler and started peeling potatoes.

"They don't have the money to go to the movies."

"Really?" Rob raised his eyebrows.

"Yeah. That's why they're here. Do you think they'd be at our table if there was a big Thanksgiving dinner waiting for them at home? No way."

"I didn't know that. It's nice of you to have them here."

"They appreciate it but would rather be in their own homes."

"I get it."

She turned to face him. "Do you?"

"Oh yeah. After my parents passed our big Thanksgivings went out the window. Gramps did what he could, but he wasn't much for cooking. Sliced turkey from the deli, stuffing, and canned cranberry sauce was what we had."

She reached out to touch his arm. "I'm sorry. I didn't know. You always looked so happy. Gramps seemed successful, bragging about deals he cut all the time."

"I was a good actor even then." He finished up the peeling, threw the peels in the trash, then dumped the potatoes in the pot and turned on the flame.

She laughed. "I guess so."

Rob went to check on the fire. After a poke or two with the tongs, he closed the screen and returned to the kitchen. He pricked the potatoes with a fork.

"They're done," he said and poured the water into the sink.

"Add butter and milk," Rachel said.

He did as he was told and mashed the life out of them. She looked over, peeking into the bowl.

"They look good. That's enough. Add another pat of butter and put the bowl on the table with a spoon for serving."

One by one, the dishes appeared. Rob went into the bathroom to wash his hands. The cleaning crew had been there. The room sparkled. He looked around the small living quarters and there wasn't a speck of dust or dirt anywhere. The upstairs of the store was divided into two bedrooms, a kitchen, a bathroom, and a combination living/dining area. The extended table squeezed the living space down a bit.

The delicious aromas from the sweet potato casserole and the pumpkin pie baking filled the air. A hint of onion from the green bean casserole added a touch of spice to the scent. Rob's stomach growled. A hunger he hadn't felt in years gripped his belly. Damn, he could eat the entire turkey!

Finally, Rob did his last task, putting the turkey on a lovely ceramic platter and placing it on the table.

"Rob, get your grandfather. He's downstairs," Rachel said. While Gramps rode up the chair elevator, Rob climbed the stairs. The kids took their places at the table.

"Here, Gramps. You sit at the head," Rob said, holding out a chair for the old man.

Gramps grabbed Rob in a bear hug. "Thanks for comin', Bobby."

Everyone held hands while Gramps said grace.

"Rachel calls you 'Rob', and Gramps calls you 'Bobby'. What is your real name?" Simon asked.

"Bobby is his real name, but his stage name is Deke," Gramps said, loading mashed potatoes and green bean casserole onto his plate.

"Stage name? You famous or sumthin'?" Simon asked.

"His latest movie is playing right in Oak Bend," Gramps said, adding some sweet potato casserole onto his plate.

"You got a movie out?"

"You made a movie?"

"I don't believe it," Simon said, casting a skeptical look at Rob.

"Yep. Say, when we're finished here, why don't we go see the movie?" Rob said.

Simon shook his head. "No money for a movie."

"Well, how about if I treat?"

"All of us?" Bianca asked.

"Yep. All of you," Rob replied.

"I think there's a seven o'clock show. We could come back for pie after the movie," Rachel added.

"Great idea. What do you say?" Rob looked at the eager faces.

Each one agreed. They lit up as if it was Christmas and Rob was Santa Claus. Warmth suffused his body for the first time in a long time. He couldn't remember the last time he'd done an act of kindness or generosity for anyone. He'd forgotten how good it felt.

"Rachel, will you go along as a chaperone?" Rob asked.

"Sure, sure. But let's finish the meal first."

"This is the best Thanksgiving dinner I've had in a long time. Thank you all," Rob said.

The conversation turned to school topics, then politics, and then dating. Rob listened carefully to the kids. He smiled at their insightful observations. When the main part of the meal was over, they bustled around like bees, getting the leftovers put away and the dishes washed.

At six-thirty, they were ready. Rob drove some in Gramps' rickety old car and Rachel drove the others in hers. They made it with five minutes to spare.

"Anyone want popcorn?" Rob asked.

A collective groan told him they were all too full for popcorn. Rob bellied up to the ticket window where an older man sat. The man counted the heads and said, "Twelve adults. That'll be a hundred twenty bucks, mister. Say, look who's here, Martha!" He turned to face a woman standing behind him. "It's that lady. A teacher, aren't you?"

Rachel nodded. Her face changed color. "Yeah. Can we just have the tickets, please?"

Rob slid his credit card under the window. He glanced at Rachel and again at the ticket man.

"What about her?"

"Why, she's seen this movie at least five times already, haven't you, miss?"

Rachel mumbled something Rob couldn't hear.

"Say, aren't you the fella in the movie?? Martha, come here. Isn't this Deke Walsh?"

"Why, now that you say it, sure looks like him," Martha said.

"Well, son-of-a-gun," the older man said. "Imagine that. The movie star and his biggest fan meet. Here at our little theater. Martha, ain't that somethin'?"

"The tickets, please?" Rachel said. When the man slid them toward her, she snatched them away and strode toward the door. "Come on."

As they went inside and found seats, Rob settled into a chair next to Rachel.

"So, you saw my movie five times, eh? Liked it that much?"

"Wanted to be sure of the parts I didn't like."

"BS, Rachel. You don't hate me."

"Never said I did. Sshh. The movie's starting."

Rob's grin stretched from ear-to-ear. Rachel liked him. A lot. No chick sees a guy's flick five times unless she's super hot for him. He chuckled to himself.

"Sshh," she said.

He settled back into his seat. Things in Pine Grove were looking up.

Chapter Three

After the movie, Rob offered to drive the kids home. While in the car, the inquisition began.

"So, you're a big movie star? Do you live in a mansion?"

"If you're super rich, how come Gramps lives in a crummy apartment?"

"You got a fancy car? Girlfriend?"

The questions from the kids kept coming. Seemed nothing was out of bounds for the curious young minds.

Rob wasn't too preoccupied to notice the shacks the kids called home. He saw trailers in need of serious repair, tiny houses with peeling paint, and overgrown postage-stamp lawns. Some properties looked like junkyards with rusting cars in various stages of disrepair parked amid sparse grass and weeds.

Now he understood why Rachel invited these teens for Thanksgiving. Didn't look like they had much happening at home. When he arrived back at the store, he fell onto the sofa. After stretching out his legs and resting them on the coffee table, he rubbed his belly.

Still flat, though it wouldn't be for long if he continued to stuff his face the way he had. But the food had tempted him beyond reason and delivered a scrumptiousness surpassing expectation. He ran the tip of his tongue over his lips and swore he could still taste the tender turkey and zesty cranberry relish. He closed his eyes to recall the outrageous creaminess of the pumpkin pie and the piquant flavor.

After he dodged most of the personal questions from the kids, they bombarded him with requests for the secret path to success in the movies with untold riches to follow. Sheepishly he hung his head. He'd fallen into the movies by accident—through no plotting or planning on his part. He'd been discovered by a passing motorist who had been waylaid by a flat tire in front of the store. Rob had changed it for free.

Grateful, the man had chatted with him.

"Ever think of a career in the movies?" he'd asked.

"No. Not really."

The man had taken a couple of pictures of Rob and said he'd be in touch. He gave him his card: Huntington West, director. Figuring the guy to be a bullshit artist, Rob nodded politely, then forgot about it. He shoved the card in the back of a drawer and went on with his life.

But the man had been sincere.

"I showed your picture to a couple of people out here in L.A. and they want you to come for a screen test. Interested?"

"Sure."

"I'll send you a plane ticket."

"Okay. Thanks."

He'd passed the screen test and got an agent and after appearing as an extra in several movies, he clinched a supporting role. His career took off when the star of an adventure movie died of COVID-19. Using the name Deke Walsh, Rob stepped into the role and hit success. He owed everything to Mr. Huntington West's flat tire and his own good looks and hard work.

He told the kids to forget about the movies. His opportunity had been a fluke, and he'd not get their hopes up that every flat tire meant the road to money and fame. Instead, he advised them to get good grades, then they could write their own ticket in life. They trained a jaundiced eye on him.

"You sound like Rachel. Same bullshit."

"Yeah, that's all adults ever say. Same shit over and over."

"Study, study, study. Do your homework. Stay out of your way, you mean. No one cares about us and grades have nothing to do with it."

"But with good grades, you can change that. Get ahead," Rob said.

"Sure, sure. Same old, same old."

Thinking back, he noted how hard the kids had worked. How proud they were of either the bathroom they made gleam or the delicious green bean casserole they concocted. The students weren't strangers to hard work. They had impressed him, which he never expected. Funny, but he wondered if a few of them would have beaten him out in the success category had it not been for that flat tire. Rachel interrupted his thoughts.

"I'm going to bed," she said, heading for the stairs.

"Wait."

"What?" She stopped and faced him.

In two long strides, he was beside her. He drew her into his arms for a giant hug. "Thank you."

"For dinner?"

"For everything. For coming to get me. Everything."

She stayed in his embrace for a few seconds before stepping back. "I didn't do it for you."

"I know. But thank you anyway." He ran his thumb down her cheek before she pushed it away.

"Stop that."

"What?"

"That seduction thing you do. Don't touch me. I'm not one of your Hollywood idiots, hanging on your every word, waiting to jump into bed with you and bask in reflected fame. I'm a real person with a life. I don't need you, and I don't want you."

Rob lurched back a step as if he'd been slapped.

"I don't mean to be mean, but you can't just turn on the charm and expect me to forget everything. Everything you've done, and especially the stuff you haven't. That's not going to happen."

"Okay. I get it. Yes, you're right. I've been a selfish bastard."

She nodded once.

"But I sent money to Gramps. Every month."

"If you did, he never said a word."

"If? If? You calling me a liar? I can show you bank statements that prove every month ten grand from me went into his account." If Rachel had been a guy, he'd have slugged her. He may be many bad things, but a liar wasn't one of them.

"If you did—not saying I believe you—why didn't he say anything?" She raised her palm.

"You'll have to ask him. I'm done here." In two quick steps, he was walking down the stairs to the tiny back room and slamming the door. He plopped down on the narrow bed and kicked off his shoes.

His mind went back to the advice of the therapist he saw in high school.

"What's your takeaway on this experience, Bobby?" Dr. Carlin had asked.

"Yeah," Rob said aloud to himself. "What's my takeaway?"

He stretched out on the meager bed, lacing his fingers behind his head. "Okay, Dr. Carlin. My takeaway on this is that I kinda brought it on myself. I coulda done more."

He shut his eyes and brought up the image of the Thanksgiving table. It had been such a joyful meal. The kids snarfing down huge quantities of food, the conversation entertaining, and the sense of belonging overwhelming.

"No more. No more," he muttered to himself. No way could he return to his lonely existence, rattling around by himself in his huge home. He wanted, no needed, a family. It was time. Time to get married and start having kids. It was the only way to fix his lonely life.

He forced himself to stand and undress. Back in bed, underneath a warm, homemade quilt, he closed his eyes and ran through the list of eligible females on his contact list.

"Wendy. Wendy Cochran. Yep." Wendy Cochran would make the perfect wife and mother. And then he was asleep.

RACHEL BARELY MADE it to her cottage behind the store before tears spilled down her cheeks.

How dare he be nice? Even though she watched Deke Walsh's movie five times, she knew the real man, Rob Walsh, was no hero. All puffed up with years of pent-up anger, hostility, and resentment, she'd be damned if she'd let his charm unnerve her.

He was a selfish bastard, plain and simple. Sure, he could be nice when he wanted. He'd turned on the charm for the kids and they fell for it, swallowed it whole. But she knew the truth. She knew he was acting the whole time. Okay, maybe not when he was eating. His compliments on the food were genuine. But the rest of the time...

Treating the kids to the movie was another phony stunt. Just buying more fans. He couldn't care less about those kids. He'd leave, and they'd still be stuck in their miserable lives. Leave. The word stopped her. Yes, he'd be leaving on Sunday night. She had less than three full days with Rob Walsh. She sighed. Why did she care? Why did she want to be around him? Why did she get so mad when he was nice to her?

She plopped down at her tiny kitchen table. The truth washed through her brain. She didn't want him to leave, knowing she'd probably never see him again. Oh yeah, maybe at the reading of Gramps' will. But that would be it. And he'd be gone forever.

Having him around brought her heart right back to those days so many years ago when they'd ride bikes together or play catch or kickball. The days when, unbeknownst to him, she'd given him her heart and never took it back. He'd been her hero, and today he'd reprised that role, touching her heart with his simple acts of kindness, reminding her of who he had been once upon a time.

But the loving boy Bobby disappeared when he became Deke. Was it possible to totally change who you were inside? She'd never thought so, except when it came to Bobby—no Rob, as he was known by now. Her disappointment grew with every month that went by with no word from him. Every holiday he ignored and every birthday for Gramps he'd missed was another nail in his coffin and another arrow to her heart.

But today, Bobby had come back and melted her heart all over again. Disgusted at her own weak will, she stomped over to the stove and put the kettle on for a cup of tea. She wiped away her tears with a vengeance.

"Haven't you cried enough over this man?" she asked herself.

Of course she had. And Bobby Walsh—the memory—had interfered in every relationship she'd had with a man ever since. Not that there were many, but no one measured up to Bobby. No one could love her the way he had. And so, she was alone.

The whistle of the kettle caught her attention. She poured a cup of Earl Grey, added milk, and sat at the kitchen table. As she thumbed through the small pile of mail, she couldn't focus or concentrate while Rob Walsh slept nearby, alone in his bed.

She sighed and took a sip. How she'd wanted the chance to spend just one night with him. One night. Was that asking too much? All those Hollywood airheads had managed to warm his bed for years. But not her. Nope. She had iron pride that would never quit. She'd never admit to him how she wanted him, craved his touch, his praise, his love. Never. She'd promised herself it would be her secret forever.

Her sharp words and nasty attitude kept him at bay. It might have been different if she'd seen any glimmer of the affection he'd once shown. Instead, he seemed the callous, insensitive man who'd hop into bed with any woman. Rob lived up to his public image. She didn't want that man. Secretly she feared the guy she'd loved for so many years had disappeared, consumed, swallowed whole by this shallow shadow of a man.

And so, she lived alone, wanting, needing so much, and getting by on so little. She finished her tea, cleaned up, and crawled into bed for a restless night.

IN THE MORNING, AFTER breakfast, Rob took a walk around the property. Sitting down on a wood bench in the sun, he zipped his jacket higher against the cool air. Totally forgetting about the time difference, he called Wendy Cochran, his flavor-of-the-month. It was seven-thirty in Pine Grove and four-thirty her time. The grouchy greeting told him he'd woken her up.

"Hey, babe. Sorry to get you up."

"Who is this?"

"Deke."

"Oh yeah. Hi, Deke. I don't have a shoot until this afternoon. Why are you calling me?"

"I want to see you."

"Yeah?"

"Yeah. Say, can you cook?"

"I can fry an egg. Why?"

"Can we do dinner when I get back? I want to ask you a question."

"Can't you ask it now? I want to go back to sleep."

"It's personal."

"Come on, Deke. I'm tired," she said with an edge to her voice.

He closed his eyes. "Okay. Okay. Do you want kids?"

"A family?"

"Yeah. Do you?" He held his breath.

"Eventually."

Eventually? That would have to do. Good enough. He'd convince her to start sooner rather than later.

"Is that it?"

"No." He shifted his weight. Somehow, he had envisioned this going differently.

"Come on. I'm tired."

His throat closed for a second as sweat broke out on his forehead.

"Okay, okay. Will you marry me?" He wiped his face on his sleeve.

"What?"

"Let's get married."

"You're proposing to me long distance? Over the phone?"

"You're the one who didn't want to wait until I got back." Rob pushed to his feet and sauntered toward the store.

"This is crazy. We've only been dating for like a couple of weeks."

"Months, actually. Months, Wendy." Rob's brow wrinkled.

"Are you sure you want to marry me? It's Wendy here."

"I'm sure. And I want to have kids. Like right away."

Silence.

"Wendy? You there?"

"You want to turn me into a baby machine while my career is going full speed?"

"Yeah. So?"

"I'm not going to ruin my figure because you want some brats around to make you feel like a man."

"You said you wanted kids. A family."

"Yeah. Like maybe when I'm forty."

"Come on, Wendy. You can retire and raise our children. I'm rich. We'll have a nice life."

"I don't know what fantasy you're living in, but you've got the wrong girl, Deke. I like you. You're a nice guy. Good looking. Sexy. But I'm not going to sacrifice my life for your dream of a storybook family life. Never gonna happen."

Embarrassed, she'd seen through him so quickly, he fumbled, unsuccessfully, for words.

"So the answer is 'no'?"

"Yep. It's all right, Deke. I'll still sleep with you. But no more talk of babies. Okay?"

"Okay."

The phone went dead. If he had been in her place, he probably would have said the same thing. He stopped to flip through the contacts on his phone.

"Amy? No. Beth? No. Tiffany? Definitely not. Angela? Nope. Sarah? No." He couldn't come up with one woman who was not connected to the movie, television, or modeling industry in some way.

None of them had any strong connection to him. An occasional party, dinner out, or a publicity event was fine. Even warming his bed when they were in the mood. But nothing beyond that. They had been his revolving door women. Whenever he needed a date or wanted to get laid "his ladies" as he called them, always accommodated.

He entered the store and sank down on the chair by the door, staring out the window and watching clouds form. A gritty day, cold, overcast, with the threat of snow. Even though he was indoors, he raised the collar of his shirt. The years spent in Los Angeles had eroded his ability to deal with winter weather.

"Where have you been?" Rachel's voice cut through his thoughts.

He faced her and shrugged. "A walk?"

"No time for that. Don't you know what day this is?"

"Yeah. Day after Thanksgiving. So?"

Rachel tugged on his arm. "It's Black Friday! We're opening early, in fact, in like five minutes. Don't you see people waiting in their cars? It's our biggest sales day of the year."

"Here? People buy this shit for Christmas?"

"Yes! We have lots of stuff. Gifts, lights, replacement bulbs, all kinds of holiday junk. And the local folks eat it up. They like shopping here. It's a monster day for me. You have to help."

Rob smiled. "Really? You want my help?"

"Damn right I do. Get up. Let's get started. Remember anything about the store?"

He closed his eyes for a split second and was back twenty years ago. "I sure do. I used to help Gramps. I knew where everything was."

"Some things have changed, but not everything. Let's go."

He smiled. Something important to do—what a blessing.

He pushed to his feet and touched her shoulder. "Show me what you want me to do."

The clang of the electric elevator chair interrupted his thoughts.

"Rachel! Rachel! Where are you? People are waitin' girl," shouted Gramps.

"Rob's going to help," she said, moving to help the old man stand.

"Rob? Oh yeah. Rob. Good, good. We need him."

"Sit down. You be the supervisor," Rachel said, guiding Gramps to the chair Rob had warmed.

"Okay. Let's go. Time's a wastin.'"

Rachel thrust a canvas apron at Rob. "Here. I'm going to open the doors. You help people, okay? I'll ring up sales."

Rachel unlocked the door and people wandered in.

"Happy Holidays!" Rob called, offering his hand to customers. "How can I help you?"

He smiled to himself. Right out of *It's a Wonderful Life*, eh?

"Two penny nails? They're probably two for a buck now. I think they're over here," he said, leading a customer to the right place. It was like he'd never left.

"Say aren't you that movie star Deke Walsh?"

"Rob. The name's Rob. Nice to meet you. What can I get for you?"

AT EIGHT O'CLOCK, RACHEL locked the front door. After the twelve-hour workday, she ached all over. Having reheated leftovers, Gramps had toddled off to bed.

"Are you hungry?" she asked Rob.

"Starving. You?"

She nodded. "Come on. Cold turkey and leftover stuffing and potatoes." She motioned him to follow her upstairs. Quietly, they threw together a delicious meal.

"Sometimes I wonder if the leftovers aren't even better than the first time," Rob said, digging his fork into an impressive mound of stuffing. When they finished, Rob took Rachel by the shoulders, turned her around, and walked her over to the small sofa.

"Sit. I'll clean up. You've done enough."

"No argument there." She sat down, leaning back and resting her feet on the coffee table. Reaching up she rubbed her neck to work out the kinks. She was surprised how much Rob had done: helping customers, talking people into buying more stuff..."If you put this on your Christmas table then you surely need some holly to go with it. And we have it right here." She'd heard him suggest that to a customer in the store.

Pleased to ring up more sales than ever, Rachel didn't mind sore fingers from working the old cash register and the credit card machine all day long.

When he finished drying and putting away the dishes, he joined her, but he sat on Gramps' lounge chair instead of snuggling up with her on the couch. She eyed him.

"That was quite a day. How'd we do?" he asked.

"I'd say probably 30 percent more today than our usual Black Friday take."

"Really? That's great."

"I was surprised you remembered stuff like where everything was." Rachel massaged her shoulder.

"Cramp?" he asked.

She nodded.

"Here. Let me." He moved over to the sofa and turned her to face away from him. His large hands covered her shoulders as he massaged her gently, adding pressure with his thumbs.

"Damn! You could have a second career doing massage." But the tingle she felt wasn't strictly about relaxed muscles and it traveled down to her private place.

"You have off tomorrow?" he asked.

"Are you kidding? I never take off on Saturday. It's our biggest day of the week. From now until Christmas, we're open every day. Gotta make as much as we can."

"Why the hustle? Gramps has the money I send him."

"I don't know what he does with that, but according to him, we're always running behind."

"I paid off the loan. What's the hassle?"

"Electricity, water, propane, wood for the stove, real estate taxes. Oh, and I like to buy food every now and then too."

He dropped his hands. "Do you have to be sarcastic *all* the time?"

"Maybe if you'd stop being condescending and treating me like a moron who doesn't know what bills she has to pay, I wouldn't."

"How should I know what you have to pay? I haven't been here in ages and never as an adult."

Rachel turned to face him and narrowed her eyes. She poked her forefinger into his chest. "That's it! You hit the jackpot! You haven't been here. That's the whole point. Not for Gramps' birthday, not Thanksgiving, not Christmas. Nothing. Nada. No-show. So, you wouldn't know diddly-squat about our expenses. But you're just arrogant enough to think you know more than I do. Some effing attitude!"

Rob sat back as if he'd been slapped.

"I'm sorry."

Once she started, she couldn't stop. Emotion flooded her veins.

"Sorry? You're sorry? I've been here manning the fort by myself. Taking care of Gramps, schlepping him to a million doctor appointments, running the business, cooking, cleaning, stocking shelves, doing the books—BY MYSELF! Just me! He's not been well enough to do much for the past three years. So, it all fell on me."

"Why didn't you tell me?"

"Would you have come?"

Rob's face turned red. He cast his gaze on his hands, fidgeting in his lap.

Silence.

Rachel forced back her tears with every ounce of strength she had.

"That's what I thought. Waste of time to tell you. You were living the good life."

"I'm sorry."

"No, you're not." Rage, which was trapped in her chest building a head of steam, bubbled up. "You're not sorry one bit. I bet you're relieved to have missed all that."

Rob's face paled and then two angry spots of red appeared on his cheeks. "I am not! Don't you dare tell me what I'm feeling!! Back off!"

Rachel swallowed the bile in her throat. She took a deep breath and then another. Calm washed over her. She'd said what she'd needed to say for the past three years.

"He's my grandfather, not yours. Of course, I worried about him. But he sent me letters. Said you had everything under control. I focused on my career. Hollywood is fickle. You can fizzle in an instant and be out of work and on the train home in the blink of an eye. I had to work while the series was hot. Didn't know if I'd get another chance at anything else. Even my agent didn't hold out hope. She said I should take all the movies planned for the series and be grateful."

"Under control?" She laughed. "If you mean on the verge of a nervous breakdown, no, wait, nervous exhaustion for three years as being under control, then I guess he was right."

"I'm truly sorry, Rachel." Rob turned soft eyes on her. "Is there some way I can make it up to you?"

Rachel clamped down on her brain. *Don't go there.* "What's past is past. I'm tired. I'm going to bed."

Rob reached out and grabbed her forearm. "I'll work my ass off tomorrow and Sunday too. Every minute I'm here, I'll be your slave."

She nodded. "Great. A slave for a day-and-a-half. I'm a lucky girl. Good night."

He stood up and drew her into his embrace. "I'm sorry," he murmured into her hair. "I'll make it up to you. I promise."

The warmth of his arms melted her. She slid hers around him and buried her face in his chest. Tears refused to be denied. She simply couldn't contain her feelings any longer.

"Tears?" he whispered.

"It's been so damn hard...and lonely," she muttered, the truth flowing from her lips.

"I'm so sorry, honey. So very sorry. Things will be better."

She didn't believe him, but for the moment, it soothed her to have his sympathy. Even if nothing changed, and she doubted it would, at least he knew, and he'd help when he could. Maybe that would mean he wouldn't leave for good. Probably not, but she could hope, couldn't she?

Chapter Four

The sun woke Rob at daybreak. Seven a.m. He wrestled his covers down to the foot of the tiny bed and swung his legs over the side.

"Sweet Jesus!" Since when had Rachel substituted an ice rink for the wooden floor? He glanced down, just to make sure he wasn't dreaming. It was wood all right, but colder than the frozen Cedar Lake.

Hopping as quietly as he could, he made it across the floor, dressed in a flash, and then tiptoed up the stairs. Sure enough, the wood stove was stone cold. He shrugged on his jacket and headed for the back door.

After depositing a good armful of logs near the stove, he shoved a couple in and got it started. It was only late November and already he was frozen to the bone. He lost his capacity to deal with cold weather and couldn't imagine how frigid the place must get in January. His heart filled with sympathy for Rachel and his grandfather.

He wondered how much it would cost to add real heat to the old store. Would it be worth it? Probably not. From the looks of his grandfather, he wouldn't be around much longer. After he passed, Rob would sell the place and return to L.A. permanently. He'd give the proceeds to Rachel to start over.

Once the stove did its job, he headed for the kitchen. Least he could do was get breakfast going. He turned on the coffeemaker and opened the fridge. Plenty of eggs and some bacon. Things were looking up.

Just as he set a pan of bacon on the old stove, Rachel came around the corner.

"Good morning," Rob said. "Milk and sugar? Black?"

"Coffee?"

"Yep."

"Milk, please," she said.

Her smile added warmth to the room. Funny he hadn't noticed it before. Maybe it's because she never smiled. He prepared a mug and handed it to her.

"Thanks." She took a sip. "This is good."

"I'm a whiz at coffee," he said with a chuckle.

"How do you want your eggs?" Rachel asked, putting her mug down on the counter.

"Sit. I'm doing breakfast."

"Really?" She raised her eyebrows.

He nodded and opened the fridge door. "So. How do you like your eggs?"

Rachel's grin lit up the entire kitchen. "Any way you choose to make 'em."

Before he put on the eggs, Gramps, dressed in pajamas and a robe, shuffled into the kitchen.

"Who's cooking bacon?" he asked.

"Your grandson is our breakfast chef this morning."

"Rob, you can cook?" He faced his grandson.

"I live alone, Gramps. I do have to feed myself."

Gramps chuckled, his lips spread into a sly grin. "I thought all those ladies of yours would be makin' you breakfast every morning."

Rob's cheeks heated. He turned toward the stove. "Not every morning."

Gramps laughed and helped himself to a mug of coffee.

After breaking the first yolk on the fried eggs he was preparing, Rob opted to switch to scrambled and hide his mistake. Sure he could put food in front of his face, but he was no French Chef by any means.

"I'd turn off the eggs if I were you. They'll burn. The bacon's gonna take longer."

Rob nodded and did as Rachel suggested. She disappeared with her coffee and returned a few minutes later dressed in jeans and a flannel shirt, hair brushed, and toting the newspaper. She handed it to Gramps.

"Ah, thank you, sweetheart. Today's news. Probably all bad, but still. A man's gotta keep up with what's happening in the world." With the paper under his arm, he picked up his mug and tottered into the living room.

Rachel returned to her seat, and Rob checked the bacon. It was almost done. He put a couple of paper towels on a plate. Rachel refilled his mug and hers. When she wasn't looking, he stole a glance at her. Sun streaming in the window kissed her dark hair, dancing on auburn highlights. Her shiny hair fell loose to her shoulders and invited touching. A few stray strands fell over her cheek. Unable to resist, Rob leaned over and tucked the naughty locks behind her ear.

"Thanks," she said, turning dark chocolate eyes on him, her lips in the shape of Cupid's bow curled into a brief smile. Why hadn't he noticed how beautiful she was? He swallowed and snuck a peek at her breasts, surprisingly prominent under the baggy shirt she wore. *Nice.*

"You can turn the eggs back on now," she said.

"Oh. Yeah. Right." He'd better keep his mind on the food, or he'll get tossed out on his butt. He smiled. Caution was not a word in his vocabulary.

"How come I don't remember you being this pretty when I was in Pine Grove?" The minute he said it, he regretted it. No taking it back now.

Fortunately, Rachel laughed. "King of the backhanded compliments, eh?"

He shrugged, forcing himself to keep quiet.

"Yeah. I was kind of a scrawny thing with wild hair in those days. It was a long time ago. Even childhood...uh...friends grow up. Eventually," she said.

He faced her, his gaze zipping up and down her form. "You grew up great if you don't mind me saying," he said, feeling the heat in his face grow.

"Thanks." She met his stare.

He'd seen that hungry look in a female's eyes before, but it shocked him to see it in hers. But she hated him? No, he must be wrong. Couldn't be that she wanted him. No. No way. Uh-uh. Not Rachel.

"The eggs?" she said.

"Oh damn!" He turned off the stove and removed the pan.

Gramps entered the kitchen and asked, "Something burnin'? This place is a damn tinderbox. Be careful."

"I think he got to them in time," Rachel said.

Rob shot her a grateful glance.

"Why don't you get plates and divide up the bacon? I'll handle the eggs," she said, giving him a look.

He swallowed and followed her advice. Rachel scraped most of the overcooked eggs onto her plate and some on Rob's, and the ones cooked correctly she placed onto Gramps' plate.

"Looks mighty tasty," the old man said, sitting his bony butt on a chair at the table.

Rob mouthed "thank you" to Rachel behind his grandfather's back. They all ate in silence.

When they finished, Gramps rose, mumbled something about lying down, and left the room.

Rob checked his watch. "It's eight. Why don't you open the store? I'll clean up."

"Okay. Thanks. Good breakfast."

"Yeah, right." He pulled his lips into a half smile and shook his head.

Rachel slipped quickly downstairs. Rob heard the creaky old lock turning and her voice greeting customers. Damn, she's right. They're waiting for that door to open. He washed and dried the dishes, then cleaned up himself and headed downstairs.

"I think we have whole wheat flour in the back in the baking section," Rachel said.

"I didn't see it there," the customer replied.

"I think I saw it yesterday. Follow me," Rob said, leading the lady to the back of the store. Sure enough, a small sack of whole wheat flour had been shoved behind the white flour. Guilt flashed through him for a moment. He'd done that to make room on the shelf for more items.

"Here you go." Rob handed her the sack.

"Thanks, mister." She headed for the counter.

Rachel flashed him a grateful glance as she stood at the cash register, ringing up a sale and taking a credit card.

Rob looked around. Things were in disarray from the flurry of buyers the day before. He set to work reorganizing the shelves.

At noon, Gramps appeared at the top of the stairs and yelled, "Lunch!"

Rob put a hand on Rachel's arm. "You stay here. I'll take care of it."

She nodded. "Thanks."

"I'm looking for a hammer for my single daughter. She just moved into her own place and doesn't have any tools. Can you show me one that wouldn't be too heavy?" a woman asked Rachel and then eyed Rob. "Say, young man. Are you married?"

Rob's eyes widened. "My grandfather needs help." He gestured to the stairs and made a quick getaway. As he took the stairs two at a time, he heard the conversation between the woman and Rachel.

"He's not married? Rachel, you should do something about that!" And the woman laughed.

Sweat broke out on Rob's brow.

"You're going to make my lunch? I don't want you. I want Rachel. She's a better cook than you. She wouldn't have burned the eggs."

"Rachel's busy. I'll make you a nice turkey sandwich."

"I'm sick of turkey. Don't we got anything else?"

"I'll look. How about a cup of tea?"

"Okay, okay. I know she's gotta work. She usually makes my lunch early and leaves it up here."

"Sorry. We missed that today. One lunch coming up."

Gramps put his hand on Rob's arm. "Don't forget Rachel. She's gotta eat too."

"I won't. I won't."

Rob put on the kettle and held out a chair for the old man. Then he opened the fridge and peered inside.

"Doesn't look like we have much," Rob said.

"What about the leftover turkey?" Gramps asked.

Rob straightened up and stared at his grandfather. Hadn't they just discussed that?

"Yeah. We have turkey."

"Well, whatcha waitin' for? The next millennium? And I want Russian dressing too."

"What?"

"Mayo mixed with ketchup. Okay?"

"Yeah." Rob set about getting the tea set up and lunch made. The realization that his grandfather's brain wasn't what it used to be hurt. He'd never imagined Gramps losing his marbles or not being as sharp as always. Obviously, things had changed. Regret for not spending more time with him when he was less cantankerous pricked at him.

Rachel had Rob pegged. A selfish, insensitive bastard who only cared about his own life. And now he'd lost some good years with his grandfather...his only family. Years he'd never get back. Tears stung at the backs of his eyes. This isn't who he was, was it? Shame flooded his heart. Maybe it was. But it's never too late to change, right?

AFTER LUNCH, GRAMPS went downstairs to the store and perched in the chair by the door, greeting customers. Rob noted the old man remembered people's names but couldn't recall what he had for lunch. Wasn't short-term memory the first to go? Rob wondered.

It was a busy day. Rob swore he wore a path on the old wood floor from the stockroom to the shelves. On his last trip of the day, he made a note of which shelves would need to be restocked. The store had run out of Christmas decorations, wrapping paper, flour, sugar, and other food staples. He shook his head. It was crazy to run a general store, there are so many different items. The big stores had it all over Gramps' little operation when it came to price. Rob figured locals weighed the cost of time and gas to drive twenty miles or more to a bigger store vs. paying more at Walsh's General.

The space was big, having been a barn many years ago. And then Gramps had added on to it when Grandma was around. They'd sold her homemade pies and cookies too. He'd built a chicken coop and sold fresh eggs. But now they could not compete with the rock-bottom prices of the huge stores. Rob scratched his head. How had they remained open and where did these customers come from?

At seven p.m., Rachel locked the door and leaned against it.

"Best Saturday in a long time," she said, closing her eyes and smiling.

"Do you know you're out of a lotta stuff?"

"Delivery comes on Tuesday." She took her time climbing the stairs.

"Is that restaurant near the lake still in business?" Rob asked.

"Homer's? Yeah. Why?"

Rob took her arm. "Come on. I'm taking you out to dinner."

"What about Gramps?" She raised her eyebrows.

"He had a bowl of soup, turkey, and the last of the stuffing."

"You do that?"

He nodded. "He's gone to bed. Come on. You deserve a night out."

She stopped for a moment. "We'd better hurry. The kitchen closes at ten."

"Well, what are we waiting for?"

"I should shower and change," Rachel said.

"Bag it. Let's go." Rob grabbed her jacket and his from the hooks by the door and took her hand. "Are you open tomorrow?"

"Only in the afternoon. People have church in the morning."

"Oh right." He opened the front door and then the car door. Rachel pulled out her keys and drove to Homer's Restaurant.

When he saw the fire burning in the fireplace, Rob's heart lifted. His grandparents used to take him there when he got a good mark on his report card. He loved to warm himself in front of the fire. His frugal grandfather kept their place cool in the winter to save money. Rob loved L.A. because it was warm all year round.

"Two for dinner?" Homer asked.

"Yes. Table by the fire?" Rob raised his eyebrows and shoved a ten in the man's palm.

"For our favorite Pine Grove movie star? You bet. Keep it," Homer said, pushing the bill back at Rob.

He pulled out Rachel's chair and then sat down. Raising his hands to the flames, he ordered a beer. Rachel ordered a glass of red wine. They were silent until the drinks arrived.

"You're holding up pretty well," she said, taking her first sip.

"This is just like a workout at the gym. I'm fine."

"Good. We have tomorrow afternoon until the limo arrives."

"Yeah. What time is it coming?"

"Didn't you arrange it?" she asked, panic in her voice.

"Oh yeah." He laughed. "I did." He pulled out his phone. "Six. Red-eye flight is at nine-thirty."

"Should give you enough time, right?"

"Yep." He changed the subject. "So, what's your most popular item?"

"Food and hardware. Small hardware purchases. I raised the prices on those. I know our customers aren't going to drive twenty miles to the big stores for a couple of screws or nails."

"Pretty smart."

"They're most expensive, but not a fortune. You can't charge ten bucks for a nail."

Rob laughed. "Nope. If you could, Gramps would have done it."

"I learned pricing from him. He's a retail genius."

"I wouldn't call him a genius..."

"I would," she interrupted. "He kept the place going in spite of all the bigger, cheaper stores."

"What's the secret?"

She leaned over, grinning. "Don't tell anyone."

"I swear," Rob said, raising his hand.

"We have specialty items."

"Like what?"

"Like the old penny candy stuff, cinnamon sticks, clove gum, Australian licorice, and shortbread cookies from Scotland. Little indulgences. Stuff you don't buy a lot of, but when you want it, you can only find it online. Then you have to pay for shipping and buy a minimum quantity. But we have that stuff, and you can buy one cinnamon stick if you want."

"And you make money on the one stick?" Rob raised his eyebrows.

"Nah. But it's like a loss leader. Once someone comes into the store for that lone cinnamon stick, they usually find at least five other things they want or need. And that's where we make our money."

Rob nodded. "Smart."

Rachel sat back. "That was my idea."

RACHEL STARED AT HIM. The light from the fire kissed Rob with an irresistible glow. Rachel gripped her wineglass to keep from touching him. But it wasn't easy. *He's leaving tomorrow.* She tried to shove it out of her mind, but her practical, protective side wouldn't have it. She had to accept he'd be gone in less than twenty-four hours. And then she'd probably not see him again until Gramps' funeral.

Leaning back in her chair, she cradled the wineglass with both hands before raising it to her lips. She sensed his gaze lingering for a moment on her mouth. A trickle of sweat inched down between her breasts. The heat between them rivaled that coming from the fireplace.

Chemistry! Damn, she hadn't counted on that. Slowly, her disdain for him dissolved. He'd been amazing. Helping, encouraging, laughing, and brightening her days. She'd dreaded yanking him off the set and forcing him back to Pine Grove, expecting to have a sullen, hostile guest who would expect to be waited on and would drag down the holiday. But he'd surprised her. His willingness to do everything, and his warmth, had turned it into a delightful surprise. It was the best Thanksgiving she'd had in years. And she hated to admit it was all because of Rob Walsh.

Soon she'd be back to her old melancholy self. Why did she insist he come home? It was her idea, and it had backfired. He was leaving, and she wanted him to stay. Stay now. Stay forever.

Never gonna happen. Guys like Rob—Deke Walsh—didn't settle for frumpy little nobodies hiding out in a small town. *Shut up and enjoy the time you have.* She blew out a breath. Time to listen to her smarter side and make the most of every minute.

He picked up the menu. "What's good here?"

"I love the blue cheeseburger or the burger with sauteed onions."

"Onions. Sounds great."

They ordered burgers and sweet potato fries.

Rob pulled out his phone. *There he goes, probably texting his two dozen stunning girlfriends.*

"I made some notes. Stuff people wanted, but we didn't have."

We?

"Thought you might be interested."

"I am." She leaned forward as he read the list.

"I can send it to you. Or do you want me to write it down?"

"Write it down. I'll talk it over with Gramps," Rachel said.

"Okay. I'll do it on the plane and drop it in the mail."

"Fine. Thanks."

"Thought you'd want to know." He tucked his phone into his breast pocket.

"I do. Anything I can do to keep the place going."

He smiled. Food arrived, and the discussion drifted over to his grandfather's condition and the buildings.

"I know the place is in need of repair..." she said.

"Ya think? You'll be lucky if the damn roof doesn't cave in this winter! One good, heavy snow and you guys are done for," Rob said, then took a bite of his burger.

"It's not that bad."

"Have you had it inspected?"

"Well, no," she admitted and put a fry into her mouth.

"Because you know what they'll say. 'Replace it or else.' Right?"

"Probably. But that'll cost thousands, which we don't have."

"Do you want to save it? I mean, Gramps looks like he's on his last legs." Rob raised his palm. "Not that I'm wishing death on him. But we have to be practical. Do you have plans for after he's gone?"

She shook her head. "Oh, I've thought about it. But nothing leaps out at me. I'm hoping to go back to teaching."

"In Pine Grove?" he asked.

"Yes. I'll stay in the guest house until I have enough money to buy a place of my own. It's what I know. I have friends here." She lowered her gaze to her food. She didn't want him to know she didn't expect to inherit the place or have any plans otherwise. But he'd asked and she couldn't think up a plausible lie fast enough.

"If Gramps leaves everything to me, you can stay in the guest house, rent free, for as long as you like. In fact, I might gift it to you."

She raised her head and met his stare. "Really?"

"Why not? What would I do with it?"

She shrugged. "Sell it?"

"I haven't seen the inside, but if it's in the same shape as the store, who would buy it anyway?"

"I would."

Rob covered her hand with his. "You don't have to buy it. It's yours for as long as you want it. If I were to sell everything, I wouldn't include the guest house."

Emotion closed her throat. His fingers squeezed hers and she responded, but not with words. They wouldn't come. Her eyes filled, and she looked away, gently easing her hand from under his. After years of building up a reservoir of serious anger, she simply could not handle his kindness and generosity.

"Honestly, Rachel. You've meant so much to the old man. Been like a daughter. Taken care of him and the store. I'm grateful. Really."

As if an icy knife had sliced into her heart, the word "grateful" cut her to the quick. Grateful? He was grateful? Of course he was. He wouldn't do something for her because he actually liked her, would he? Not *the* famous Deke Walsh. He didn't see her as a woman, only as a caretaker for his grandfather.

Hard to believe she'd actually lost ground with him. Being invisible before to being less than human now. A robotic caretaker, could she get any lower? She picked up her fork and pushed some fries around on her plate. Anger seeped into her neck and crept up to her face.

"What's wrong?" he asked.

What happened to his brain? Couldn't he figure it out? "Nothing. I didn't do it for your gratitude. I did it because I like Gramps. He's like family. So take your gratitude and shove it."

Rob's eyes widened. "What did I do? One minute you're like all warm and sweet, and the next you're a shark biting my head off. I don't get it."

"Correct. You don't. Finish and let's get outta here."

ROB'S CHEEKS HEATED up. "I don't think so."

"What?"

"You heard me. I'm not leaving here until you tell me what's going on." Rob sat back, arms crossed over his chest, his eyes riveted to hers.

Her face hardened. Defiance sparked in her eyes. "Oh yeah?" She pushed her chair back from the table.

"Don't you dare get up."

"What?"

"Don't you dare get up!" Rob said, rising slowly from his seat, stopping halfway. "I've been nice to you. Did your bidding without complaint. Worked my fuckin' ass off for you and Gramps this week. And this attitude is what I get?"

"I appreciated what you did."

"Pull your chair up to the table."

"And if I don't?"

"I will do it for you," Rob said, his voice deep, vaguely threatening, and barely audible.

As if she realized she'd gone too far, she did as he demanded.

"That's better. Now we're going to get to the bottom of this. Are you not grateful for my help?"

"There's that word again. That ugly word. Grateful."

"What's ugly about gratitude?" He uncrossed his arms and leaned on the table.

"If you're going to put it like that, nothing."

"So?" He raised his eyebrows.

She shifted in her seat.

"You wanted more? Maybe I should get down on the floor and kiss your feet for letting me work myself into the ground doing menial labor?" His voice rose.

"No."

"Then what?"

She covered her face with her hands to hide her tears. He saw her shoulders shake. In a flash, Rob was on his feet and next to her. He wrapped an arm around her shoulders.

His voice softened. "Tell me. Tell me, honey. What's wrong?"

She wiped her eyes on her napkin. Avoiding his stare, she mumbled, "I wanted you to like me."

"What? Like you? Of course I like you. I love you for what you've done for Gramps...and me."

"No. I wanted you to like me for me." Her voice trailed away, and the tears returned.

Rob picked her up in his arms, slid into her seat, and transferred her to his lap. He hugged her tightly.

"I do like you for you. I remember that little girl who looked up to me. Who made me feel like a superhero..."

"You were my superhero."

"Not exactly. I was just an awkward boy standing up for a girl I liked. And still do. A girl who deserved to be protected."

She quieted down.

"You're amazing. I mean, when you were little, so cute and adoring. I loved you like a little sister. Nobody was going to mess with you. But now? Oh my God. The things you do, the way you handle people: the kids, Gramps, customers. The way you keep it together and stay in control and calm. I'm amazed. Impressed. You're the most capable woman I know."

"Just capable?" she squeaked out.

"Capable and sexy," he whispered before lowering his mouth to hers.

Rachel slid her arms around his neck and kissed him back. The most amazing kiss he'd ever had. When he raised his head, he took a deep breath. Of all the things he'd expected, Rachel wanting him was last on his list. He'd hoped she'd stopped hating him and remain neutral. But this? This was beyond his wildest dreams. Wouldn't a woman like Rachel, a woman of substance, see him simply as a cardboard cutout? But she saw the real Rob Walsh, and it warmed his heart.

Homer stopped at their table. "Hey, folks. I'd ask you if you wanted anything else, but I know the answer. No charge. Get a room, okay?"

Rob looked up.

"Sorry, Homer," Rachel said, straightening her shirt.

Rob deposited her on her chair and quickly returned to his seat. He placed his napkin in his lap to hide his growing affection for Rachel. "Maybe we'd better go."

"Yeah, yeah. Right." She pushed to her feet.

"Why don't I write out that list for you when we get home?"

"Good idea."

They put on their coats, thanked Homer, and left. When they got home, the store was quiet. They crept up the stairs softly and met in the kitchen. Rachel opened a drawer and pulled out a small pad and pen.

"Here. Write down the list of items people want."

"I'll put how many people asked for these too, in parentheses."

"Good idea."

If Rachel had been anyone else, they'd be kissing their way to the bedroom by now. It wasn't that he didn't want to, and his dick had ideas too, but he couldn't treat her so callously. What would the future hold for them? He was leaving tomorrow and who knows when and even if he'd be back. Although only another two weeks of shooting remained for his current film, he had a commitment for another movie as soon as this one wrapped.

No stranger to recreational sex, Rob couldn't do that to Rachel. The kiss, their conversation, had touched something he'd buried a long time ago: affection, genuine feelings for a woman. He'd put his career before anything and anyone for so long, that he'd forgotten what it was like to care, deeply care, about a woman. Until now. Feelings flooded back into him like Niagara Falls.

"Rachel, I...I..."

She put her hand on his arm. "I know. You're leaving tomorrow. I get it. I totally get it."

"It's not like I don't want to. I do want to, but I want to be fair to you. I don't know when we can see each other again."

"Yeah, well, I don't do one-night stands, anyway. So forget about it. It's okay."

He cupped her chin and brushed his lips over hers before picking up the pen and pulling out his phone.

Chapter Five

S unday passed in a blur. They spent the morning taking care of
Gramps, who had had too much excitement the day before, and
straightening up the store. By noon, the door opened, and people
flooded in.

Preoccupied with customers, ringing up sales, and packing gifts
in bags, Rob and Rachel barely had time to smile when passing each
other. They closed at four. The limousine was due to arrive at six.

Rob packed up the meager belongings he'd acquired since arriving and stopped to say goodbye to his grandfather.

"Be good, Rob. Win an award or something."

"I'll do my best. Take care of yourself. I expect to come back and
see you hauling ass up and down those stairs."

His grandfather patted Rob's cheek. "Let's not kid each other.
This is probably our last time together."

"Don't say..." Rob started, but Gramps held up his hand.

"Don't kid a kidder, son. It's life. No false expectations. No lies
now. We've never lied to each other. I don't want to start now. You're
the best grandson in the world. I love you. Go out and conquer the
world. And please take care of Rachel after I'm gone."

"Will do. You're the best mother, father, grandfather in the
world. I love you too." Rob stopped as emotion choked him. He
hugged his grandfather as tears dribbled down his cheeks.

The honking of a horn brought back reality.

"I know. I know. Time for you to go. Be well, son," Gramps said.

"I will. You too."

The old man made a shooing motion with his hand, then pulled a handkerchief out of his back pocket and wiped his eyes. Rob skittered down the stairs, gripping his backpack with one hand and the railing with the other.

He poked his head out the door. "Coming!! Just a minute, okay?"

Two feet away, Rachel stood, eyes full, attempting to smile. He grabbed her in a huge bear hug. "I'm coming back."

"Yeah right," came her reply, muffled by his shoulder.

"I am. And I expect to find you here. And Gramps too."

"Good luck with that." Rachel rested her palm on his cheek for a moment. "I'll miss you."

"I'll miss you too."

"Sure, sure. Your sheets won't be cold for five minutes after you get home."

Rob summoned all the sincerity he had. "That's not true. No one is like you."

She laughed.

"Really." He pulled her closer and kissed her with everything he had, hugging her so tight he lifted her off the floor.

The horn honking grew more insistent. "If I don't go, I'll miss my plane."

She nodded. Her eyes glowed.

"You're the best, Rachel. Really, I mean it."

"I'll miss you, Rob."

He nodded, then pushed through the screen door and ran down the driveway. He jumped into the back seat and shut the door hard. As the car took off, he opened the window and waved. The sight of Rachel with a hanky to her face, waving, about broke his heart.

Rob sat back against the seat. He stared out the window, absorbing the scenery, committing it to memory. Would he ever be back this way again? He had no idea. The lake looked beautiful, but cold. Its frozen top turned slightly whitish. Lights glowed in the little homes hugging the shore. Rob pictured the roaring fires keeping families warm as a winterish wind whipped up off the lake.

Only a day after one holiday and people had already put up colored lights on their homes. Trees and shrubs sported solid colors or flashing ones. Even the ones without holiday lights had single candles in each window. A tingle shot up his spine as he remembered holidays past.

Although he and Gramps didn't have much, the old man had managed to save enough to get Rob the one toy he'd craved every year. The colored lights ramped up his spirits as fantasies of a storybook Christmas danced in his head.

Of course, the holiday had never been like the ones in movies or books. They didn't have a tree inside but did decorate one right outside the door. Gramps had some ornaments he'd saved over the years. He and Rob strung them up in the store and their private quarters.

As the car passed by small town after small town, Rob spied a bicycle resting against a garage. He remembered his best present ever. Secretly, Gramps had bought a second-hand bike at a garage sale in the fall and repainted it. He'd added streamers to the handlebars. It was red, white, and blue. Gramps had called it Rob's "freedom bike." Once he had wheels, Rob was everywhere. Foregoing the free school bus, Rob rode his freedom bike to and from school to football practice to the store...everywhere.

He sighed. Days of simple pleasures were far behind him now. His life had become incredibly complicated since everything he did made the news. As the car turned onto the highway, Rob sighed and glanced out the back window, bidding a silent farewell to his old town, the grazing cows, weathered barns, emerging holiday celebrations, and the easy days of childhood.

He spoke out loud. "I'll be back for Christmas."

"Pardon, sir?" the driver asked.

"Nothing. Just talking to myself." He sat back, smiling, closed his eyes and slept until the vehicle pulled into the airport.

"I'M GOING OUT FOR COFFEE, Gramps," Rachel said, giving her nose one last swipe and reaching for her jacket.

"Going to The Cozy Café?" he asked, hitching up his pants.

"Nope. Java the Hut."

"Powwow with Winnie Briggs?"

Rachel smiled. "How'd you guess?"

"You always go to her when you have man trouble."

"Who says you're not a sharp old man?"

"Not me!" He laughed.

"Want anything?"

"If they've got a cinnamon bun, grilled and buttered, I'd be grateful."

"You got it." She zipped up her coat and slipped quickly through the door, closing it firmly behind her to keep whatever heat was emanating from the wood stove in the store. With a heavy heart, she drove slowly through the streets of the small town. Java would be open, but not for much longer. She stepped on the gas.

Spotting Winnie's car as only one of two cars in the small parking lot, Rachel smiled. Her friend was still there. Thank God. She needed to talk.

She opened the door and a wave of warm air smelling delightfully of rich coffee and cinnamon met her nose. Waving briefly at Winnie, she moved her gaze to the small glass case holding baked goods. Ah yes, there was one cinnamon bun left.

"Hello, stranger!" Winnie called, wiping down the counter for Rachel. "What'll ya have?"

"The usual. And that," she gestured toward the cinnamon bun, "grilled and buttered for Gramps."

A lone customer sitting in the corner got up and brought his bill to the counter. Winnie rang up the sale, wished him a good day, and then prepared a hot mocha latte and sliced the bun in half, buttering it and putting it on the grill.

She poured herself a cup of regular coffee, then leaned against the counter in front of Rachel.

"So, who is it this time? Brady at the hardware store?"

Rachel shook her head. "You'll never guess."

Winnie's mouth fell open. "No! Not him?"

Rachel nodded. "Him."

"Did you sleep with Deke Walsh?"

"No, silly!" Rachel said.

"Oh damn. I was going to ask for a blow-by-blow—" she said, then howled with laughter at her own joke. "No? Because you hate him?"

"No."

"Okay, then I bet you wanted to," Winnie said before taking another sip of coffee.

"Yeah, well, kinda," Rachel said, feeling heat in her cheeks.

"Why not? You've known him forever."

"He didn't want to. Didn't want to have a one-night stand. Said he doesn't know when he's coming back."

Winnie shrugged. "True that."

Rachel burst into tears. "I know. I know when he'll be back. For Gramps' funeral. Then I'll never see him again. I won't have Gramps and I won't have Rob. I'll have no one." Rachel folded her arms on the counter and put down her head.

Winnie came out from behind the counter and eased an arm around Rachel's shoulders. Rachel turned into the older woman's embrace. Confusion and mixed emotions caused laughter one minute and then tears the next.

"You're confused, honey. That's all. You'll always have a life here. So many people here love you."

Rachel cried until spent. Taking a big breath, she stepped back, picked up a napkin, and wiped her face. "I'm sorry, Winnie."

"Pish tush. Don't apologize," Winnie said, waving her hand.

"I didn't think he could still matter to me. But inside, he's the same Bobby."

"People don't change, Rach. Honestly. Inside they're the same. Even if they're famous on the outside."

"You're right." Rachel nodded and sat back down.

"Gotta get the bun," Winnie said and disappeared behind the counter.

Rachel gazed out the window at the frozen lake and the cozy little houses hugging the shore. The sight of Christmas lights made her smile. Pine Grove residents still rushed the holiday. She chuckled to herself, but she didn't mind. While folks awaited impatiently for December 25th, she had Hanukkah to celebrate and tide her over until the town lit up with holiday celebrations. Holiday spirit always cheered her up. This might be her last Christmas with Gramps.

Winnie returned with the bun wrapped and ready to go. Rachel finished her coffee.

"Yeah, I know. Christmas already?"

"Hanukkah first," Rachel said, pushing to her feet. Winnie handed her the bag, then grabbed her arm.

"In case this is Gramps' last Christmas, make it real jolly. Okay?"

Rachel smiled at her friend. "Okay. And thanks." She picked up the bag and opened the door, bracing for the cold air awaiting her.

ROB SLID INTO HIS WINDOW seat in first class and fastened his seatbelt. The flight attendant gushed over him, offering him drinks. He turned down everything. Alcohol couldn't fix the hurt in his heart. He looked into the blackness out the window. The one thing he'd been seeking had been in Pine Grove all along. If Rachel didn't hate him anymore. He'd left behind the only family he'd ever had. The warm feeling suffusing his body slowly dissipated, seeping out of him as the hours went by.

In Los Angeles, a limo awaited him at the airport. It dropped him at the front door of his obscenely huge home. As he looked at it—empty room after empty room—shame washed over him. What a waste! He thought about the kids he'd met at Thanksgiving and the rundown, broken, inadequate places they called home.

After his first three huge paychecks, he'd vowed to buy the biggest house he could afford. Now he realized all the show was simply a sham, a cover-up for the fact that his life was vacant, hollow, and meaningless. He had no one but himself to occupy this monstrosity.

He opened the front door. The echo of his footsteps in the foyer only repeated his solitary status. Loneliness engulfed him. He missed Rachel, Gramps, and even the kids. There was no laughter, no sound of any kind. Total silence blanketed him. He threw his keys on the small table. As he trudged through the garish foyer and up the ridiculously hideous ornate staircase, lugging his backpack to his room, his stomach turned at the over-the-top décor that simply wasted a ton of money and brought no beauty, no peace, no satisfaction.

He'd sell this house and buy something more modest. Hell, how many rooms did one man need, anyway? Exhausted, he ripped off his clothes and plopped naked onto the bed. First thing in the morning, he'd call a real estate agent and put his house on the market. Lacing his fingers behind his head, he stared at the ceiling and racked his brain, thinking of what he could do to improve Pine Grove with his profit. So physically tired he could hardly move, his mind got a second wind. Ideas raced through his brain. He lurched out of bed and pulled a pad and pen out of his desk drawer.

Back in bed, he let his mind go big.

"If I had a million dollars to spend, what would I do? How about five million?" he muttered to himself, jotting ideas down as quickly as they entered his brain.

With the profit from the sale of the house, he'd have enough money to do some of it. Maybe over time, he could add to it. For as long as he could keep his eyes open, he scribbled. Finally, exhaustion caught up with him. He fell sound asleep, pen in hand, pad propped up on the pillow next to him.

The next morning, the relentless Los Angeles sunshine woke him up at seven. Holy hell, he had to be at the studio at eight! The limo would be waiting in twenty minutes. He threw the pad on his desk and jumped into the shower. By the third blast from the limousine, Rob was racing out the door, sucking down orange juice and shoving his arm through the sleeve of his T-shirt.

At the studio, actors and the crew milled around on the set, waiting for Rob. He found Luke sitting alone in a corner. Tears ran down the boy's cheeks.

"Hey, buddy, what's wrong?"

Luke turned away from him.

"Come on. We're pals. You can tell me. I won't tell anyone."

The boy continued to look away. Rob touched his chin and gently turned his head to face him.

"My parents won't let me do travel baseball even though I made the team."

"Why not?"

"Because I have to do the next stupid movie, that's why."

"You mean, *The Emperor's Ring* with me?"

Luke nodded. "I don't want to be an actor anymore. I want to play baseball."

Rob nodded. "Oh, I see. Are you sure?"

"Yeah."

"And you've told your parents?"

"We had a big fight. I locked myself in my room."

Rob nodded. "Oh, one of those. I remember."

"Do you? Did you ever want something so bad?" The boy's eyes widened, pleading.

Did he ever want anything so bad? Hell yeah, like right now. He wanted to change places with Luke's father. That's what he wanted. But it would never happen. He doubted any of the women on his contact list would be interested in marriage and starting a family. If they didn't, Rob would be out of luck.

"Yeah. I have."

"So you get it?"

Rob chucked the boy on the shoulder. "I get it."

"What does it matter? You can't help me. No one can help me," Luke said, turning away to hide his tears. Luke put his finger to his lips. "Don't tell anyone."

"Okay."

"Promise?"

"I promise," Rob said.

Their conversation was interrupted by everyone gathering together for an announcement.

"Let's hustle. Be on time. Know your stuff. We can wrap in two weeks and be finished before Christmas if everyone does their part."

A cheer went up from the crew. Rob couldn't believe his ears. He was free for Christmas. Luke ran back to his mother. Rob headed for his dressing room. He couldn't stop smiling. With trembling fingers, he dialed.

Rachel answered.

"Don't change the sheets. I'm coming home for Christmas!"

Chapter Six

Rachel answered her phone. She could count the number of times she had been speechless in her life on the fingers of one hand. And this was one of them. It was Rob.

"I'm coming home for Christmas."

"What? Aren't you finishing the movie? What happened?"

He gave her the rundown, then paused. "Hey, it's okay...me coming home, right? I mean, it's your holiday. I didn't think..."

"Of course it's okay. It's more than okay!" Excitement bubbled up in her chest. She tamped it down as best as she could.

"It's just until January," he said. "New movie starts shooting sometime in January."

She couldn't stop smiling. "When are you arriving?"

"I need a couple of days to do stuff. Say Friday before Christmas? You're sure this is okay?"

"Of course it's okay. You said it. This is your home too."

"Don't tell Gramps? I want to surprise him."

"Might give him a heart attack."

"Oh. Never thought of that."

"It would be good for him to have that to look forward to. And to make plans for."

"Then tell him. First Christmas home in years."

"We'll make it memorable," she said.

"Gotta go. See you then."

"Right."

Rachel clicked off her phone. Could it be true? Was Rob really coming home for Christmas? Santa worked in mysterious ways.

"Oh my God, there's so much to do!" She jumped up from her chair.

"To do for what?" Gramps limped into the kitchen and opened a newspaper on the table. "Tea?"

"Sure." Rachel put on the kettle. "Rob's coming home for Christmas."

Gramps' head snapped up. "What? My hearing ain't so good. Did you say Bobby's coming home for Christmas?"

"Yes. And you have to start calling him Rob, Gramps. He'll be here the Friday before Christmas."

"Holy Christmas!" The old man pushed halfway to his feet before Rachel's hand on his shoulder eased him back down.

"Yeah. We've got a lot to do."

"Gotta find those ornaments Martha collected. They're around somewhere."

"I moved some of the Christmas stuff out to the barn last year."

"Those were in the attic, I think. I'll get 'em."

"No, no. You stay here. We've got to decorate the store," Rachel said.

"And the house."

Rachel frowned. "Gramps, you sold the house years ago. The store is the house."

"Oh yeah. Forgot."

The old man's grin spread from ear to ear. "My boy's coming home for Christmas. It's a miracle."

"You can say that again," Rachel mumbled under her breath. As happy as she was, a little part of her wondered why he'd be returning. He'd made it plain he'd moved on from dusty old Pine Grove. What did he want? She gave her head a little shake. She had to stop looking for the negatives in life. Hadn't she already dealt with a ton of bad things?

"Be happy, girl! He's coming home. Gonna be the best Christmas yet!" Gramps slammed his palm down on the table, making the teacups dance.

Rachel laughed. "Damn right, Gramps. Damn right!"

"Get a pencil and paper, Rach. We gotta make a list. I don't want to forget nothin'."

She pushed to her feet and rummaged through a drawer by the sink. Plucking out a pen and an old pad, she refreshed their tea, then joined him at the table.

"Got any more of them scones left?" he asked.

"One left. With your name on it." She fetched the confection and put it on a plate.

"Start writin', girl. Christmas ornaments," he said, breaking off a piece of the goody.

"Check."

"Tree."

"Oh yeah. A tree this year?"

"Yeah. No more decorating that wimpy little pine outside. Biggest tree we can get in here."

"Don't think I can carry something that big," she said, taking a sip of tea.

He placed his hand on her arm. "Don't have to. He'll be here. Rob'll be here. He can do it."

The thought of having someone big and strong to help with all the work at Christmas brought her tears of relief.

"Yep, that's right. You ain't gotta do it all by yourself this year." He turned a penetrating stare on her. "And if you play your cards right, you might have someone here to help you every year." The old man laughed, his eyes glistening with mischief.

Rachel waved him away. "Go on. None of that. He's got his own life. Plenty of women are a whole lot prettier and fancier than me."

Once again, Gramps wrapped his fingers around her forearm. "None of them are half the woman you are, sweetheart. If I'd been twenty years younger, I'd have married you myself."

"How about forty years younger?" She laughed.

A WEEK LATER.

With all the excitement about Rob coming home and Christmas, Rachel almost forgot about Hanukkah. This year it fell a couple of weeks before Christmas. Rachel climbed the stairs to the attic and searched for her special box with her menorah and candles in it. It was small, easy to overlook in that mess up there.

"Found it!" she said aloud. She tucked the rectangular box under her arm and tromped down the stairs.

"Whatcha makin' all that racket fer?" Gramps called from his room.

She entered the kitchen, set the box on the table, and went to the window. After carefully removing her plants from the windowsill, she sponged it off. The sound of Gramps' uneven gait met her ears. After opening the box, she looked up to spy him in the archway.

"That time already?" he asked, pulling out a chair.

"Yep."

"What color do you have this year?" he asked.

"I don't remember. Why don't you take a look?" She pushed the box toward him.

As she wiped off the menorah and placed it on the sill, she remembered a scene from a few years ago. She'd always lit the candles and said the Hanukkah prayers alone, but this one time Gramps showed up and asked, "Whatcha doin'?"

She'd explained.

"I wanna do it too."

"You do?"

"Yeah. You do my holiday, I wanna do yours." Hands on his hips, he clamped his jaw shut firmly and stared at her. There would be no dissuading him.

She chuckled at the memory. They'd agreed he could forego memorizing the prayers but could take a turn lighting the candles.

"Just one tonight," she said.

"This is a mess. You got too many colors in here," Gramps said, rummaging through the box.

"I like it like that. We can make different color combinations for each night."

Gramps snorted, coughed, then picked out two candles. "You only got two of these pink ones."

"Perfect for tonight. We'll have a matched set," she said, gently taking the slender candles from his grip.

"Won't have any after tomorrow. All mixed up."

"That's fine. God doesn't care what color they are, just that you light them and say the prayers."

"I s'pose. Seems kinda messy to me."

She set up the two candles and pulled a box of wooden matches out of a drawer by the sink. Gramps' hands were too shaky to use the match, but he could light the one for that day with the shamash, or helper, candle.

He limped over to the window and gave a nod. Rachel struck a match and lit the shamash. She recited the prayers and then touched Gramps' arm. He picked up the lit candle and used it to light the other candle. She steadied his hand with her own.

"There," she said, standing back. Gramps smiled. The darkness outside caused the burning candles to be reflected in the window.

"Tea?" she asked.

"Yep. Wait a minute," he said, hustling as fast as he could out of the room. He returned in a flash with a small package. "This came for you. I found it on the ground by the front door."

She raised her eyebrows as she took the parcel. It had had a rough trip. The wrapping was torn in places and dirty. Rachel opened it carefully. Wrapped in tons of bubble wrap was a small box and a card. The box read "*Encore Une Fois*".

Gramps looked over her shoulder. "What the hell does that mean?" he asked.

"It means one more time in French," she replied.

It was an exquisite small bottle of Coty perfume. She opened it and took a sniff, then offered it to Gramps.

"Never mind that. Who's it from?"

Rachel ripped open the card. It read "*Happy Hanukkah, Love, Rob*."

Emotion rose in her chest, stealing her words. She handed it to Gramps.

He beamed. "That's my boy. Real class act," he said.

She had to agree.

TWO WEEKS LATER. SATURDAY afternoon.

Rob called Barbara Holmes, his agent.

"Hey, Barbara, I'm going to New York on the red-eye Saturday night."

"To the city or that little hick town."

"To Pine Grove."

"Oh okay. Do they have cell service there?"

"They do."

"Good because I'm in final negotiations for your next movie. I'll need to reach you. I want this signed, sealed, and delivered right away. They want to start shooting right after the new year."

"Sounds good. I'll be around."

"Your movie's doing well. The new one will be a blockbuster too. We're in a strong position."

"Don't close the deal yet," he said.

"Oh? Why not?"

"There's something we have to discuss."

"Break it to me gently," she said.

"Well, it's about Luke..." he began.

"What about Luke?"

"I want him replaced," Rob said.

"What?"

"I won't do the movie with him."

"Why?"

"I can't say. Please just tell them to find someone else, okay?" Rob said.

"That's crazy. You and Luke have great chemistry."

"Yeah, I know. I can't say why. I promised. Trust me."

"You sure you wanna do this?" Barbara asked.

"Absolutely."

"Okay. It's your funeral," she said and ended the conversation.

Rob searched his closet for any cold-weather gear but didn't find any. Hell, he'd buy new stuff out there. After tossing underwear, toiletries, and two pairs of jeans into a backpack, he checked his watch. Limo was due in ten minutes. He scanned the three rooms he spent the most time in for anything he might have forgotten. Oh yes, the small, silver-framed photo of his parents. Gramps might like to see it. He tucked it tenderly into a safe place.

At the toot of a horn, he jumped, zipped up the bag, shrugged his old suede jacket on, and strode to the door. On the ride to the airport, he looked out the window. So many mansions, homes of the rich and famous. But he had no clue who his neighbors were.

He'd never been invited, even for drinks. Of course he'd never invited them either.

Nope, he had his own life. Skiing in Switzerland for Christmas and New Year's, or he was with his Swedish actress girlfriend outside of Stockholm. He'd been a world traveler. And an outsider. He'd stock up on generic gift items during the year, so he'd have something to take during the holidays when he'd stay with a girlfriend and her family or friends. What friends?

No, he didn't really have friends. He had acquaintances in the business. No invites for Christmas dinner, but he was sought after for New Year's Eve parties. A single, good-looking, wealthy guy in his thirties? Who wouldn't want him milling around their guests—hungry, single women—on New Year's?

He boarded the plane and took his seat in first class. Too excited to sleep, he looked out the window and mentally ticked off all the things he'd have this year. Snow, check. A big, real Christmas tree, check. Turkey or ham for Christmas dinner, check. Christmas cookies, check! Carols, music, presents, roaring fires...his mind spun so fast he got dizzy.

"Are you all right, Mr. Walsh?" The flight attendant put her hand on his arm, her brows knitted.

He wiped the silly grin off his face and turned innocent eyes to her.

"Thinking about Christmas is all."

She shot him a sexy smile. "Seems like Santa's already been good to you."

Ordinarily, he would have jumped on her invitation to chat and get cozy, but not tonight. Getting in touch with his inner child who craved a storybook Christmas, he simply could not let it go. "We'll see about that."

Her smile dropped. "Enjoy the flight," she said, walking away.

Favorite Christmas music played in his head as he closed his eyes.

"Visions of sugarplums danced in his head," he mumbled as sleep took him.

The announcement over the loudspeaker about fastening seatbelts and descending woke him. He yawned and did as the pilot asked. The plane flew into daylight. He'd pay for taking the red-eye flight, but the desire to get to Pine Grove and start creating central casting's version of the perfect Christmas caused him to throw caution out the window.

Since he only brought a backpack, he'd be first off the plane. He planned to buy a suitcase and winter clothes in Pine Grove. Checking his phone, he saw his limo was already there. Excitement bubbled up inside him. Adrenaline flowed, propelling him out the door of the plane and whizzing through the terminal to the pickup spot. There'd be plenty of time to catch up on sleep once he got to Pine Grove.

"Hi, Hank," Rob said. It was the same driver he'd had last time.

"Hi, Mr. Walsh. Back again so soon?"

"Please call me Rob. Yeah."

"Staying for Christmas?" The driver pulled away from the curb.

"I am." Rob could hardly sit still. He shifted his weight in the backseat.

"You're in for a treat. Christmas in Pine Grove is beautiful." Hank maneuvered the car deftly onto the highway.

"I remember."

"Traffic shouldn't be too bad at this hour. And we're going against it."

"Good. What time do you think we'll arrive?"

"My GPS says in about an hour forty-five."

Rob settled back in his seat, smiled, and closed his eyes.

SUNDAY MORNING. TWO weeks before Christmas.

It was eight o'clock. Even though the store wouldn't open until after lunch, Rachel was up, bustling about, dusting, arranging, rearranging, and fussing over displays. When Gramps entered from the back door, she started.

"You're jumpy today. What's up?" he asked, shuffling his way to the cash register.

"Nothing."

He grunted. "Bullshit."

"Time to update the inventory figures. You up for it?"

"Lemme at 'em. I love numbers," the old man said, rubbing his palms together.

Rachel smiled and shook her head. "No one would ever know you're not really a farmer at heart."

"Nope. It was Martha's thing. I kept the books."

She turned the laptop over to him. He hiked himself up on the stool and went to work. Rachel looked at her watch for the tenth time in fifteen minutes. She didn't want Gramps to know how she felt about Rob. First, he'd tease her, then he'd try to strong-arm Rob into a commitment or something, which was the last thing she wanted.

Not one to turn away help when she needed it, this was different. Now that she and Rob were speaking and had shared a kiss—a bone-melting one at that—she had to fend for herself. He had to come to her because he wanted her—on his own. Nothing less would work.

Being alone, except for Gramps, had become a habit. A comfortable one. Why rock the boat just to get your heart broken? She took the duster and headed for the holiday shelf.

As she worked, she spoke softly to herself. "I have one shot. One chance. Maybe never again. Be smart. Go for it. He may still be what you want."

Fear mixed with desire coursed through her veins. If she gave in and he dumped her, she'd be crushed. "Stop that!" she chided herself.

While the old man worked on the computer, Rachel rummaged around the crawl space that was their attic, looking for the store decorations. She pulled a cardboard box toward her and then sneezed. The cloud of dust threatened a sneezing fit. Quickly, she yanked down the box, located the second one, and closed the door.

Taking her time descending the stairs, she tried to remember exactly what decorations were in the boxes and which ones were in the barn. Would they be good enough for another year?

She hauled the boxes into the kitchen and plopped them on the counter. Opening the first one, she pulled out a dusty, fake garland. Some of the bogus pine needles had fallen off in the box. It looked scruffy.

"Not sure this will last another season."

Gramps looked up and waved his hand. "Throw it out. Throw 'em all out. I've put aside some money. Let's get all new decorations for the store."

Rachel's eyes widened. "Really?"

"Yep. It's about time. We're a proud general store. We've got to strut our stuff."

"Exactly how much did you have in mind to allocate for decorations?" She cocked an eyebrow.

"Don't know. You and Rob decide. Just give me the bill."

"I'll put it on the debit card."

"Better make it the credit card. I've spent the money in the checking account on inventory."

She glanced out the window at the thermometer nailed up by the back door. It read twenty-five degrees. She shivered. "Okay. Done. Time to see what's squirreled away in the barn," Rachel said, shoving the boxes into the storage room and reaching for her down jacket.

The sound of tires crunching on the gravel driveway interrupted her. She rushed to the window. The toot of a horn signaled the arrival of a limousine. Rob waved. Rachel didn't bother to wave back. She made a beeline for the door.

"Rob's here!"

She flew through the store, yanking her jacket over one arm. He exited the car, dropped his backpack, and took her in his arms. Burying her nose in his shoulder, she inhaled his scent—all man with a touch of pine. How perfect! He even smelled a bit like Christmas.

When he let go, he lowered his mouth to hers for a deep, probing kiss, sending heat all the way to her toes.

Gramps had made his way down the stairs. "Enough of that. Get over here. Give this old man a hug."

With a wink at Rachel, Rob did as he was told.

"Glory be, boy! You can't run around here dressed like that! In your fancy California clothes? Hell no. You'll freeze your balls off."

Rachel looked him up and down.

"I don't have any winter clothes," Rob said.

"You've come to the right place," Gramps said, throwing an arm around his grandson's waist. "Rach, get a couple of those flannel shirts. And the heaviest jacket we've got."

Chapter Seven

By the time they got Rob outfitted and served lunch, afternoon shadows crept in.

"So, when do we get started on Christmas?" Rob asked as he stacked soup bowls and carted them to the sink.

"I'm gonna lie down," Gramps said. "You kids take care of it." He shoved the paper under his arm and limped off to his room.

"We should go through the boxes of decorations for the store and see what's worth saving."

"Okay."

They tromped down the stairs and into the storage room. Rob rolled up his sleeves, grabbed them, and hauled 'em up the stairs. Rachel followed.

"Put them here," she said, indicating the kitchen table. He set them down. One by one she pulled out dusty wreaths, scrawny swag, red, silver, and gold balls, once shiny, that had lost their luster, and mistletoe with berries whose red paint had peeled off.

"This is pathetic. You used this to decorate the store? Are people here blind? Who can get in the spirit with moldy old crap like this?" Rob sat back.

"It isn't moldy."

"Yeah? I bet it is." He pushed to his feet, grabbed the boxes, and strode to the back door. After jerking it open, he loped to the massive garbage cans and stuffed the old boxes in an empty one.

"There. Problem solved," he said, rubbing his hands together.

Rachel stood in the doorway, hands on hips, staring. "Really? So what are we going to do for decorations now, genius?"

Rob checked his watch. "Stores are open late this time of year, right?"

"Uh, yeah. So?"

"Where are the car keys?"

Rachel pulled the ring out of her pocket. He snatched it from her and grabbed her hand. "Come on. Let's go."

"Where?"

"I don't know. Do they still have Mason's in Oak Bend?"

"Yeah."

"They always had the best stuff."

"And who's paying?" She raised her eyebrows.

"I've got this," he said, opening the passenger door for her.

She yanked the keys from his grasp. "No way. I drive my car. Get in."

He gave a short bow, then followed her instructions.

She pulled into a space near the entrance. More cars seemed to be leaving than arriving. After all, it was dark and almost six. The sign on the door said, "Open 'til 9 p.m."

Without a word, the couple entered the store. Rachel took charge of a cart.

"Oh no. Man pushes cart," Rob said, nudging her out of the way.

"Okay, okay. Go all Tarzan on me. You can push the damn cart."

"You're pretty grumpy for Christmas shopping," he said.

"I'm Jewish, remember? This stuff doesn't come naturally to me," she said. "By the way, thanks for the perfume."

"You got it? Good. I wasn't sure they could deliver out here."

"It's not Mars, you know," she said.

"I remember you and your brother used to come over before Christmas to eat my mother's cookies and gawk at our tree."

"So?"

"I even saw you rearrange a few ornaments."

She raised her hand. "I plead the Fifth."

Rob grinned. "Come on. Where's the good stuff?"

"Back of aisle four, I think," Rachel said.

"And you know this how?" He cocked an eyebrow.

Rachel felt her cheeks color. "I remember from the last time I was here."

"Yeah, sure," Rob said, shaking his head. He directed the cart toward aisle four, and they proceeded in silence.

Canned Christmas music played softly over the loudspeaker. Rob whistled along to Burl Ives "Holly Jolly Christmas."

When Rachel moved closer, he smelled something good, like lilacs in springtime. But it was winter. He leaned down, his nose almost touching her neck, and took a stronger sniff. It was coming from her—damn.

"What? What?" She swatted at him.

"You smell good. Must be 'Encore Une Fois," he said.

"How many ways do you think you can embarrass me?"

"I dunno. Maybe a dozen?" He smiled.

"Look! It's Deke. Deke Walsh! In person!" a woman shrieked. She ran over, dragging her teenage daughter along. She gushed over him. Before long, everyone in the store crowded around. He smiled and signed autograph after autograph. Rachel cooled her heels in the corner, waiting.

When the last person finished pumping his hand and tucking the autograph into her purse, he sighed. "Sorry." He resumed pushing the cart slowly down the aisle.

"I know, I know. The price of fame. Come on, Brad Pitt, let's go."

"Oooh. Jealous?" He cocked an eyebrow.

"In your dreams. I wouldn't want to be famous for anything."

"Really? Most people would give their right arm to change places with me."

"Yeah? Well, I'm not one of 'em."

Rob stopped to face her. "Exactly what do you want, Rachel?"

"What's on my Christmas list?"

"Okay, if you want to put it that way. Yeah." He couldn't keep the impatience out of his voice.

"First, I want your grandfather to get better. And I want the store fixed up, back to the way it used to be. And I want to own the little cottage, so I can decorate it the way I want. Deer heads are not my idea of great decor. I want steady work. To earn a living. To stop worrying about money."

"Is that all?"

"The rest is personal and none of your business. Can we move on?" She nudged the cart.

"You are my business," he said, stopping the cart.

"Let's get one thing straight. You are here to give your grandfather his dying wish—to have a couple of lousy holidays with his grandson. Not for me. Not because I want you here. You're just a thorn in my backside. I'm putting up with you for Gramps. Just so we understand each other."

Rob stepped back and raised his palm. "I get it. I get it."

"I hope you do. Now, can we get those stupid decorations and get home?"

"Aye, aye." He pushed the cart a little faster as they approached aisle four.

RACHEL BIT HER LIP. What a liar she was! Sure, she'd dragged Rob back to Pine Grove for Gramps, but for her too. She had to know if he'd help. Weary of pinching every penny until it screamed, she needed relief. He needed to step up to the plate where his grandfather was concerned. Pour some money into the old broken-down store so they could sell it when Gramps passed. And help fix it up and put it on the market. And be there, just be there to hold her hand as she watched her whole world disappear.

But she never truly believed he would. Still, she'd give him one last chance to be a mensch and do the right thing. So far, the jury was out as to his shouldering much of the burden. Things were heading in the right direction, but she was too afraid to hope.

He pulled up short in front of a display of colored balls. "What's your favorite color?"

"I don't know. I'm Jewish. What do I know about Christmas decorations?"

"Don't give me that BS. Haven't you decorated the store for the last umpteen years?"

She shifted her weight from foot to foot. "Maybe. Yeah. Okay I have."

"Figured. You were doing it when I still lived here. I saw you," he said.

"You were spying on me?"

"No. Just keeping an eye on the store."

"I bet you loved seeing the pathetic little Jewish girl struggling to figure out how to unravel a ton of lights and wrestle with swag."

Rob stepped right up to her, nose to nose. "I didn't see a pathetic girl."

"Oh?" She rested her hands on her hips.

"Yeah. I saw a smart, funny, cute little girl struggling to help two old men put up the decorations. Making them just so."

Her eyes filled.

He continued. "The little girl who struggled with unruly hair and being short. Still got it done." He ran his fingers through her soft, curly locks. "You tamed the hair. Looks nice. Real nice."

She melted against him, hiding her face in his shoulder. "I didn't know anyone noticed. You never said anything."

"I didn't get it...until now."

He wrapped his arms around her. She let go of the tight grip on her emotions, and her body shook slightly with sobs. He rubbed her back.

"Don't you know you were way above the others?" he asked.

"No," came a tiny sound, muffled by his flannel shirt.

"Well, you were. And you still are. If you'd just drop the snarky shit and be real."

She pushed away from him and tilted her head back. Her red-rimmed eyes searched his face. "You mean it, don't you?"

"Of course I do." He pulled a handkerchief out of his back pocket and shoved it in her hand. "Come on. We've got stuff to do. What colors do you want?" He stood back and gestured to the display.

Rachel wiped her face with the hanky. She sniffled once, then looked over at the display.

"I've always had a thing for blue and silver."

"Then blue and silver it is." Rob loaded a couple of packages of balls into the cart. He put his arm around her shoulders and kissed the top of her head. "Let's make this the biggest and best Christmas yet."

She smiled and hugged his middle.

They picked out fake swag for the front door and two wreaths, one for the front door of the store and one for the cottage door. Rob added four packages of colored lights.

"Gotta have a couple of nutcrackers," he said, squeezing two into the overflowing cart. He turned the corner and faced a big display of individual ornaments of various sizes.

"Okay. What's your pleasure?" He nodded toward shelf-after-shelf of brightly colored ornaments, and white angels, dogs of various breeds, and Santas in five different sizes.

"How many?" she asked.

"Whatever you want."

"Really?" she asked, going up on tiptoe for a moment.

"Really."

She pushed up to kiss his cheek, then approached the display. "This may take a little time."

"I'm not going anywhere," he replied.

When they finished loading all the bags into the back of the SUV, Rob opened the passenger door for Rachel and then climbed behind the wheel. "Okay if I drive?"

She nodded. "Anyone willing to shell out five hundred bucks for decorations has earned the right to drive my car."

Her stomach rumbled.

"Just what I was thinking." He glanced at his watch. "It's dinnertime. Let's check on Gramps and if he's still sleeping, I'll take you to Homer's for dinner. We can get a burger to-go for Gramps."

"You don't have to."

"Stop saying that. You're really beginning to piss me off."

"Okay, okay. Thank you."

They pulled up in front of the rickety old general store and tiptoed inside. There was no need to go upstairs because the sound of Gramps' snoring was loud enough to be heard at the front door. Rob motioned to Rachel, and the couple slowly closed the door and jumped into the car.

The winterish wind whipped up over frozen Cedar Lake, stinging her face as she approached the restaurant. On the walk from the car to the restaurant, Rachel's cheeks felt frozen. Rob opened the door, and she scooted into the welcome warmth.

"Something near the fire. She's half frozen," Rob said.

Homer nodded and gave them the table adjacent to the roaring fire. Rachel held her hands close to the heat.

"I'll drive. What do you want to drink?" he said.

She ordered a glass of red wine, and Rob ordered a beer.

When she cocked an eyebrow at him, he said, "One won't be a problem."

Homer brought their drinks and then they ordered burgers and fries.

"I can't believe you spent five hundred bucks on decorations. This'll probably be the last year we decorate. After Gramps goes, the place will be sold."

"Sold?" Rob raised his eyebrows.

"Yeah. Ya think? I mean, are you going to walk away from your fabulous career to run a rundown general store that's losing money?"

"When you put it like that..."

"What other way is there to put it? It's the truth. I'm so damn tired of pretending."

"Pretending."

"Yeah. I lie to Gramps because if I tell him the truth, he gets depressed. Then he yells at me for wrecking the store. Says I'm not doing enough to drum up business or not dusting the shelves. I'm sick of it."

Rob took her hand in his. "It's been rough?"

Tears welled in her eyes. "You have no idea."

"I'm sorry." He slipped his arm over her shoulders, drawing her close. She nestled into his shoulder. "You shouldn't have to do that alone."

She clung to him for a moment. "Thanks," she said, sniffling and wiping her eyes. "It won't be for much longer."

HER WORDS ECHOED IN his heart. Gramps was failing. There was no doubt about that. Soon there would be no holiday traditions to come home to. Not that he'd been there for all the holidays. Somehow in his mind, just knowing he could go back and have everything the same before he became Deke Walsh soothed the rough edges of his life.

The sting behind his eyes reminded him of what Gramps meant to him. She was right. Soon this would be gone, and he'd be cut loose, floating with no home base, nothing to come back to, no family, no traditions, no safe harbor. He'd be just Rob. A shudder shot through him.

Rachel raised her eyebrows. "You okay?"

Emotion closed his throat. No. He absolutely wasn't okay. How did this happen? How did life get away from him? When did he forget what was important and ride the fleeting tide of celebrity into an emotional vacuum?

"Rob?" Rachel squeezed his arm.

Her touch bounced him out of the downward spiral of reality. "What?" he croaked out.

She grabbed his chin and turned his face toward hers. Her eyes searched his. Then she moved closer and pressed her lips to his for a brief moment.

In a low voice, she whispered. "Don't worry. You'll always have a home here. With me."

"You'll find someone. Go off, get married, and have a dozen kids."

She laughed. "Uh, no."

"Why not?"

Rachel pulled away. "Wherever I am, there will always be a place at my table for you."

Rob pulled her close and closed his mouth down on hers for a passionate kiss. As his control slipped, a loud male voice cleared his throat.

"Burgers anyone?" Homer stood holding two plates loaded with burgers and luscious-looking fries.

The words penetrated the fog of desire circulating in Rob's head. He let go of Rachel and sat back. Slowly, she opened her eyes. He saw astonishment mixed with lust. He grinned.

"Right here, Homer. Boy, am I hungry."

"Yeah. I figured," Homer said, grinning as he placed the dishes on the table.

Rob picked up his burger and took a big bite. Rachel munched on a fry. She watched him from under hooded eyes.

"What?" he asked.

"What the hell was that?"

"What?"

"That kiss," she said.

"It was the kiss to end all kisses," he said, laughing.

"But me?"

"Are you kidding? You're the most real person I've ever met. In all the years since we were kids, you haven't changed. You haven't become cold. You still care for others like you did when you were a kid."

"What do you mean?"

"When you were little, you put out leftover food for the crows. A bowl of milk for the feral cat. You bandaged the knees of the local kids and gave away half your Halloween candy to kids who didn't have any. It's who you were. And who you still are."

"You remember that stuff?"

"Are you kidding? If you ran in the world of phonies and fakes, like I do, you'd remember every unselfish act you ever saw." He took another bite of his burger, then picked up two fries.

When they finished eating, Rob paid the check. They placed the to-go burger safely in the back seat of the car and drove back to the store.

Gramps was awake.

"Where the hell have you been?" he asked, rubbing his eyes.

"We bought new decorations, Gramps. And food."

"Food? Good. I'm hungry."

"A burger from Homer's," Rob said, setting the bag on the table.

"What kind of decorations did you get?" the old man asked as he tucked into the food.

Rob and Rachel schlepped bag after bag of decorations up the stairs. They showed everything to Gramps.

He chuckled. "Place is gonna look mighty fine when you've got all these doodads up. Be a big boost for business."

Rachel glanced at Rob, who met her stare.

"You'll see, Rachel. We'll have the best Christmas sales ever!" Gramps took the last bite and washed it down with tea. "Get going. We don't have time to waste. Christmas is almost here. I got my radio program. Thanks for the burger," Gramps said, pushing to his feet. He swayed for a moment but grabbed a chair before Rob could get to him. "I'm all right. Stop fussing. Just get it done."

Rob found Christmas music on his phone. The pair set to dressing the old store in bright, colorful, shiny Christmas decorations. They worked together seamlessly. First, they set the fake tree in the corner. Then they hung swag around the front door. They strung lights around doorways and colorful balls around windows and put a battery-powered candle in each window.

"Gramps is gonna love this. Let's get him."

Eagerly, Rob took the stairs two at a time. When he rushed into the room, he saw his grandfather snoozing in his chair. Rob switched off the radio.

"Help me get him into bed," he said to Rachel, who stood in the doorway.

She pulled down the bedclothes as Rob gently picked up the frail old man and undressed him.

"He'll wake up to Christmas in the store," Rachel said. "He'll love it!"

When they finished, they went back downstairs. Rob stopped at the front door to take a breath.

"Relax, we're not done yet," Rachel said.

"Your place?"

"Yep."

He picked up the remaining bags of decorations and headed for the door. "Let's go."

Grinning, she held it open. Together, they hurried through the freezing night air to the small cottage at the back of the property. Fumbling with the keys with frozen fingers, she managed to open the lock.

"Quick, I'll light a fire," she said, rushing to the fireplace.

Rob put down the bags. "Got any wine?"

She gestured to a cabinet. He popped open the cork and poured two glasses.

"Where should we start?" he asked.

Chapter Eight

Rachel knelt in front of the small fireplace, lit rolled newspaper and stuck it up the chimney to create a draft. Then shoved the burning paper under her little pile of logs. They caught quickly.

Rob turned on the Christmas music on his phone and rested it on the small dining table next to the bags of decorations.

"Not a lot of room here. Where do you want this stuff?"

Rachel moved over next to him and opened each bag. After peeking inside, she stood back, crossed her arms over her chest and surveyed the room. Rob handed her a glass of wine.

"Sit. Be the director," Rob said. He put his hands on her upper arms and eased her down into a chair. He pulled out each item and asked her where to put it. She sat there, sipping wine and giving instructions.

Rachel chuckled. "I guess one thing you've learned in your shiny career is how to take direction."

"Yep."

They finished the living room and kitchen, then moved to the bedroom.

"These last ones go in here?" he asked.

"Yeah. Only place left," she said.

"The wreath?"

"That's for the front door."

"Got it." Rob took the wreath and a hammer to the front door. In the bedroom, Rachel grabbed a string of lights and climbed up on a chair. Rob barged through the door, knocking into her. She went flying, landing on the bed, flinging the lights behind her.

"Oh my God! I'm so sorry! Are you okay?" He knelt on the bed.

Rachel reached up and grabbed his shirt, pulling him down on top of her. "Now I am."

In a moment of silence, the faint strains of Christmas music wafted through the air.

Rob's eyes lit up. "Merry Christmas," he said, then lowered his mouth to hers. Rachel softened under his kiss. She wound her arms around his neck. When his tongue pressed against the seam of her lips, she opened. Slowly, he took possession.

He pulled up on his knees and increased the pressure. Heat sparked, warming the very air around them. Rachel opened her knees, cradling him between them. As their hips met, passion flew through her veins. Her skin grew sensitive, longing for his touch.

He pushed up. "Rachel," he moaned, kissing her neck.

Her breath quickened as his lips lit a hot trail down her flesh. Rob opened her shirt with one hand and kissed down until her bra got in the way. He reached up and squeezed her breast, and she closed her eyes and moaned.

"Yes," she whispered, arching her back.

He reached around with one hand, popping the garment open, and then shoved the strap and shirt off her shoulder, baring her breast to his eyes and mouth.

"Sweet," he said, lowering his lips to her peak. He cradled her breast with one hand and rolled over on his side, pulling her over. Lying on their sides facing each other, their eyes met.

"I want you," he said, reaching up, losing his fingers in her silky locks.

At the sound of the words she'd longed to hear for what seemed like forever, she whispered, "I want you too."

She fussed with the buttons on his flannel shirt. When they were open, she tugged his tee up from his pants, slipping her hand underneath. Closing her eyes, she glided her fingers through the hair on his chest, then rested her palm on his warm skin. His muscles moved under her touch, sending desire straight to her core. She needed him inside her right now.

"Please..." she whispered.

Rob pushed up on his knees. He stripped her shirt off and tugged her pants down to her knees. She kicked off her shoes, and he peeled her socks down and off, then ripped off the pants. Sitting back on his haunches, he stared. She covered herself the best she could with her arms.

"Stop staring. Just do it."

"No way," he said, coaxing her arms away.

"What do you mean?"

"I've been dreaming about this body and I'm going to look at it as much as I want."

She pushed up on her elbows, her brows drawn in mock anger. "Yeah? Says who?"

"Says me," he said, his hand on her shoulder, easing her back down. "You're beautiful, Rachel. Inside and out."

She felt a blush steal into her face. "Stop."

"Why? Why can't you take a compliment?"

"Because it's not real. You date hot women, poised, sexy, and famous. Not like me."

"That's right. They don't come close to you."

"Yeah right."

"Right," he said, leaning down to kiss her. "You're real. Smart, hard-working, caring, funny, and generous. You're everything I'm not."

She laughed. "Right!"

"I mean it. I've led a shallow existence for a long time. You're the only real thing in my life. You and Gramps. And he won't be here much longer."

Rachel raised her eyebrows. "You expect me to believe this? You don't have to give me a line to get me into bed. I'm already here."

"I would never do that to you. It's the truth."

"Deke Walsh isn't really you. Underneath his shiny surface lives Bobby Walsh, the world's most decent guy. My hero."

Rob laughed. "I'm nobody's hero."

Rachel reached up to palm his cheek. "You're mine."

For a moment, Rob's eyes filled. He blinked back the tears, bowed his head, and kissed her breast. "You make too much of nothing."

She yanked his chin up. "It's not nothing to me. And you're not nothing."

Their gazes met. "That's the nicest thing anyone's ever said to me," he whispered.

"That's a shame. How about this? I love you," she said. Yep, it simply slipped out of her mouth. She covered her lips with both hands. "Oh my God," she said.

His eyes filled again. "I love you too, Rachel."

"You don't have to say that just because I did."

"I know. I mean it. You're amazing. Now shut up. I'm in pain."

She glanced down to see a major erection straining against his jeans, needing to be freed. Rachel squelched her desire to laugh. She unsnapped his pants and pulled down the zipper. He pushed to his knees and shoved the pants and boxers down at once. An erection like Rachel had never seen before sprang loose.

"Holy shit!" Her eyes grew wide.

"Yeah. I'm hung," he said, chuckling as he shucked his clothes.

Rachel's gaze roamed over his body. Damn, it was perfect. Broad shoulders, muscled chest and belly, slim hips, meaty thighs, and strong arms.

"Do I pass inspection?"

"Holy crap. Are you kidding? I'm gonna come just looking at you."

"Don't do that!" He raised his brows, then dove down, spreading her legs and nestling his face in her core. When his tongue touched her hot flesh, she arched her back. "Holy shit! Oh God. Oh, Bobby!"

"Rob," he said, lifting his head for a moment.

"Okay, okay. Rob. Rob. Damn!" She closed her eyes.

He swirled his tongue over her flesh, then flattened it against her clit and circled. Rachel gripped the bedclothes. Her breathing sped up. She squeezed her eyes shut and panted while he worked his magic.

"Oh God!" she moaned.

Then he stopped and inserted one finger and then another inside her.

"Please, oh God, please. Do it. Do it!"

"Just a sec." He reached over and snatched a condom from his pants pocket. She stared at his erection and folded her fingers around it. Bending over, she closed her lips over his dick and moved her mouth up and down a couple of times. He put his hand on her head.

"Stop!"

"Really?" She sat up.

"Yeah. I won't be able to hold it," he said.

"Okay." She closed her hand around his erection again. "Velvet-covered steel," she said.

He laughed. "Now you're a writer!" He unrolled the condom over his dick and got into position. But first, he went back to swirling his tongue over her.

"If you want to know if I'm ready? I was ready ten years ago."

He laughed, then mounted her, rubbing his dick up and down her slippery slit before gently inserting it.

She gasped.

"Are you okay?" he asked, his brows coming together.

"It's been a long time."

"You're tight as hell."

"Out of practice," she said, breathing heavily.

"We'll have to change that," he mumbled, slowly pushing himself into her until he filled her completely.

Again, she drew in a deep breath.

"Are you sure you're okay? I'm not hurting you, am I?"

"No, I'm okay." She bit her lip gently.

"We need to get you used to this."

"Lovely." She smiled and took a few deep breaths, relaxing. The initial discomfort melted away, and they became a perfect fit. She wound her arms around his chest and drew him closer. He bent and kissed her hair, then started a slow in and out.

Her nipples tightened and heat grew inside her. He dropped his head down until his mouth was level with her ear. She felt his warm, moist breath.

"Oh God, Rachel. It's so good. Damn. Sooooo good," he muttered as his hips moved faster.

Moving with him, she opened her mouth and latched onto the fleshy part of his shoulder near his neck. He tasted good. She ran her nails up and down his back.

"That's awesome. Don't stop," he said.

As he increased his speed, an orgasm built up inside her, like a small tornado, picking up speed quickly. She let go of his shoulder and groaned into his neck. In an instant, the heat grew too unbearable. Tension ratcheted up inside her until it reached a breaking point. Her body exploded into a massive orgasm, and she groaned loudly, muttering unintelligible words. She closed her eyes, her hips, on automatic pilot, rocked with his.

Suddenly, his body stiffened. He grunted and swore as his hips gave one hard thrust and stopped. He clutched her shoulders, burying his face in her neck.

Heavy breathing accompanied the Christmas tunes drifting into the bedroom from Rob's phone.

He pushed up on his arms and looked down. Then he bent down and kissed her nose. "I love you, Rachel."

She ran her palm down his cheek. "And I love you too."

"I've never had sex like that before," he said, easing his dick out.

"What do you mean?"

"I mean, it's usually been kinda quick and kinda cold. Not this time." He shook his head. "It was all about you. Doing it with you."

Her eyes filled and tears ran out of the corners and down into her hair. He wiped one away with his thumb.

"Don't cry, honey. It's all good."

"It was amazing." She leaned up to plant a sweet kiss on his lips.

"For me too." He smiled, pushing to his feet and hightailing it to the bathroom.

Rachel rolled onto her side and pulled up the blankets to warm her skin, which went cold after he left.

When he returned, he slipped on the flannel shirt and turned off his phone.

"It's late," he said, climbing in beside her.

Rachel leaned over and turned out the light. Rob folded her into his embrace. They rolled over on their sides. He spooned her. She raised his palm to her lips for a moment.

"Good night, Rob."

"Good night, honey."

Smiling, Rachel slipped into a peaceful sleep.

COLD AIR ON HIS FACE woke Rob early. He pulled the blankets up over his shoulder and snuggled closer to his sleeping lover. Sunlight gently crept over the frozen world outside. He exhaled and swore he could see his breath.

"Jesus," he said quietly. He buttoned his flannel shirt and stole across the ice-cold floor to the bathroom. After putting on boxers, he rubbed his hands together, placed logs in the fireplace and her small wood stove, then looked around for any other heat source. He spied a small space heater, plugged it in, and got back into bed. Rachel rolled over, opened her eyes, smiled, then closed them again.

It was six-thirty. As heat slowly chased away the frostiness in the air, Rob grew sleepy. He inched over to Rachel and drew her naked body up against his. A sense of peace flowed through him, and he drifted off.

The soft caress of lips on the back of his neck woke him. He grinned. No one had ever woken him up that way before. The few women he'd actually spent the night with were dressed and halfway out the door by the time he woke up. The rest were a nameless, faceless blur.

"Hey you," Rachel whispered.

He turned to face her. Sporting a flannel robe that fell open, she glowed with the satisfaction of a well-loved woman. He reached up and threaded his fingers through her soft hair.

"Good morning, beautiful."

She laughed. "You're funny."

"Stop. Stop, Rachel. You are beautiful."

"No, you're beautiful," she said.

Rob pulled her on top of him and wrestled her underneath. "No, YOU'RE beautiful."

She giggled and tussled with him until they got so tangled in the sheets they couldn't move.

"Stay just like you are," he said, reaching down to his pants. Like magic another condom appeared. Scooting to the bottom of the bed, he flattened his tongue against her core. She bucked and whimpered. After sliding on the condom, he mounted her. After last night, it was easier to get inside her. One good push and she was his again.

The warmth of her love surrounded him. Oblivious to the chill lingering in the air, his body heated, sweat beaded on his forehead as he pumped into her. Tension grew, and his balls tightened. He increased his speed, but he needed to get her off first.

"Oh my God!" she yelled as her hips bucked, then joined his rhythm.

He grinned. Yeah, now it was his turn. He loosened his control and let his climax overtake him. The power of it almost knocked him off the bed. He howled, then collapsed on her, panting, hiding his face on her shoulder. The combination of fierce desire and heart-melting emotion had sapped his energy, leaving him totally wrung out.

"Some people just say 'good morning,' ya know," she said, pushing up on her elbow, a twinkle in her eye.

He palmed her cheek, brushed his lips against hers, and replied, "Yeah? Well, some people don't wake up to you."

She backed up and slid off the bed to her feet. "Come on. I've got bacon."

"Oh no," he said, following her. "We're going out to breakfast." He trotted off to the bathroom. When he came out, the smell of fresh coffee met his nose.

"One cup here. Then off to The Cozy Café," Rachel said.

"Time for a shower first. Come on." He held out his hand.

"Really?"

"Save water, shower with a friend," he said, winking.

She laughed, slipped off her robe, and joined him.

ROB OPENED THE DOOR and Rachel scooted through. Was everyone staring at her? Did they know about last night and this morning? Or was she just glowing like an incandescent bulb? Maybe it was the gust of frigid air that drew their attention. That must be it.

"Good morning, kids," Laura Dailey said. "Coffee?" She raised the round, fat, steaming glass carafe.

"Sounds great," Rob said. "Where should we sit?"

"Anywhere," Laura said.

Rob took Rachel's hand and led them to a table by the window.

"Might be a mite drafty there today," Laura said, following them to the table. "It's twenty outside."

"It's fine," Rachel said. Usually sensitive to the cold, she had no idea the temperature had dropped so low. Rob held out Rachel's chair. She sat down, and feeling eyes were still on her, cast her gaze to the silverware. Couldn't be the cold air inside, could it?

Laura turned over each mug on the empty table, one at a time, and filled them with the hot brew.

"I'll be right back with menus," she said, bustling off.

When Rachel dared to raise her gaze to the counter, she spied Laura whispering something in the ear of the other waitress, who looked over at Rachel's table and giggled.

"Everyone is staring," Rachel whispered.

"Yeah," Rob said, adding milk to his coffee from the small pitcher on the table. He raised the mug to his lips.

"You may be used to it, but I'm not." She added milk to her beverage and took a sip.

"Get used to it. When you're with me, it happens a lot."

"Swell." She raised her eyes to his.

Laura returned. With pen poised over a pad, she said, "Whatcha having?"

Rob gestured to Rachel.

"A couple of scrambled eggs and bacon."

"Aw, come on. Have something fancy," he said.

"Like what?" Rachel perused the menu.

"Uh..." Rob studied it. "Eggs benedict?"

Rachel laughed. "Okay. I'll have eggs benedict."

"And a side of home fries," Rob added.

"And you, Deke?" Laura asked.

"I'll have a short stack of pancakes, three scrambled eggs, bacon, sausage, and whole wheat toast," he said.

Rachel's eyes widened. "Really?"

"Great lovin' always makes me hungry," he said with a grin and took her hand between his.

Laura laughed. "Breakfast of lovers! Got it." She scooted away.

Rachel touched her cheek. Could her skin simply combust?

"You're embarrassing me," Rachel said. "Not everyone in Pine Grove needs to know what we did last night."

"And this morning," he added.

"What we did, we do, is our private business."

"Not when you're in the movies. The press follows me around. They write about everything I say and do. Even the stuff I buy. If I buy one brand of jeans and the press gets wind of it, sales of that brand spike."

"Really? Do you like being so public?"

"No, but I'm used to it. It's the price I pay for success."

"I s'pose."

Laura breezed by to refill their coffee mugs. "You two an item?" she asked Rob.

"An item? Laura, this is the 21st century," Rachel replied.

"Yes, Laura, we are," Rob said, picking up Rachel's hand and bringing it to his lips. "I've finally come to my senses."

Despite her age, Laura giggled. "You got that right, Rob. She's a gem. A home-grown peach."

Rachel snatched her hand away. "What are you doing? That's gonna be in the papers before morning."

"So what?" He sat back in his seat and narrowed his eyes. "Am I not good enough for you?"

Rachel laughed. "Now you're a comedian?"

Rob cleared his throat and stared at Laura.

She shifted her weight. "Oh. I guess you want some privacy," and she hurried back to the kitchen.

Rob leaned forward. "Look, Rachel. I know you're way smarter than me. Educated. Know all the fancy words and math, and you're a great speller. Don't think I don't see it."

"Don't tell me you feel second rate to me? That's a laugh. I've always been way below you. Always so far under your radar, I was subterranean."

"See? There you go using big words." He sat back and finished his coffee.

"You're in a different stratosphere, Rob. Admit it."

"There you go again! Your fancy words are pissing me off."

She took his hand in both of hers. "I don't mean to. I've always felt so beneath you."

"And I've always felt so beneath you," he replied, pulling his hand away.

The sound of Laura's footsteps caused the lovers to draw back and dummy up. She smiled and placed plate after plate on their table until there was no more room. Then she scraped the hash browns onto Rachel's plate. "Bon appétit!" she said and disappeared into the kitchen.

Rob added butter and maple syrup to his flapjacks.

"You were beneath me...last night," Rob said with a chuckle before filling his mouth with pancake.

"Very funny," Rachel said, making a face.

They ate in silence for a while. Rachel mulled over what to say next. Should she be totally honest with him? If not now, when? She washed down a mouthful of eggs with coffee.

"Okay, here goes," she said softly to herself, then she took a deep breath. "I've always loved you. I loved you when you were Bobby and I was a little kid."

Rob stopped his fork in midair and stared. "You did?"

Unable to speak, Rachel simply nodded.

"Even when you were a kid, and I was mean to you?"

"Yes." She picked up a piece of his toast.

"Even in middle school when I wouldn't talk to you?"

"Yes."

"Why?" He stabbed a potato.

"Because you cared enough to protect me. You were there when I needed you."

"That's all?"

"Isn't that enough?" she asked, cutting into her eggs benedict.

"And after I left town?"

"I followed your career. Read every story about you in every gossip column. Watched gossip TV so I could see what you were doing."

"You were obsessed?"

"I guess so. But I loved Bobby, not Deke. The real person, not the image."

"But I treated you badly when we were kids," he said, then put his fork in his mouth.

"Only sometimes. Not when we were alone," Rachel said. "I understood. You had an image to protect. Big bad Bobby. I got it."

Rob grinned. "Yeah. Even back then, I was acting. I was never as tough as everyone thought. I was scared shitless most of the time."

"You hid it well."

He laughed. "I learned early to bluff. If you got really good at bluffing, no one knew you were afraid." He cut a piece of pancake with his fork.

"You weren't bluffing when you stood up for me and my brother." She shoved a piece of egg into her mouth.

His face clouded. "I hate prejudiced people. They need to be taught a lesson." Rob's fingers clenched into a fist.

"And you did." She picked up her coffee.

"I wasn't scared then. How could you be afraid of people who push around little kids, people too small to stand up to them? They're bullies."

"You were my hero," Rachel said, stabbing some home fries.

"You were always the smartest girl in school. I never would have graduated if you hadn't helped me with math." He shoveled in the last piece of pancake and then drained his coffee.

Rachel sensed a flush stealing up her neck. "Yeah, well, math always came easy to me."

"Like standing up to bullies and beating the shit out of idiots always came easy to me."

She reached over and squeezed his hand. "I never forgot." She finished her food and wiped her lips with her napkin.

"Neither did I. I'm still here. Still protecting you if you need it. I love you too, Rachel. Always have. Always will." He glanced over at the waitress. "Check, please."

Chapter Nine

C hristmas Eve.

The days before Christmas flew by in a blur. Packed with crowds of shoppers, the little general store rang up more sales than ever. Rachel and Rob hopped back and forth, gift wrapping packages and restocking the shelves. While Rob and Rachel ran their butts off, Gramps sat in an armchair directing traffic and chatting with shoppers.

Rachel had never seen the store so crowded.

"It's Bobby," Gramps said. "Newspapers wrote he's here for the holiday. I bet he's given out a thousand autographs already."

"More like two thousand," Rob muttered, shaking his sore hand.

Rachel didn't stop to talk. It was Christmas Eve and they had to finish sales and close up shop. Gratitude for the bountiful season flowed through her. She appreciated Rob's star power drawing customers. She and Gramps needed the money.

Too busy to note how Gramps had slowed down, Rachel pushed scary thoughts about his mortality out of her mind. She'd put off looking into a nursing home until after the new year. She had fires to put out now and sort through the confusion in her own mind about her relationship with Rob.

When they finally closed the store at nine o'clock, they sank down on the small sofa and sipped their last cup of tea. Crumpled up almost into a ball, Rachel blew out a breath and stretched. She rested her feet on the coffee table. Rob wiped his forehead with the sleeve of his sweatshirt and yawned.

"How much did we take in today, Rach?" Gramps asked, putting his empty cup in the sink.

"Lemme check," she said, her voice weary. Slowly, she mustered the strength to push up and go to the computer. After a few minutes and some keyboard action, she spoke. "Looks like fifteen hundred. I think there are some more transactions that haven't gone through yet."

"That's a record for one day," Gramps said, grinning. "And we have Bobby to thank for it."

"It was a group effort, Gramps," Rob said, glancing at Rachel and patting the sofa.

She stood up and trudged over to him. Falling down onto the seat, she snuggled into Rob's shoulder. He wrapped his arm around her and drew her close.

"How long you stayin', Bobby?" Gramps asked.

"Gotta be back by the first week of January," he replied.

Gramps clicked his teeth and shook his head. "Won't be the same here without you."

"I'll be back."

Gramps' rheumy eyes bored into Rob. The old man opened his mouth to speak, thought for a moment, and shut it again. Rachel silently thanked him for not voicing what they were all thinking. Would Gramps still be around when Rob got around to returning?

How long would she have to wait to see him again? Would he remain faithful? She gave a quiet little snort. Hell no! She'd hoped against hope that his new movie would be delayed, and he could stay longer—like forever. But it seemed unlikely. All she could do was pray for a big snowstorm that would delay his outbound flight.

Now that Christmas was almost over, the future looked bleak. All she had to look forward to were gray, overcast days of bone-chilling, unrelenting cold and snow. Movie images of pristine snow-covered cottages with huge wood-burning fireplaces and never-ending pots of hot cocoa didn't happen to her. Not in Pine Grove.

Gramps got more cantankerous in the winter. He, too, would be affected by the drab, sun-less days and freezing weather. The older he got, the thinner he became. Cold winds blew through him like he was made of paper. Would he be able to withstand another brutal winter? She refused to ask that question.

Rachel had been preparing to be alone for a long time. She'd watched Gramps grow more fragile every year. Each time he made it to the new year, she silently cheered. Still, the dread of his passing forced her to prepare to be alone—totally alone. And now Rob had come along and ruined her plans. He'd given her hope and a few days of love, like water to a woman dying of thirst in the desert. Rachel came back to life. Now what? Another question she tried to avoid.

"I'm going to bed," Rachel said, barely able to walk down the stairs.

"Me too," Gramps said, yawning.

"I'll close up," Rob said, turning off the light and following Rachel down the stairs.

In the darkness of winter, she had to use the moonlight and one streetlamp as a guide. She crunched over hardened snow and trudged to the front door of the cottage. Once inside, she didn't even bother to turn on the lights. Shuffling to her bedroom, she undressed along the way, dropping clothes where she shed them.

Stopping at the bed, she ripped down the covers and fell in. Asleep seconds after hitting the pillow, she disappeared into sweet sexy dreams about Rob and their imaginary life together.

RACHEL SLEPT SOUNDLY through the night. It was eight a.m. when she woke up. She was alone. Where was Rob? Why didn't he wake her? Another glance at the clock and she noticed the date. December 25. It was Christmas Day.

At that moment, church bells rang. She smiled. A day of rest, playing, opening presents, and overeating. She could hardly wait. Bounding out of bed, she threw on her robe and peeked out the window. Yes! There was fresh snow on the ground. She'd dusted off the old sled. Though the runners were darn rusty, she hoped it would still slide and take her and Rob down the old hill by the abandoned house on Marsh Street. After breakfast, she and Rob would shovel their way to the barn and get the sled.

She, her brother, and Rob used to go sledding there when they were kids. Giddy with anticipation, she pulled on flannel pants, shirt, and boots, grabbed her down coat, and headed for the store. While she trudged through the snow, she saw smoke coming from the chimney. Ah, a fire was burning. She took a deep breath and smelled the burning wood. Would there be hot cocoa? Her mouth watered at the thought, and she increased her pace, pushing harder through the deep drifts.

When she drew nearer to the store, she noticed something on the porch. Rob must have forgotten to take out all the trash from the day before. But no, this item appeared tall and skinny. A speck of sun from a crack in the porch roof gleamed off something metal. As she got closer, her eyes grew wide.

"Hot damn! A real Flexible Flyer!" She ran up the freshly shoveled steps and ran her hand over the wooden seat, then the shiny, red metal runners. Brand new. A deep voice caught her attention.

"Santa came early. You were sleeping." Rob's handsome frame filled the doorway.

"A Flexible Flyer!"

"Yep."

"Is this for me?"

"Read the tag."

Rachel yanked her mittens off and turned the tag around and read aloud. "To a good girl this Christmas. Love, Santa."

When tears flowed, she threw her arms around Rob's chest and buried her face in the shoulder of his coat. He held her tight.

"I always wanted a brand-new sled," she muttered, her voice muffled by his down jacket.

"I know."

"My grandfather got me the old one at a yard sale. I still have it."

"I saw it in the barn. It's time to put that one out to pasture. Its best days are behind it."

"I don't need it now. I have this one. Thank you so much. You've made like a thousand Christmas wishes come true."

He pulled a handkerchief from his back pocket and wiped her face. She took it and blew her nose. "I'll wash it and return it. Promise."

"Come on in. Cocoa's ready," he said, holding the door open for her.

She stood on tiptoe and placed a chilly kiss on his frozen lips. "Thank you."

The aroma of hot cocoa blended with the smoky scent of the fire and the sharp tang of pine from the fresh swag adorning the staircase. Rachel took a deep breath to fully appreciate the scent of Christmas. She bounded up the stairs.

Gramps sat with his eyes closed and a soft snore emanating from his mouth. Whew! Rachel breathed a sigh of relief. At least he wasn't dead.

"Merry Christmas, Gramps!" she said, rushing over to give the old man a hug.

He sputtered, opened his eyes, and smiled. "Merry Christmas, lil darlin'. Lookit what Santa brought," he said, pointing to the door behind her.

Stacked in the doorway was the biggest bundle of gifts she'd ever seen. Church bells rang out a Christmas song as Rob took over, handing out packages. Most were for Rachel, with a few choice selections for Gramps.

"Crown Royal, my favorite whiskey! Thanks, Bobby," Gramps said, licking his lips. He stumbled over to the cabinet and got a glass. "Anyone else?" he asked.

"Should you be getting him whiskey?" Rachel whispered.

Rob shrugged. "Quality of life."

"Got it."

Next package was for her. It was a light pink cashmere sweater. She ran her palm over the soft fabric. "I've never felt anything like this."

"Yeah? I want you to wear it," he lowered his voice, "with nothing underneath."

She chuckled and felt her cheeks redden.

Rachel had crocheted him a small blanket and knitted a scarf for Gramps. Gramps gave her a box of her favorite chocolates. And a bottle of booze for Rob. Box-after-box of designer clothes came to Rachel who was rendered speechless at the over-the-top generosity.

"I'm not used to this. You're spoiling me."

"I want to. If anyone deserves it, it's you," he said, kissing the top of her head.

The last box was small. With shaking hands, she opened it. Gramps let out a whoop. Rachel lifted out a white gold necklace with a heart made of small diamonds.

"I can't accept this," she said, but her eyes glowed.

Rob folded her fingers over the gift. "Yes, you can. You will. I want you to have it."

Her eyes welled. "Okay."

Gramps found Christmas music on the radio. The smell of roasting ham met her nose. Gramps always got a small, spiral-cut ham the grocer saved 'specially for him. Rob mashed potatoes and Rachel took roasted Brussels sprouts out of the oven and then set the ham on a carving board.

"And Laura's homemade cheesecake for dessert," Rob said.

"A feast fit for a king," Gramps said. He licked his lips.

"Merry Christmas, Gramps." Rob lifted his glass, toasting his grandfather with Crown Royal.

"Merry Christmas, son. You too Rachel. This is the best Christmas ever!" He raised his glass.

Rachel toasted with a mug of cocoa.

"Definitely the best Christmas ever," she said, shooting a warm look at Rob.

GRAMPS TODDLED OFF to bed early. Rob and Rachel carried the gifts to Rachel's little home. Rob made a fire, and the lovers snuggled close. After making love with great difficulty on the small sofa, they fell asleep.

Chilled by the frigid winter air, Rachel woke up first.

"Jesus! It's freezing in here!" she poked Rob. "Come on. In bed."

"Wha? What are you doing?"

"Getting you out of this refrigerator and into a warm bed," she said, pulling down the covers.

"It's not warm yet," he muttered, stretching out.

"It will be," she said, joining him.

With their arms wrapped around each other, they fell back to sleep until eight. Rob opened his eyes first. He yawned, stretched, and then skipped over the icy floor to cram some wood into the wood stove.

"Time to get up," he said, tugging on her arm.

She rolled over, pulling the covers over her head. "Not yet."

"Yes yet," he said, yanking the blanket down.

She sat up. "Why?"

Rob pointed to the window. "Because we have fresh snow and a new sled. So get your butt up. Let's get breakfast and get out on that hill."

Rachel rubbed her eyes and stared out the window. The scene was perfect. The snow, all powdery and glistening, looked like the set of a Disney movie. Memories of childhood days when she and her brother could hardly shove food down fast enough before they ran outside and trudged their way through the heavy snow to the hill by the abandoned house on Marsh Street.

After spending the entire day sledding down that magnificent hill, they'd disperse into teams for a gigantic snowball fight. Rob always picked Rachel for his team. Taking her first because she was the smallest and certain to be chosen last if he didn't step in. One time, Dylan Smith "washed" Rachel's face in the snow. Rob grabbed the boy, washed his face, and then gave him a black eye.

She chuckled and sighed as the happy memories floated through her brain, recounting the pure fun of being out in the fresh air and new snow with their best friends. They didn't have many material things or live in a big house or eat fancy food, but they had the same outdoors as everybody else.

"Get a move on, girl! The sun's coming out. Snow'll be melting," Rob said, throwing some clothing at her.

They dressed quickly. Rachel threw together breakfast, while Rob woke up Gramps.

"Leavin' the store closed today," he said. "You kids need some time off. Go play in the snow."

"Thanks," Rob said, handing a plate of bacon and eggs to his grandfather.

When they finished eating, they hurried down the stairs. The sled was still propped up against the side of the store. Rachel raised her hand. "Stop! Wait!"

She stood stock-still next to the shiny red sled. She took off her mitten and ran her palm along the smooth wooden part, then slid a finger over the shiny red runners, so perfect, no nicks, no dents, no chipped paint, staring and staring at it.

When she was a child, she'd never owned anything like it. Her parents weren't poor, but they didn't spend much money for new toys. Her parents shopped at garage sales and thrift stores.

"What do you need a new sled for? It's just gonna get banged up anyway. This one is fine. Still works, doesn't it?" her father had said.

She couldn't argue with him. No, her old worn sled wasn't as shiny as Dylan Smith's, but it got her down the hill just as fast. When she looked back, she was amazed at the things you could find to please or clothe a child for just pennies.

"Are you gonna have an orgasm over the sled or can we get going before the snow melts?" Rob shifted his weight.

"My aren't we impatient," she said with a grin.

"Well?"

"Okay, okay. Let's go."

"Do you wanna carry the sled?" he asked.

"Nope. You can."

"All right then." He picked it up as if it had been a mere tooth-pick, took her hand, and turned them toward Marsh Street.

They stayed out for hours, hauling and riding, hauling and riding, until their fingers and toes grew numb. When they went inside, they put their wet socks and mittens on the wood stove to dry and stretched out with their feet close to the fire on the first floor of the store.

While Gramps napped in his chair, Rob and Rachel kept their voices low.

He took her hand and rubbed it between his two. "Gotta get your circulation going."

"Time to talk."

"About?" he asked.

"You know. Where do we go from here?"

Rob frowned. "On January 2, I fly back to the coast."

"Okay. Then?"

"I've got a couple of conferences about the next movie. Things I have to straighten out."

"When do you go on location?"

"I don't know. They're pushing to get going. Maybe January 15 or 20?"

"Where does that leave us?" Rachel swallowed. She didn't want to ask, didn't want to know, but could not stop herself.

"I don't know, Rach. I haven't thought that far ahead."

"We need to have a plan. You can't just take my heart and leave and never come back."

"Who said I wasn't coming back?"

"It must have slipped your mind."

"Don't get snarky with me. I hate when you do that," he said, pushing to his feet.

"Yeah? Well, I hate when you fuck my brains out and disappear." She turned toward the window.

"I'm not leaving you. Not leaving what we have."

"Oh yeah? Pretty hard to keep something alive three-thousand-miles away."

"Okay, okay. I get it. I haven't figured it out yet. But you're the one I want."

"Now."

"Forever."

Her eyes welled up. "Stop it. Stop it. Don't lie to me. You never lied to me before. Don't start now."

He approached her, but she shrank from his touch. "Why do you say I'm lying?"

"Because I know Deke. Deke goes out with every movie star or model he can. He screws them all, then leaves. Don't. Don't do that to me. Please. God." She shook her head slowly.

"I'm not Deke."

"Yes, you are."

"Okay, maybe I once was. But I'm not anymore. I don't want that anymore. I want more. I want a real life. A family. Kids."

Rachel raised her eyebrows. "You want kids? Deke, the movie star, wants kids?"

"Yeah. Is that so hard to believe?"

She let out one brief, dry laugh. "Not hard to believe. Impossible."

"I saw Luke run off with his family at Thanksgiving. I wanted to be his family. But I wasn't. I'm not. I'm just an actor he knows. Maybe a friend. At best." He sank down next to her.

"You had it here. I had to drag you back."

"I know, I know. I was an asshole. A few months ago, truth penetrated my thick skull. A family. Kids. That's life. That's where it's at. That's what you have when they turn off the lights and stop the camera."

"Duh."

"There you go again." He frowned. "I even proposed to some of my old girlfriends."

Rachel raised her eyebrows. "You did? When?"

"On Black Friday. Remember that early morning walk I took by myself?"

"Yeah, so?"

"I called someone..."

"You proposed over the phone?"

He nodded.

"Long distance?"

"Yeah," He shifted his weight.

"Really? How romantic."

"Okay, okay, it wasn't ideal, no candlelight and roses."

"And what did the woman of your dreams say?"

"She turned me down."

Rachel snorted. "Not exactly surprising."

"Actresses, models, they don't want to ruin their bodies having kids. Don't want to lose their careers. Hah! Someday they'll be old, like Gramps. If they're lucky. And they won't have their stupid careers anymore. But they could've had kids. You have kids, you're a family forever."

Rachel shifted in her seat and cast her gaze to her hands.

Rob rubbed the back of his neck and then ran his hand down over his face. "Sounds idiotic, doesn't it? I mean, some people would say I have everything. I say I have nothing."

"I don't think it's idiotic. It's what I've always wanted," she whispered.

Rob's face lit up. "That's right! I knew that. I mean, I know. That's why this is so perfect for me. Because you and I want the same thing."

"Yeah? With you on the coast and me freezing off my ass here?"

"Not forever. I'm gonna quit after this next movie. I've got enough money." He faced her.

"You're gonna quit the movies to come back to this broken-down store? Are you feeling all right?" She placed the back of her hand on his forehead. He pushed it away.

"Yeah. We'll do something cool with the store. We'll start over. Build something. Together."

"You, me, and Gramps?"

"Gramps might not be around for this makeover. I doubt he'd approve, anyway."

She smiled. "He loves this old barn-of-a-store. Never figured out why."

"I want it all, Rachel. And I want it with you. You know me and you love me, anyway. You're real."

"Maybe. We'll see what happens when you go back."

"I know what I want. I know what I'm doing. Will you wait for me?"

She laughed. "That's funny. Me wait for you? Is there a line of men I don't know about waiting here in this god-forsaken place for me? You're the one who has to fend off the opposite sex. Not me."

"Will you?"

"The question is, will you?"

At that, he took her in his arms and kissed her. The fire crackled. A log burned through and fell, releasing a shower of red sparks against the screen, but Rob and Rachel didn't notice.

Chapter Ten

A *week later on the plane.*
Rob fastened his seatbelt and stared out the window. He flew first class, on the studio. Good ole Liberty Pictures.

"Oh my, Deke Walsh! Can I have your autograph?" The flight attendant smiled and flirted with him. Even though he signed, he didn't say much. Sure, she was pretty, but his promiscuous days were over. He had to smile to himself. In the old days, he'd have had her number in his phone before he even buckled in. Now, he couldn't care less. He had the best woman in the world and didn't need to keep looking.

Staring out the window, he hadn't started his search for the right one until recently. He'd approached everyone—well, almost everyone—there was that whack job in Las Vegas, but she was another story—on his contacts list. By the time he'd reached the Ts, he probably sounded pretty desperate.

He sat up a little straighter. Still, who would turn up their nose at a marriage proposal from Deke Walsh? A whole lot of women, he discovered. The wrong women. He hadn't proposed to Rachel—yet. One more movie and he'd be on his way to a new life, a better life, with Rachel in that god-forsaken town. As he closed his eyes, his phone rang. It was Barbara Holmes, his agent.

"You didn't sign the contract yet," she said.

"Nope. Did you tell them about Luke Keller?"

"I'm waiting for you to give me a good reason why you won't work with him again."

Deke shifted in his seat. Not totally convinced refusing to work with Luke had been a good idea, he remembered the look in the boy's eyes, the tears. Although he hadn't helped Rachel much, he did have the chance to help Luke. Perhaps this would be Rob's first unselfish act in years. He had his dream and Luke deserved to have his. And it wasn't the movies, it was baseball. Decision made. "I don't have to. I won't. That's it. Take it or leave it. Find someone else to play my part. Either Luke goes or I do."

"I don't understand. His parents will go batshit."

"So what? I don't care."

"Why don't you like the kid?"

His eyes grew moist. If she only knew how much he cared about Luke. For the first time, he put someone else's wishes ahead of his own. He swallowed. This wasn't easy.

"It's not a matter of not liking him. I just don't want to work with him. Please, Barbara. No more questions. Okay?"

He swore he could hear her shrug over the phone.

"You're the boss. I'll make the call now. We need to get this wrapped up."

"I agree."

The flight attendant brought him whiskey and soda. He took a sip, then put his drink down and picked up his phone. He sent a text to Luke.

My agent is calling Liberty today. The shitshow is about to start. I hope you're ready.

He got a reply right away.

Thanks, Deke. Yeah. I'm ready.

He shut his eyes to avoid thinking about what would happen when Liberty got the news. Fan magazines would pick up the story. Deke was about to be the bad guy publicly. Putting himself in harm's way to do the right thing for someone else was new to him. Luke hated acting. He wanted to play baseball, and he was good enough to make the travel team.

Avoiding sleep, Rob allowed his mind to wander over that fateful encounter with Luke about changing his life. After their first conversation, Luke approached him.

"You're the only one who can do anything," he'd said.

"Yeah? What?" Deke had asked.

"You can refuse to act with me. Get me fired."

Deke's eyebrows had shot up. Be the bad guy? Have everyone hate him? Think of the bad press? What would that do to ticket sales and his reputation as the hottest guy on the big screen?

"Please?" Luke's tear-stained face had touched him. He remembered how hard it was to be a kid, especially when no one listened to what you wanted. Sure, the kid had acting talent, but also athletic ability. He wanted to be a kid, do kid things, enjoy childhood, and not be a disciplined adult at age ten. Deke couldn't blame him.

"Okay. But there's gonna be a ton of fallout," Deke had said.

"What do you mean?"

"Well, bad press, people saying nasty things about me, maybe even you. And I'm not sure the studio would do it."

Luke sighed. "That's okay. I didn't think you'd do it, but thought I'd ask, anyway."

Deke had placed a hand on the boy's shoulder. "Hey, wait a minute. I didn't say I wouldn't do it. I want you to be aware of what's gonna go down."

"So you will?" Hope brightened the boy's face.

"Yeah. I will. You have the right to be a kid."

Deke stood up, and he and Luke shook hands and made a pact to keep it a secret. Deke knew he could carry it off. After all, he was an actor, wasn't he?

Now the plan was in motion. He couldn't back out now, could he? Nope. He'd made a promise. How bad could it be? He figured they'd use Luke's understudy and rehearsals could begin immediately. Deke had looked over the script in Pine Grove and on the plane. Ready to begin, he grew anxious, wanting this part of his life to be over so he could move forward with his plans for his future.

After landing, Deke found his limousine pick up, also courtesy of Liberty, and arrived home. His big house had grown a bit dusty in his absence. He confronted Nora, his housekeeper.

"Yes, Mr. Walsh. I have a crew coming in here tomorrow morning. It will be shipshape within the week."

As he wandered from room to room, he shook his head. What an ostentatious waste! A gazillion rooms for one man? Look how Rachel lived. In a tiny cottage, but it had everything she needed.

Nora had left his dinner warming in the oven. He checked the fridge, pleased to see it was fully stocked. He opened a beer, stretched out on his luxurious sectional sofa, and dialed Barbara.

"Hey, Barb, can you give me the name of a reputable real estate broker? I want to sell my house."

"Sure, Deke. There's a firestorm brewing. Liberty hated the idea. They don't want to do it."

"So? Let them find another leading man."

"Don't press your luck. They've agreed. They're auditioning Luke's understudy tomorrow. But they're pissed. You don't know the heat I took."

"They'll get over it. Thank you for getting this done."

"I always thought you were an easy-going guy. Not one to pull a stunt like this."

"You don't know the whole story."

"So enlighten me."

"I can't. I promised. At least not yet. Maybe in six months."

"Suit yourself. Rehearsal starts Monday. Don't be late."

"I never am. Thanks again."

"Oh, by the way. Someone at Liberty leaked this to the press. You're already on TV news as the meanest man in Hollywood. Your social life might take a hit."

"What social life? I'm not serial dating anymore. I'm a changed man."

"That's one point in your favor. Seriously, you might want to hunker down. Don't answer the phone. Press will be relentless."

"Okay. Thanks for the heads up. I'll manage."

"Still don't get it. But you're my client."

"Thanks again, Barb. You're the best."

"Yeah? You might change your mind when Luke's parents hit you with a lawsuit. Good luck."

The minute he hung up, he noticed a slew of missed calls. Three from *Hollywood Press*. Two from *Gossip Today*. And the rest from *Celebs 'R Us*. He swallowed. It was happening. The press would be dogging his steps to find out why the big, bad movie star had ditched his little sidekick. Who knows how long this would go on? Maybe he made a mistake?

What's done is done. But he needed something to say, some justification. Without spilling the truth. A lawsuit? Didn't he have the right to decide who he wanted to work with? Maybe he bit off more than he could chew? And maybe this new persona—Mr. Self-less—wasn't going to be so easy to live with.

He decided he'd break his silence to get some advice from the wisest person he knew. He picked up his phone and dialed. The call went to voicemail. He left a message.

"Rachel? Have you seen the news? Call me."

AFTER THE HOLIDAY SHOPPING frenzy, the cleanup took days.

"What the hell did Bobby do?" Gramps' raspy voice boomed down the stairs to interrupt Rachel as she swept the store.

"What?" she called up to the old man.

He threw a newspaper down the stairs. It landed at her feet.

"See for yourself. Stupid idiot," the old man said, shuffling off to the kitchen.

Rachel picked up the paper and sank down on a box to read it. The headline made her catch her breath.

Deke Walsh Kicks Out Co-Star

Her eyes skimmed down to read the article. Wow, they skewered Rob. Said he was responsible for destroying Luke Keller's career, killing his college fund, breaking his heart, and putting the kid on the unemployment line.

"Isn't ten too young to collect unemployment?" she muttered to herself, then kept on reading. When she finished, she sat back, blew out a breath, and chewed her lip. Gramps appeared at the top of the stairs.

"Are you done? We've got to open the store," he said.

"Cleaning?"

"Yep."

"Not quite."

"Well, shake a leg, lady. We've got customers!" he said and toddled his way to his room.

Rachel glanced at the door. It was nine o'clock and there was no one outside and no car in the parking lot. Customers? Uh no. People coming to return stuff? Probably after five.

She pushed to her feet and sat down again to reread the article. What had happened to Rob? Convinced he'd shed that selfish, egotistical shell, she had a hard time believing the words on the page in front of her. But could they print a lie? Probably not.

When he left, her heart had been full. She'd pushed away doubts about his returning and starting a new life. She believed him. Was that because she wanted to believe him? Still, this didn't seem like the man she knew. The way he'd interacted with the kids at Thanksgiving showed her a different man than the cold, heartless one she'd just read about.

Rachel returned to her cleaning, filling a garbage bag with dust, dirt, crumpled-up wrapping paper, and other debris and hauling it to the curb. Back inside, she climbed the stairs and hurried to the kitchen to put the kettle on. Damn, it was cold outside. She needed a cup of tea.

"Tea, Gramps?" she called into the other room.

When she didn't get an answer, she figured the old man had either fallen asleep or was simply too hard of hearing. She took down another mug and tea bag and then popped two pieces of bread from a loaf Gramps had picked out at the food pantry into the toaster. Toast went so well with tea. And Gramps needed to eat to keep up his strength.

Stopping at the fridge, she listened. Silence. Her stomach churned and her pulse raced. No sound came from Gramps' room. Damn! He's probably sleeping. She raced in to find him slumped, unconscious, in his easy chair. She shook him.

"Gramps! Gramps! Wake up!"

But he didn't open his eyes.

"No, no, no, no..." she said, picking up her phone. She dialed 911. "Come on, Gramps. No dying today. Okay?" She again attempted to wake him.

This time, he stirred. He mumbled something she couldn't make out, and his eyes opened gently. The sound of the siren died as the ambulance pulled into the parking lot.

The bell over the door tinkled as someone entered the store.

"EMS! What's your emergency?" a masculine voice called out.

"Up here! Up here!" Rachel shouted. At that moment, the tea kettle screamed. She raced to the stove and turned it off. Two EMS people tromped up the stairs.

"He's in here," she said.

"Gramps?" Hailey, one of the EMS people, said. "What happened, Rachel?"

"He was unconscious. I couldn't wake him."

"Huh?" Gramps muttered. "What are they doing here?"

"Come on, old feller. Let's take you to the hospital to be checked out," Hailey said, nodding to her partner. "Get the stretcher."

"I'm fine. Don't need no stretcher," Gramps said.

Rachel stood feet apart, hands on hips. "Yeah? Fine? I don't think so. You scared the crap out of me. You're going to the hospital."

"Says who?" Gramps jutted out his chin.

Hailey helped the old man down the stairs where her partner waited with the stretcher.

"Says me, that's who. And you—just be quiet, okay?" Her eyes blazed.

Gramps' gaze met hers and he allowed the EMTs to get him on the stretcher and wheel him to the ambulance.

"Get in Rachel," Hailey said.

"I'll follow along in my car, so I have a way to get home."

"Okay."

Rachel's mouth felt dry. Her hands trembled a little until she tightened her grip on the steering wheel.

"Don't die now, Gramps. Please," she whispered to herself, steering the car onto the street and shadowing the ambulance. With Gramps' life hanging by a thread, and Rob being vilified by the entire world and his career in jeopardy, could life get any worse? Maybe, if he was guilty of such a heinous act, could she still love him?

"Get the facts, mom used to say. Innocent until proven guilty, dad used to say," she recited in the car. The new year was only a few days old and already trouble banged at her door.

ROB PACED IN HIS HOUSE, avoiding the media camped outside in his driveway and filling the street. After grabbing a cup of coffee, he went out the back to his lush, fenced-in yard. He sat at the patio table.

"Hey, Deke. Is it true you got that kid fired?" a voice yelled from his neighbor's property.

Rob hurried inside, shut and locked the door. He stood at the window watching birds at the feeder, like a prisoner in his own house.

"This is what I get for doing a good deed," he muttered.

For the hundredth time in the last two hours, he looked at his phone. No call from Rachel. He paced. When he finished the coffee, he sat on his luxurious sofa, grasped his phone, and called her again.

"Rob?"

"Yeah. Where have you been?" Damn, he didn't want to sound angry, but he'd needed her, and she had disappeared.

"At the hospital."

"What?" He jumped to his feet.

"Yeah. Gramps has congestive heart failure. He passed out this morning."

"Oh my God. I'm so sorry. I didn't know."

"Yeah, I know."

"Is he gonna be okay?"

"They gave him some medicine. He's gonna be there for a couple of days while they do tests."

"Okay. He is eighty-nine. I guess we can't expect him to last forever."

"No," she said, her voice low.

Silence.

"Have you seen the papers?" he asked, hoping she hadn't.

"Yep. Gramps read the story and then passed it along to me. You made the front page."

"Please, Rachel. Don't judge. Let me tell you the truth." He sat back down and launched into his story.

When he finished she, asked, "That's the truth?"

"So help me God."

"Only you could be in such a sticky situation."

"I know. I'm almost regretting it," he said.

"It'll blow over. Meanwhile, you have Luke's undying gratitude."

"Yeah, maybe. Is it worth it? I've got the press camped out here on my front lawn."

"We need to concoct a story to get rid of them. How about the truth?"

"I promised Luke I wouldn't. I shouldn't even have told you."

"I'm not going to spill it. Let me think. I'll call you back later and we can discuss it."

"Okay. Thanks. I knew you'd help."

"Don't thank me yet. I haven't done anything," she said.

"Yes, you have. You believe me."

She laughed. "Yeah. I do. Sounds wacko enough to be something you'd do."

He laughed. "You know me too well."

He put down the phone. Relief flooded him. Rachel knew him only too well. She was so smart she'd come up with something to reduce this heat he was feeling. His cell rang. It was his agent.

"Whatever possessed you to get Luke fired, the studio has turned it into a P.R. bonanza. They are having open auditions for Luke's part."

"Really?"

"Yeah. And they want you to help."

"Me?"

"Read with some of the kids who make the first two cuts."

"Great."

"Hey, you opened this door. Now you have to walk through. They got rid of Luke. Now you have to help with the auditions."

"How soon will they hire someone?"

"As soon as they can find a kid who can take direction and has good chemistry with you. So get ready to spend long days at the studio."

"Great."

"You reap what you sow, buddy," Barbara said and hung up.

The front door opened. The housekeeper managed to squeeze through without letting any of the press inside.

"Mr. Walsh. It's a zoo out there."

"I know, Nora. I'm sorry."

"Can I fix you some lunch?"

"That would be great." With all his anxiety, he'd forgotten to eat breakfast and was now starving. He watched a raccoon attempt to rob the bird feeder. What a mess he'd made. And Rachel was alone dealing with Gramps, who was probably dying. Rob paced in front of the window overlooking the back yard.

"Doing the right thing isn't easy, is it?" he asked himself. But he didn't bother to voice the answer because he knew what it was. He sat down and picked up the phone.

"Rachel, whatever you need for Gramps, let me know. I'm sending you some money. Hire any help you need, buy food, medicine, whatever you need. Okay?"

"You don't have to..."

"I do. I want to. I can't be there right now."

"No?"

"I have to be in the auditions for Luke's replacement. But I'll send a check. I wish I could be there myself. Use every penny to make life easier for you and Gramps."

"I will. Thank you."

He strode into the den, grabbed his checkbook from a drawer, sat at the desk, and wrote a check out to Rachel for twenty-five thousand dollars. He put it in an envelope, sealed it, and stamped it. He sat back, resting his feet on the wastepaper basket. It didn't relieve him of all responsibility, but it would give Rachel a chance to hire whatever help she needed. He smiled. At least he did something right.

Once again, he picked up his phone. This time, he dialed Barbara.

"What was the number for that real estate agent?"

"I'll text it to you."

"I want to sell this barn as soon as the film is through shooting."

"Buying a bigger house?" she asked.

"Nope. Moving back east."

"You're kidding, right?"

"Never been more serious in my life."

"Texting you her contact info."

"Thanks, Barbara. You're the best."

"I hope you know what you're doing."

"So do I." He chuckled and hung up the phone.

Nora poked her head into the den. "Lunch is ready, Mr. Walsh."

"Thanks, Nora." Suddenly, he had an enormous appetite.

Chapter Eleven

L*ate January.*
After ten days of grueling auditions, Rob returned home. There were no more reporters camped out in his driveway or on his street. The auditions diverted attention and his evil act took a back seat. Who would be Deke Walsh's new sidekick?

Rob stretched out on the sofa to watch a movie and unwind. Snoring peacefully, the tone of his cell woke him up. It was Barbara.

"You're a sly one. Pretty cagey. Selling your house to move back east? I don't think so. Why didn't you tell me?" she asked.

"Tell you what?" Rob asked, rubbing the sleep from his eyes.

"That you're getting married."

"What?"

"That's why you're selling your house. You're getting married."

"How do you know that? I haven't even asked her yet," he said, now fully awake.

"Come on. It's me...Barb. You can be straight with me."

"I don't know what you're talking about."

"It's on the news! It's in every gossip column, on every front page. She's holding a press conference in like ten minutes."

"Who?"

"Wendy Cochran, your fiancée, of course. Don't be silly. This acting like you don't know what I'm talking about is beginning to piss me off. Call me back when you're feeling truthful," Barbara said and hung up.

Rob sat up and retrieved his remote control. He channel surfed until he had the right one. Leaning forward, he rested his forearms on his knees. Totally alert, adrenalin pumped through his veins. This had to be a nightmare. He prayed he'd wake up soon, but then there she was. Wendy Cochran, big as life, gushing about her love for Deke.

"And I was so surprised. I mean, I just didn't expect Deke to propose."

"Were you shocked?" the reporter asked.

"Shocked? No. Happy, yes."

"And you said yes on the spot?"

"Who wouldn't say yes to a proposal from Deke Walsh?" Wendy cooed, grinning at the camera.

Anger pumped through Rob. He yelled at the screen, "You! You wouldn't say yes!! You, you fucking moron!! You didn't say yes. What the hell?"

"Did he give you a big ring?"

"It's being resized for my small finger," she said, waving her slender digit at the camera.

Again, Rob shouted at the screen. "No! NO! I didn't give you ANY ring! You said no!! What are you doing?"

Sweat broke out on his forehead.

"When's the wedding?" the reporter asked.

"Deke's doing a new movie, so we have to wait until that wraps."

"And then?"

"I'm scouting venues now. I'm sure we'll be ready to go when the shooting is over."

"Well, good luck to you, Wendy. That's it," the reporter faced the camera. "Another beautiful movie star opts for marriage. This is Lisa Mahoney for Silver Screen News."

Rob turned off the television. "Liar!!" He sank back in his seat, deflated. What the hell was he going to do now? A small thought improved his mood. Rachel would never watch Silver Screen News. She probably hadn't seen the broadcast.

But it would be in the newspapers soon too, right? He wiped the sweat from his brow with his sleeve. He had to talk to her before she read this crap. But what could he say?

"Uh, Rachel, you're going to read a story about me being engaged, but it isn't true."

Nope. That wouldn't work. Or would it? He pushed to his feet and paced. Think. Think! Maybe if he proposed to Rachel? Over the phone? What would he say?

"Rachel, will you marry me? You will? Great. Don't believe anyone who tells you they're already engaged to me, okay?"

That scenario made his stomach queasy. The only way he could fix this was to get Wendy to recant her tale. Just as he went to the phone, it rang. It was Barbara again.

"I just got a call from the studio. They are thrilled about your engagement announcement. They're getting a ton of free publicity for you and the new movie. And they're even considering writing in a small cameo for Wendy."

"No! No, no, no!! No cameo for Wendy. We are NOT engaged!"

"You don't have to yell. I can hear you just fine. What do you mean, you're not engaged?"

"Sorry. We are not engaged."

"Did you propose to her or not?"

"I did. Months ago. And she turned me down flat. She said no, and I dropped it. A week later I was relieved she'd turned me down."

"So you're not marrying her?"

"No."

"You didn't give her a ring?"

"No."

"Oh boy. This is one big mess."

"You're telling me? I have someone I do want to marry."

"Have you proposed to her yet?"

"No."

"What the hell are you waiting for?"

"For Wendy to go away."

"Oh, she's not going away. This is great publicity for her career."

Rob sighed. "Yeah, I know. Can you help me fix this? When Rachel hears this, she'll be crushed. Everything I have will be gone."

"So you really are selling and moving back home?"

"Yes. Have I ever lied to you?"

"No. But there's always a first time."

"Not for me. Not with you. I need help. How can we fix this?"

"I don't know. Let me think about it."

"Thanks. Let me know if you come up with something."

"At least this story has pushed the Luke Keller story off the front page. You're no longer the monster who kicks dogs and fires little boys."

"But this is far worse."

He put down the phone and sank back into the sofa. How could his life have been so good half an hour ago? How could he have had it all, only to lose it? As soon as Rachel sees that, it will be over for Rob. His dreams shattered, his future dry, cold, and lonely. He put his head in his hands and cried.

EARLY IN THE MORNING, Rachel took Rob's check to the bank. She deposited it, then returned to the store. Sitting at the kitchen table with a cup of tea and the calculator on her phone, she added up expenses. Gramps was still in the hospital, but he'd be coming home in a day or two. She made a note to ask the doctor what the old man would need at home. Should she order a hospital bed? How about nurses? Round-the-clock?

Rachel knew she couldn't take care of him and run the store at the same time. Thank God for Rob's money. She'd hire people to be with Gramps so she could conduct business. Mentally patting herself on the back for getting the store cleaned up after Christmas, a few tasks still lingered. Reordering popular stock and restocking a few shelves topped her to-do list.

After she made a list of phone numbers to call for home health care, the bell on the front door sounded. Ah, customers! Were they here to buy or to return unwanted Christmas gifts? She took a final sip of tea and hurried down the stairs.

Only one return. A new mother perused the children's bookshelf and picked out two books. Rachel rang up the purchase and three more to boot. When she finished, she bagged up the garbage from the weekend and toted it outside. On her way back in, she picked up the newspaper from the front stoop.

Once inside, she returned to the kitchen and reheated her tea. She sat down and opened the paper. She read the headline. "Hollywood's Sexiest Man Engaged!" There was a picture of Rob and some blonde woman, grinning like the Chesire Cat.

Rachel read the story.

"Rob? They're talking about Rob?" she muttered to herself as she continued to read. "This can't be true." But the more she read, the more convinced she became that the story was true and that the love of her life had played her for a fool.

She rested her forehead on her arms on the table and cried. Within five minutes, the tinkle of the bell summoned her again. She spent the rest of the morning busy ringing up sales and handling returns.

When she finished, she scooped up the slips she'd made out for merchandise reorders and placed them. After that, she finished restocking the shelves. By three o'clock, she collapsed onto the sofa. After realizing she hadn't eaten anything, she took twenty bucks from petty cash and headed to The Cozy Café for lunch.

Laura greeted her. "Hi, Rachel. Just you today? I've got a small table by the garden. Nothing's growing there, but you can watch the birds at the feeder."

"Perfect," Rachel said, following the waitress.

"Coffee?" Laura asked.

"Please."

Laura returned with the pot and a mug. "Did you see the paper?"

"I did."

"Looks like Deke's getting married. Boy, you could have fooled me. He didn't act like he was about to get engaged. Engaged to anyone but you, that is," Laura said, filling the mug.

Rachel's eyes welled. "Yeah. That's what I thought."

Laura patted Rachel's arm. "There must be some mistake, don't you think?"

"I don't know, Laura. I'm no grand prize and that Wendy person. Wow!"

"Don't sell yourself short. I saw the way he looked at you."

"Thanks," Rachel said, hoping to stop the conversation before her tears overflowed.

"Call him, honey. I bet there's more to the story."

Rachel nodded, added cream to her coffee, and raised the mug to her lips to avoid talking.

Laura patted her arm. "Just pouring salt into the wound, aren't I? I'll shut up now."

She hopped over to the front to seat new customers.

Rachel watched the chickadees take seeds and fly away to eat in privacy.

"That's me. Eating alone," she whispered to herself.

Rachel felt the frigid wind all the way to her bones. Her insides seemed hollow as the cold crept into her heart. How could Rob have been so two-faced?

"Maybe it's not true?" Rachel fingered the diamond heart from Rob she wore around her neck.

"Maybe I should call him? What will he say? What can he say? And I'm not going to beg." Her heart hardened. She pulled her mouth down in a frown and conjured up the conversation in her mind.

"Sorry, Rachel, you were just a fling, just a holiday fuck. All the time I was in love with someone else."

Sure, sure, but that didn't make sense. Why did he buy her the diamond heart? Why did he send money for Gramps? Feeling guilty? Probably. Still, he'd never done anything like that before. They'd been on the phone every other day, catching up on each other's lives. Yet he'd never mentioned a fiancée or even a girlfriend. Still, if it wasn't true, the papers wouldn't print it, would they?

Confused, she didn't know what to believe. Laura returned with the BLT Rachel had ordered.

"If I was you, I'd call Deke. Get to the truth. Or maybe to give him a piece of my mind. Anyway, I'd call. But that's just me. Here's your sandwich, honey. Enjoy," Laura said, then walked back to the kitchen.

Enjoy? Really? Rachel took a bite and hardly tasted it. Would she ever enjoy anything again? Probably not, but she had to eat. One thought nagged at her. Why would he call her and admit the truth about why he had Luke Keller fired? That would be a juicy piece of gossip that could blow the whole deal apart. And she had it. Would he trust someone he didn't love with that information? He told her because he didn't want her to think he was a rotter.

It didn't add up. Simply didn't add up. When Laura showed up with the check, Rachel faced her. "You're right. I need to call him."

"Atta girl. Get the facts from the horse's mouth," Laura said, pocketing the cash.

Rachel pushed away from the table, and with a determined gait, strode through the café to the parking lot. Her foot hit the gas pedal harder than usual. She needed to know, and she needed to know now.

Chapter Twelve

Rob left his house early. He drove to the closest newsstand and bought all the different papers. He was looking for the one Rachel subscribed to. *Sullivan County Gazette.* "Of course they didn't have it in California," he cursed and drove home.

Sucking down his third cup of coffee and it was only nine o'clock, he looked it up online. Certain his groan could be heard across the country, he put his head in his hands. Sure enough, he'd made the front page. Why not? Successful, famous local guy gets engaged to a hot model. That was news even for the big New York City papers. The local paper would be shouting it to the rooftops for a week.

His phone rang and his heart rate doubled as he checked the screen. Thank God it was only Barbara because he hadn't figured out what to say to Rachel yet. He'd have to call her. He knew it in his gut. But he needed to have a plan mapped out. Maybe Barbara could help.

"Hi," he said, sinking down into his chair and picking up his mug.

"Hey, newly engaged newsmaker."

"Don't call me that," he said.

"What's wrong? You are on the news everywhere. The studio is tickled to death. Thrilled beyond belief. This great, happy story has pushed the one about you being a nasty, selfish, egotistical narcissist who fires children off the front pages."

"If you're trying to make me feel better, you're not succeeding. Goodbye,"

"No! Wait! What are you so upset about? This is great publicity. The public is eating it up. The studio figures you've generated about two hundred grand's worth of publicity for the movie for free. They're now planning how they can dovetail your wedding with the release date for the movie."

Rob groaned again.

"What? I don't get it?" she asked.

Rob pushed to his feet, pacing, anger building in his brain. "There's not going to be a wedding. We're not engaged! I don't love her. Don't want to marry her. And what's more, she doesn't want to marry me!"

"That's not what she's saying now."

"That's what she said when I proposed to her."

"You did propose?"

"Ages ago. When I didn't have anyone. She turned me down. Flat. And that was fine with me."

"I guess the girl has changed her mind."

"Well, she'd better change it back again."

"If you dump her, you're going to be the meanest man in Hollywood. You'll never get another picture contract. They might even have cause to fire you from this one."

Deflated, Rob sank down in his chair again. "What can I do? I don't want to marry her. I'm in love with someone else. The right one. The one I want to marry. And Wendy ain't it."

"You throw her over for someone else. Not going to look good, Deke."

"I don't give a damn how it looks. Wendy took advantage. She did this for the publicity, to punch up her sagging career."

"I bet she's getting all kinds of calls."

"What can I do, Barbara?"

"Have you tried talking to her?"

"No."

"That might be the first place to start," Barbara said.

"What about Rachel? What can I tell her?"

Silence.

"Barb?"

"The truth. Tell her the truth. If she's the woman you think she is, she'll believe you."

"Pretty hard story to swallow, though," he said. "But I did tell her the truth about Luke, and she believed me. At least I think she did."

"The truth about Luke? You never told me."

"Exactly. And that's the way it's gonna stay. Thanks for the advice." Rob hung up the phone before she could say anything else. After more pacing, he decided to call Wendy first. If she agreed to break it off with him, he'd have a much easier time convincing Rachel.

He slugged down the remaining coffee, now cold, sat down on the sofa, and dialed.

"Deke, baby! Isn't it great? We are front page on every paper in town. In the country!"

"It's a lie, Wendy."

"What?"

"Our engagement. Have you forgotten you said no?"

"Oh that. Details."

"Not a detail to me. You have to call off this thing."

"Not on your life. Are you kidding me? My agent's phone has been ringing all morning. I've got bookings through next month. And I even snagged an audition. Guess what for?"

He made a face. He didn't give a damn what for, but he played along. "What?"

"*Thunder and Patch*."

He stopped and sucked in air. "My new movie?"

"Yep."

"What part?"

"Some barmaid or hooker or something. Just a walk-on, but my first speaking part."

"You can't!" Panic seized Rob's chest. "You'll ruin it."

"Well, thanks a lot. I certainly can and I will. And if you don't like it too damn bad."

"Wait! Wendy. Please, please call off the engagement."

"No way. I'm riding this thing as long as I can."

"It's a lie, Wendy. Can't you see that the truth will come out?"

"Not if you keep your mouth shut."

"I can't do that."

"Oh yeah? You'll look like a serial killer if you do. Wreck your reputation. Maybe even lose this movie."

"The truth is the truth." He pushed to his feet.

"We'll see."

"Yes, we will. This is so vindictive." He paced.

"Why do you care? Is there someone who's actually agreed to marry you?"

"Not yet."

"Oh. I see. Go to hell, Deke Walsh."

The phone went dead.

ANGER PULSED UP THROUGH his brain until he thought he'd explode. What a self-centered bitch! He could hardly believe he'd ever thought of marrying her. He had to get rid of her.

"Two can play the same game," he said to himself. He went to the bar and poured two fingers of scotch, then added ice. Pacing through his house, he finally stopped at the large dining room windows. He sipped his drink and watched the birds. Then he dialed Barbara.

"Did you talk to her?" Barbara asked.

"Yes," he said before finishing the last of the drink. "And she wouldn't budge. You've got to help me."

"I don't know what I can do, but I'll do whatever I can, Deke."

"Do you believe in love?"

"Sometimes."

"Well, I'm in love and I want to get married...to the right woman. So, we need to get rid of Wendy."

"That won't be easy."

"You're telling me?" Rob strode into the kitchen and loaded the glass in the dishwasher.

"The publicity has probably given her career a shot in the arm."

"It has. It would take dynamite to blast her away from our phony engagement now."

"What can I do?"

"First, she's auditioning for some small part in *Thunder and Patch*. Tell the studio if they hire her, I'm out."

"What?"

"That's right."

"But the money?"

"I don't care. I mean it."

"Okay."

"I need you to think of some way we can get leverage against Wendy to force her to break our engagement."

"I'll try. Are you sure you want to do this? Your P.R. right now is sky high. You're a hero. A romantic hero."

"Yeah? Not in my mind. I'm a jerk who's getting squeezed by the world's biggest bitch."

"Okay, okay. I'll see what I can do. My real estate friend said she has an appointment with you this afternoon. I told her you might call it off."

"No way. I want to see her. And yes, I'm selling this house."

"Okay, Deke. I hope you know what you're doing."

Rob disconnected the call and took another swig of scotch. He had to agree with Barbara. He hoped he knew what he was doing too. His doorbell rang, and he looked through the glass.

"Avery Miller, Mr. Walsh. Hollywood Real Estate?" she called through the door.

Deke opened the door. "Come in, come in."

"You're selling this house?"

"Yes."

"Moving to a new place with Wendy Cochran?"

"Not exactly. Please tell me what we have to do."

"How fast do you want to sell?"

"The quicker, the better."

"Okay then. Would you show me around?"

"My pleasure. This is the living room," he said, taking her elbow to guide her through the big house. After dinner, he'd call Rachel. Maybe by then, he'd have a plan.

RACHEL RECEIVED THE call at nine in the morning.

"You can pick up your grandfather anytime, Rachel," the nurse said.

Rachel put the "closed" sign up on the store window and got behind the wheel of her wheezy old car. She cranked up the heat to high, but the car was so cold it wouldn't be comfortable in there for a while. The hospital was a forty-five-minute drive. By the time she got Gramps, the car should be warm enough.

She chewed her lip. Would she need any special apparatus for him? Nursing care? She'd have to talk to the doctor and get all the facts. Gramps couldn't be relied on to tell the truth about his condition. He preferred to think of himself as a younger, more fit man who still had many years ahead. Rachel had gotten a health proxy over Gramps and managed to squeeze the truth out of the old man's doctor. Gramps had heart problems. He'd been living on borrowed time for years.

Grateful Gramps took up so much of her time, she hadn't thought about Rob's treachery. Even on the drive to the hospital, she forced herself to think about the old man and what accommodations she'd have to make.

"No more beef. No sugar. Lots of veggies. Bread," she mumbled to herself, searching her brain for nutritious meal ideas that would keep him healthy. Her stomach churned and sweat broke out under her arms and between her breasts. She'd avoided thinking about Gramps dying for such a long time. Then the magic of Rob's love over Christmas gave her hope that when Gramps did take his last breath, she'd have a new life to look forward to. But now that idea grew cold. It had simply been a fantasy, and she was left with the hard reality that when the old man passed on, she'd be alone and have nothing.

When she reached the hospital, Gramps sat in the waiting room.

"What took you so darn long?" he asked, pushing to his feet.

"Wait!" the nurse said. "We have some paperwork."

After Rachel filled out the paperwork and signed it, the doctor stopped by.

"We've given him a new pacemaker. He should take it easy," the doctor said.

"Any dietary restrictions?" Rachel asked.

"Nope." The doctor took a long look at the old man. "He should gain some weight."

"Okay then. Thanks for everything."

"Take care," the doctor said, shaking Gramps' hand.

Gramps slipped his arm through Rachel's, leaned on her a bit, and made his way through the icy sidewalk to the car.

"Damn cold in here, girl!"

"Sorry," Rachel said, cranking up the heat to high. It wasn't really cold, but he had no fat on his bones and very little meat to keep him warm.

"That damn hospital! I'm never going back there," Gramps said.

"Why not?"

The minute the question was out of her mouth, she'd regretted it. Gramps launched into a litany of complaints about the place. Rachel listened with only one ear. In her heart, she figured the next time he had an incident would be the last time and it would be too late for the hospital.

"Did you tell Bobby?" he asked.

"Yes."

"What did he say?"

"He said he wished he could be here but couldn't right now. And he sent money in case we need anything."

"Generous to a fault that boy," Gramps said. "How's the store?"

"Busy. Returns, some new sales. Ordering more stock, stocking shelves. It's not like I've been watching TV all day."

"Oh yeah. After Christmas is always a busy time. Any of those new gift certificates we sold come in?"

"A few."

Relief flooded Rachel. She'd avoided talking about Rob and now Gramps tackled the happenings at the store. She loosened her grip on the wheel and smiled as she answered his questions. A light snow fell as they drove home.

When they arrived at the store, Rachel put up a pot of tea and made buttered toast. Gramps ate the toast and took one sip of the tea before he shuffled off to his bed. Rachel drank her tea and cleaned up. His snoring told her he was okay, but she checked on him, anyway. She spread an extra blanket over him to protect him against a chill in the air. How much longer would she have him? She frowned.

Although he could be cantankerous, he loved her. She knew he wanted her to marry Rob. At Christmas, she fantasized it would be the best present she could give the old man. To know the two people he loved the most in the world would be together after he was gone. But now, it didn't look like that would happen. She sighed.

She glanced out the window. The snow had intensified and accumulated quickly. No sense in shoveling the walk until it tapered off. There probably wouldn't be more customers for the rest of the day. She poured another cup of tea, took it downstairs, and perched on the window seat in the back of the store. She'd put it off long enough. With a deep sigh, she picked up her phone. Time to call Rob.

"THANK YOU FOR YOUR time, Mr. Walsh. I'm sure I'll have no problem selling your home. It's in great condition," the agent said.

Before he could reply, his phone rang. Rachel's name came on the screen.

"One minute," he said and answered. "Rach, could you wait a sec. I've got a real estate agent here."

"Okay," Rachel responded.

"I've got to take this call. Thanks for coming," Rob said, showing the agent to the door.

"You'll hear from me soon, Mr. Walsh."

"Thanks." Rob took a deep breath, headed for the sofa, and picked up his phone.

"Rachel? You still there?"

"Yeah."

"Listen, before you say a word. It isn't true."

"What isn't true? That you love me like you said? That you're marrying Miss Skinny Ass? That you lied to me? That you lied to her? That you're a fucking asshole?" She fired off the questions.

"The first one and last one are definitely true."

"Great. That's all I wanted to hear."

Rob jumped up from the couch. "No! Wait! Wait! Don't hang up."

"Why should I listen to you?"

"Because I need to tell you the truth." Even to his own ears, he sounded desperate.

"Go ahead. I'm listening," she said, a note of doubt evident in her voice.

"I'm not engaged to Wendy Cochran. I don't love her." A modicum of relief sparked through his system. He finally got out the words.

"Did you propose to her?"

He hesitated. Truth. Whole truth. He had to fess up or lose Rachel. "Yes...but—"

"Well, then you are engaged!" Rachel interrupted.

"Wait! Wait. It was a long time ago. Right after Thanksgiving. I was desperate. She turned me down. Flat. No interest." The admission relieved a weight on his heart.

Silence.

"Rach?"

Silence.

"Rachel? You still there?" His pulse doubled, pounding in his ears.

"Yeah," came almost in a whisper.

"Please believe me. I don't love her."

"But you're selling your house? To move in with her?"

"No, no, no."

"Then why?"

"To move back to Pine Grove."

A snort and a laugh greeted him. "Yeah right. Like I believe that."

"It's true. I have no interest in Wendy."

"Then why is she going on TV and in newspapers and saying she's engaged to you? If this is a lie, why does she keep telling it?"

He paced back and forth in front of his living room window. "Publicity. To give her career a boost."

"But you haven't denied it."

"No. Barbara told me to keep quiet. The studio is loving the publicity."

"And the studio's okay with this lie?"

"They don't care if it's true or not. I'm no longer the big bad wolf firing the poor innocent kid. Now everyone loves me. The studio is happy as shit to have so much free good publicity for the film. Dollar signs are lighting up in their eyes."

"Sounds like the plot for a movie."

"It's real. Barbara told me how happy the studio is. They're even thinking of picking up the tab for the wedding and televising it."

"Televising your wedding to Wendy? I thought you weren't marrying her?" He heard anxiety in her voice. Damn. If he'd been there, he could have pulled her in for a big hug. Could have reassured her. But over the phone? Not so easy.

"Please, Rachel. Please believe me. It's you I love." Tears welled. He could barely control his voice. He'd planned on a life with her. It would be his lifeline, his exit strategy, to leave the phony world he lived in. Finally, he could step out of the lonely darkness and into the sunlight with the love of his life and have a family of his own. Now his dream was dying right before his eyes.

"It's pretty farfetched. You'd make a good screenwriter."

He stopped her. "It's the truth. You're the only one I want."

"Right."

"Really. Truly."

"I'll think about it. Oh, Gramps is home from the hospital."

"Is he okay?" Rob asked.

"I don't know. We'll see. But I'm thinking he doesn't have a lot of time left."

Silence. Rob took a big, shuddering breath. "I'm so sorry."

"I'll call you if he goes downhill, so you can come and say good-bye."

"Okay. Thanks."

Silence.

"Rachel? Are you still there?"

"Yeah."

"You'll think about what I said?"

"Yeah. Gotta go."

"Love you," Rob said, but she'd already hung up.

He put his head in his hands and cried. With no help from any-one else, he'd managed to mess up his life and lose the only good thing he'd ever done—falling in love with Rachel. What could he do now to convince her of the truth?

Chapter Thirteen

T*wo weeks later.*
Rob sat by his kitchen window, watching the birds at the feeder and reciting his lines for the movie. He had a lot to memorize. The studio had picked a replacement for Luke and was preparing to shoot.

He'd turned off his phone. Since Wendy's fake announcement, it had been ringing constantly. The media plagued him for a statement. Even though he'd agreed to the studio begging him not to deny it, he sure wouldn't confirm it. There was no engagement. He'd been firm about it with the studio.

"Okay, okay. We get it. Just hang on a little longer, all right? Maybe for a couple of months? Just until we finish shooting," the head of the studio had asked.

"A couple of months? No way!"

"All right. Just be quiet, can't you? It's gonna mean a lot for the movie."

Rob had reluctantly agreed to say nothing. But he had to hold himself back from throwing his phone under a bus or telling the media to drop dead. He swore he didn't know if he could contain himself if he ever saw Wendy again.

But he did as asked. Rachel had maintained her silence. She answered his calls with a brief sentence or two about Gramps and then hung up. Rob's heart ached. He needed her support throughout this ordeal, but she froze him out like ice in Antarctica.

"Being alone is nothing new," he'd said to himself as he prepared another pot of coffee. "I should be used to it by now."

But he wasn't. He even missed Gramps and the cantankerous old man's snarky remarks. Most of all, he missed Rachel, her warm smile, her soft hands, and her kiss. Happiness was snuggling with her in front of the fire.

As the hot water dripped, he recited his lines out loud, over and over again. The fourth *Thunder and Patch* film would shoot some scenes in the studio but more on location in the desert. If he and Rachel were married, he could have brought her with him. He sighed.

"Dream on," he mumbled.

Valentine's Day approached. He'd planned to propose to Rachel then. Now, she hardly spoke to him. The next time his phone rang, he saw Barbara's name pop up. He answered.

"Boy, are you hard to reach!" she said.

"Sorry. Dodging the press."

"And doing a great job of it too. Have you seen the papers? There's tons of speculation as to why you're unreachable. Some even say you have a terminal illness."

"Idiots," he muttered.

"An email with your plane ticket and shooting instructions is coming tomorrow. Are you ready?"

"No."

"What do you mean 'no'?"

"I'm learning my lines. But that's all."

"Get with the program. This is paying you and me a ton of money."

"I know, I know. I'll get there."

"The new kid seems anxious to start. At least his parents are."

"Wonderful. A new set of pushy parents."

"You could have kept Luke," she said.

"No, I couldn't. It'll be fine."

"Once the movie comes out and the ticket sales are through the roof, you can ditch Wendy. Say something about irreconcilable differences or some such BS."

"After the movie comes out? That's next year! No way. I'm not waiting that long."

With one hand, Rob refilled his mug.

"Come on, Rob. It'll go quick."

"No, it won't. In the meantime, I'm losing the woman I really do want to marry."

"Gotta run. Bye," Barbara said and hung up.

Typical Barbara. When the discussion heated up, like when he disagreed with her, she took off. He added milk to his coffee and returned to reading and reciting his lines. The minute he put down the phone, it started to vibrate. Disgusted at the persistence of the press, he did glance for a second at the screen. It was Rachel.

He jumped to the table and grabbed it. "Rachel?"

"Yeah. Geez. I've called you like six times, and it goes to voicemail."

"I'm sorry. I've been dodging the press."

"Gramps has taken a turn for the worse. If you want to say goodbye, you'd better do it now."

Rob sucked in air. Gramps, the only person left on Earth who cared about him, wouldn't be around much longer. Emotion filled his chest. His eyes stung.

"Rob? Rob? You there?"

He took a deep shuddering breath. "Yeah. On the phone?"

"If that's the way you want to usher him out, it's up to you."

"No, no. I'm sorry. Just didn't expect this."

"You thought he'd live forever?"

"Just didn't think. I'm coming. I want to see him. I'll be on the next plane outta here."

"Okay. I'll tell him to hang on."

"Please." His voice shook.

Silence.

"Rachel? You still there?"

"Yeah. Have a safe trip," she said, her voice showing more warmth than he'd heard since New Year's.

"Love you," he said—again to a dead phone as she had already hung up.

He dialed Barbara. "Tell the studio I need a leave. My grandfather is dying. I'm flying out there today. I'm sure there will be stuff to do. So I will probably be gone for a couple of weeks."

"Oh God, really? I'm so sorry."

"He's the only family I have."

"Okay. I'll tell them. But when you get back, you'll be ready to shoot?"

"Yeah. I'm taking the script with me."

"Good. Sorry about this."

"Thanks. Me too." Rob put down the phone and chugged the cold coffee in his mug. He hurried to his desk and opened his laptop. There was a plane leaving in three hours. He booked a first-class seat and a limo to the airport, then ran into his bedroom and threw the warmest clothes he had in a suitcase.

After Rob tucked the script in his briefcase and closed up the luggage, he washed out his mug. As he finished, he heard a car honking. Running outside, he jumped into the back seat of the waiting limousine.

As the car zoomed out of his driveway, he mumbled to himself, "Hang on, Gramps. I'm coming."

A TEXT DINGED ON RACHEL'S phone. It was the flight information for Rob's flight. She tucked her phone into the pocket of her apron and picked up a mug of chamomile tea. The snoring had stopped. Gramps was up. She slapped a smile on her face and tiptoed into his room, careful not to spill the beverage.

"Howdy, Gramps."

The old man opened his rheumy eyes. "Whatcha got there? Some scotch?"

"Nope. Tea."

"Blast that damn crap. A dying man needs scotch."

"Who said you're dying?" Rachel put on her best innocent face but didn't hold out much hope it would fool the old man.

"Come on, sister. Don't lie to me. Don't pretend. We've never done that, Rachel. Always spoke the truth. Don't stop now."

She cast her eyes down to her hands.

"Okay, bring it here. I'll drink it" He exerted a huge effort and sat up, propping himself against a mountain of pillows.

Rachel sat on the edge of his bed and slowly handed the mug over to the old man. He surrounded it with the bony fingers of both hands and raised it to his lips. She reached up and combed his thick white hair back from his forehead with her fingers.

"Don't be fussing over me, Rach," he said, freeing up one hand to swat at her. The mug tipped, but she caught it before it spilled any of the hot liquid on him.

"You put honey in here?" he asked.

"Yep. Your favorite. Linden tree honey."

He nodded. "Thought so. That's why it tastes so good."

"Rob's coming," she said, clasping her hands together in her lap.

"He is?" Gramps raised his eyebrows, took another sip, then smiled.

"On the red-eye. He'll be here in the morning."

"Best news I've had in days." He took another sip. "Dang. That honey is really somethin'."

When he finished the liquid, she took the mug. He leaned back and closed his eyes.

"I'm tired, sister."

"I know. Get some shut eye," she said, rising from the bed. She unfolded a blanket from the end of the bed and added it to the ones that already covered his thin frame. It was brutally cold outside, wind chill of minus ten degrees. The frigid air snuck through small cracks in the old building and chilled the air in the store.

The hospice lady had said to keep him warm and hydrated. Rachel followed orders. Peering out the window, she spotted a car.

"Edie's here," she said. Edie was the hospice nurse.

"Okay," Gramps said, then a soft burr came from his slightly open mouth as he drifted off to sleep.

Rachel dumped the mug in the sink and hurried down the stairs to let Edie in. It was too darn cold to keep the poor woman waiting outside for long. She threw open the lock and unlatched the door.

The store was closed. It wasn't like she'd expected any customers when the brutal wind of winter cast a frozen spell on Pine Grove. Rachel welcomed a respite from the writing up sales, restocking, and tidying.

"Come in, come in. Kettle's hot. Tea?" Rachel said, ushering the woman inside and quickly shutting the door against the persistent wind.

"Thanks. It's brutal out there." Rachel took her coat and hung it behind the door. Edie, a small woman in her fifties, stomped her boots in the entryway and then followed Rachel upstairs. Warmed by a small space heater and the oven when she was cooking, the kitchen felt comfortable.

"Chamomile?" Rachel asked.

"Please," Edie said, taking a seat at the table.

"Peppermint stick? We have so many candy canes left from Christmas, I've taken to putting them in my tea."

"Sounds delightful."

Bless Edie. How the woman could maintain such a cheerful demeanor with the work she did was a mystery to Rachel.

When two mugs of tea were piping hot, Rachel joined the nurse at the table.

"How long does he have?" Rachel asked, blowing on the hot tea.

"No one can say. How old is he?" Edie asked.

"No one actually remembers. Somewhere in his late eighties or early nineties, I think."

"He's not sick, just worn out."

"His grandson is coming from L.A. He'll be here early tomorrow morning. Will Gramps last that long?"

"He might, if he has a reason to. The will to hang on can be strong."

"Oh, he does. He's looking forward to Rob's visit."

"Good. Then it's likely he'll make it," Edie said, taking a sip of her drink. "This is delicious."

"Thanks."

"Have you discussed plans with your grandpa?"

"He's not really my grandfather. But no. Every time I ask him anything, he changes the subject."

"Some people go into great detail about the plans for them after life has passed. Others, not so much," Edie said.

"Or, like Gramps, some not at all!" Rachel said with a chuckle.

"If he doesn't care, then it's up to you."

"Up to Rob, really. He's the blood relative."

"What about your life? Will you continue on at the store?" Edie asked.

Rachel raised her mug to her mouth, giving her time to think. "I don't know."

"You have no plans?"

Rachel sensed heat rising in her cheeks. Before Wendy Cochran opened her big mouth, Rachel did have plans—lots of plans. But now? Not so much.

"No."

"Do you have a copy of his will?"

"I do. Yeah, he's leaving me some money and the cottage. But beyond that? I don't know. Rob gets the store. He'll probably demolish it. There really isn't enough business here, except at Christmas, to keep it going. And his career is in Los Angeles. Not here."

Edie finished her beverage. "I'll go and check in on him. You don't have to hang around. If you have things to do, go ahead with them."

"Thanks."

"Don't mind the dishes. I'll take care of them."

"Thanks, again."

"Gives me something to do," Edie said, rising from her seat.

Rachel turned on the radio but kept the sound low so as not to disturb Gramps. The weather report said the big howling winter storm had blown over and the temperature had risen to thirty degrees. Rachel donned her down coat, boots, hat, scarf, and gloves and opened the front door.

She needed to get out of the store and breathe fresh air. And move around. Sunlight peeked around the few clouds leftover from the storm. She checked her watch. It was already four. Soon the sun would be setting.

She set out to walk on the plowed road. The landscape looked so neat and clean, tucked under a blanket of pristine snow. Sunlight caught some frozen flakes, making them glitter. No cars came along. The street was quiet. A few bird songs broke the silence, calling her attention to frozen bare branches sparkling in the fading sun.

Wandering down the street, she stopped at the junction with the road leading to the old house. She took a few steps in and stared at the decrepit old place. It was huge, three full stories. The architecture and fine finishing touches faded with time, reminded her it had once been a beautiful home, standing proud, dominating the street.

Rachel sighed. The old place with the tattered 'for sale' sign had become part of her dream with Rob. After he left for the West Coast, she'd lie in bed and dream of renovating the old place, turning it into a bed-and-breakfast where they could live and work together.

She'd looked up the price online. After she inherited some money from Gramps for the down payment, she could get a bank loan for the rest. Yes, she could buy the place. They could renovate it together, doing much of the work themselves and hiring Will Lennox to do the rest. They could live in the cottage while they renovated.

But now, with Wendy Cochran gumming up the works and Rachel doubting Rob's honesty, that dream had shattered like fine crystal knocked to the floor. She had no plans and no desire to make any. How long would it take to heal a broken heart? She had no idea but feared she was about to find out.

Chapter Fourteen

L os Angeles.
 Rob checked his bag at the curb and then headed for security. Because of the last-minute aspect of his flight, he didn't have much time before take-off. He hurried to the pre-check line and begged people to let him get to the front.

"Scouting out a honeymoon spot for you and Wendy Cochran?" a passenger asked with a smug grin.

"No. Heading home to say goodbye to my dying grandfather," Rob said, his voice curt.

"Oh. I'm sorry to hear that. Sure. You can go ahead of me," the man said.

Rob rushed through, then quickened his pace as he headed to the gate.

"Say, aren't you Deke Walsh?"

Rob ignored him.

"Where've you been hiding? What's going on? Afraid to show your face after getting engaged?"

"Shut up," Rob said and kept on walking.

"Hey, I'm only voicing the opinion of the people. Why are you hiding?"

Rob pushed past him.

"Not talking? Okay. I can report that too."

"Look, buddy. I'm trying to make a plane and I'm running late. So, would you get out of my way?" Rob's control of his temper slipped a bit.

"Just doing my job. Go ahead and be an asshole. I can report on that too."

Rob stopped and squared off. "You want some real news? Why don't I deck you? Then you'll have a story and a lawsuit!" Rob fisted his hand and took a step toward the reporter.

The man backed up.

"I'm trying to catch a plane to see my dying grandfather. So get the fuck out of the way."

The man threw up his hands. "Okay, okay. Sorry, sorry. Don't hit me." He backed up and left a clear path for Rob.

"Last call for passengers on flight 2034 for New York," came over the loudspeaker.

Rob ran the rest of the way. "Wait! Wait! I'm here!" he called, scooting up to the gate.

"Ah, Mr. Walsh. We've been looking for you."

"I'm here. Thank you for waiting."

"Come on, let's get you seated." The flight attendant threw him a warm smile and took his arm.

Relief flooded him as he clicked his seatbelt and flight instructions came over the loudspeaker. At least he'd made the flight. He sat back and closed his eyes for a moment as the plane taxied down the runway.

"Drink, Mr. Walsh?" the flight attendant asked.

He opened his eyes. "Yes, ma'am."

"What's your pleasure?"

Damn. She flirted with him. Unlike every other flight in his past, he had no interest in the flight attendant. "Gin and tonic, please."

"Lime?"

"Nope. Thanks."

She brought the drink, and he downed it quickly, then asked for another. He stretched his legs and looked out the window. It was dark. The lights in the cabin went off. Most of the other passengers were sleeping. When he got the second drink, he polished it off.

"Afraid of flying?" the woman in the seat next to him asked.

"Nope. Afraid of what's waiting for me on the ground," he murmured.

The woman tried to smile but made a face and turned her attention back to the book she cradled in her lap. Yeah, no one wants to know when bad stuff happens to you. He knew that. How many times had he changed the subject when friends, no acquaintances since he didn't have any real friends, tried to talk about their divorce or the death of a family member? He couldn't count that high.

Shame filled him. Being with Rachel had opened his eyes to his own callous, insensitive, selfish behavior. Rachel had been real. Nothing phony about her. She truly listened and remembered what he'd said. She cared about him and Gramps. He'd never seen that kind of genuine devotion before from a single woman. When it had been directed his way, he'd basked in the loving glow, like the first sunshine of spring.

She'd opened his eyes to the joy of caring about someone else. The pleasure pleasing someone could bring. Living in the warmth of Rachel and Gramps had opened him up. Some part of his personality, dormant for years, had flowered and blossomed. He'd planned to nurture that with Rachel as his guide. The life he'd seen awaiting him had given him hope to finish his film, sell his house, and move back to Pine. He'd marry Rachel, have children, and be happy. Then Wendy Cochran came along and spoiled it.

As he stared out the window, he remembered some of the lessons Gramps had taught him.

'Don't let other people tell you how to live, boy.' 'Find your own path.' 'Cut your own way through life.' 'Find happiness on your terms.'

Gramps would scold him for folding his tent and slinking away. If Rob had to stand and fight for the life he wanted, so be it. He would. He'd tasted true love and wouldn't settle for anything less. But how? How could he get rid of Wendy?

He picked up his phone to send a text to Barbara.

You know everything and everyone in Hollywood. I need help in getting rid of Wendy. I know you could help me find a way. I don't ask much of you, but I'm asking this. Help me. You've made a shit-ton of money off my acting. Now it's time for payback.

After he sent it, he leaned back and closed his eyes. A few hours later, a ding on his phone woke him up. It was a text from Barbara.

I may have found something. Remember Andrew Somers? Call me when you land.

Rob smiled and closed his eyes.

EDIE STAYED THE NIGHT, allowing Rachel to return to her cabin and perhaps get a good night's sleep. But deep sleep did not come easy. She awoke several times in the night. Once to see a raccoon attempt to open her outside garbage can and another when the wind blew down a limb from a tree.

She threw in the towel at four and made a cup of tea. Carrying it to the window, she checked out the store. Sure enough, the light was on in Gramps' room. He had been restless since his return from the hospital. He slept fitfully for a few hours here and there, but never all through the night.

Tempted to get dressed and relieve Edie, she resisted, recalling the nurse's words.

"Don't come over here during the night. This is why I'm here. So you can rest. I can handle anything he needs. Don't worry. I've got this. It's my job, and a pleasure to give you some relief."

Rachel returned to the kitchen and turned on her small space heater and poured another cup of tea. She hated to miss any time with Gramps, not knowing how much he had left. Thoughts of Rob crowded her mind. What could she say to him? How would he react?

Her feelings toward him had not changed, but anger surrounded her heart. Had he cheated or lied about loving her? What were his intentions? Confusion reigned. She wanted to believe him, but it seemed too fantastic a tale. Would a woman wreck so many people's lives just to boost her career? Rachel admitted there were enough selfish people in the world who would do exactly that.

Torn between wanting to check on Gramps and forcing herself to go back to bed to be rested enough to deal with Rob, she opted to see the old man. After a glance at the thermometer, which read fourteen degrees, she pulled on her warmest clothes. Bowing her head against the biting wine, she traipsed over the icy path from her cottage to the store.

"Edie, it's me!" she called from the door. After hanging up her jacket, she tromped up the stairs. "How's he doing?"

"He's doing fine," Gramps' voice bellowed from the tiny bedroom, followed by a round of serious coughing.

Rachel poked her head in. Edie sat in a rocking chair dozing while Gramps lay back in bed, wide awake. His pale face broke into a smile when he saw her. "When's my grandson coming?"

"His plane lands around six. He should be here at eight." Though he might arrive sooner, she didn't want to get the old man's hopes up, in case there was traffic or a delay in landing. He'd probably hobble down to the window at about eight to watch for the limousine. Many times Gramps got it in his head Rob would come, only to sit by the window hour-after-hour and be disappointed.

This time, it was true. She'd received a text when his plane was in the air. Barring a plane crash, he'd be there when promised. Wasn't that evidence of him turning over a new leaf? She wanted to believe, wanted it with every bone in her body. Fear stood in her way. Somehow, she'd decided anticipating heartbreak would make it less painful, but that never worked.

"Tea?" she asked. He nodded, then his eyes closed.

Rachel strolled into the kitchen and put on the kettle. She checked the refrigerator. There wasn't much there, but she spied bread on the counter. With the butter and eggs in the fridge, she could make a meal. She checked her watch. Five-thirty—a bit early for breakfast. She popped two pieces of bread in the toaster and opened the tea canister.

"What are you doing here?" Edie asked, yawning.

"Couldn't sleep. Thought I could make myself useful."

Edie checked her watch. "I'm on the clock until six."

"Good. Gives me time to share breakfast with you," Rachel said, buttering the toast, then popping two more pieces of bread into the toaster.

By seven-thirty, Edie had departed. Rachel returned to the cottage to change and put on makeup. Rob would be there any time. By eight, she was ensconced in a chair by the picture window. She heard the electric chair wheeze its way down the stairs. Propped up on a cane, Gramps, clad in pajamas and robe, ambled slowly toward her. He sat his butt on the other chair and faced the window.

"Where is he?"

"Anytime now, Gramps," she said.

"You always say that."

"But this time it's true."

The honking of a horn drew their attention. Sure enough, a shiny black limo drove up and stopped in front of the path to the front door. The driver got out, opened Rob's door, then retrieved his luggage from the trunk.

Rob grabbed his suitcase, waved, and strode up the walkway. Rachel's heart skipped a beat.

"He's here!" Gramps said, raising his hand.

Rachel jumped up from her chair, a broad smile on her face, and raced to open the door.

THE LANDING HAD BEEN smooth, luggage retrieval without incident, and the limousine awaited Rob at the curb. He fended off nosy reporters looking for more about his phony engagement with the truth about his grandfather. Out of respect, which surprised him, the news hounds gave him space. He smiled as the driver closed the door and then steered the car onto the highway. In two hours, he'd be back in Pine Grove.

Of course, he wanted to see Gramps, but the idea of being with Rachel raised his spirits. No matter what, she'd lift him up, soothe his wounded soul, and shower him with love—if she decided to resume speaking to him.

As the driver maneuvered the big car effortlessly through traffic, Rob chewed a nail. Would Rachel be like the frozen north or would she warm up? Not knowing what to expect made his stomach roil.

"Relax, Mr. Walsh. We'll be there soon," the driver said.

Rob sank back into the leather cushions and gazed out the window at the beauty of the frozen landscape. He spied an occasional deer peeking from behind a tree trunk and some birds poised on frozen limbs, searching for food. He'd forgotten that winter in Pine Grove could be as beautiful as it was harsh.

When the limo pulled into the store parking lot, Rob glanced at the window. Seeing Rachel and Gramps there waiting raised his spirits. He jumped out of the car, tipped the driver, grabbed his luggage, and strode quickly up the icy walk, through the frozen air that was the Catskills.

As he approached, Rachel flung open the door. He barreled through, dropping his suitcase, and pulled her into his embrace.

"Rachel. Darling. My love," he murmured, his eyes closing.

"What about me?" Gramps called.

Rob sought her mouth and kissed her with feeling. She responded. His heart beat faster. When he let her go, he turned, smiling, to face the old man. The shock of Gramps' appearance melted the smile off his face. He recovered quickly, pasting a fake grin where the real one had been. Gramps had shrunk, skinnier than when he'd left. The old man's skin was almost transparent. His old eyes had faded, the color almost a light grayish blue. Veins on his arms and the backs of his hands seemed to be all there was of him.

Horrified at how quickly he'd deteriorated in the last few weeks, Rob drew a chair next to his grandfather. "Hi, Gramps. How you doing?" He knew it was a stupid question. Obviously, the old man was existing on borrowed time.

"Great, my boy. Great. Better now that you're here. You come all the way from the coast to see me?"

"Yep." Rob took the man's cold, bony hand and held it between his two. He cast a glance at Rachel. She shrugged and averted her eyes. That couldn't be good.

"Thank you for calling me," he said to her.

"No one knows how much time they got, Bobby. I could be here another twenty years!"

Rob chuckled. He'd settle for another twenty hours with his grandfather.

"Come upstairs, my boy. You must be hungry. Tell me what's going on. Did you finish shooting your next picture? Rachel, feed this boy! He looks hungry."

"Sure, sure. Come on upstairs. Gramps, are you gonna eat too?" Her voice showed a tinge of anxiety.

"Nah. I'm not hungry. Just had breakfast."

"Four hours ago," she mumbled.

Rob lifted his grandfather in his arms and carried him up the stairs. Surprised at how light the old man felt. Pain and sadness squeezed the young man's heart. He could see his grandfather fading before his eyes.

"Okay, Gramps. But you've gotta eat too," Rob said, meeting Rachel's gaze.

"All right. Geez. Why do y'all care how much I eat?"

"Because you've got to eat to live."

Rachel pulled down cans of tuna fish and made sandwiches. Rob finished his off quickly and asked for a second one. Gramps pushed the food around on his plate but didn't take even one bite.

"I'll start with dessert. Where's that box of chocolates?" Gramps asked.

Rob passed it to him, and he took two pieces. After quickly finishing the treat, he yawned. Pushing to his feet, Gramps wobbled for a moment, then slowly shuffled toward his room.

Rob moved to stand, but Rachel put her hand on his forearm and shook her head.

"See ya later," the old man said.

"See ya," Rachel replied.

When he was out of the room, Rob rubbed his hands over his face. "I didn't know he was this bad."

"He's in hospice care," Rachel said. "The hospice nurse comes at six and leaves at six in the morning."

Rob gave a slight nod. "So, this is the end?"

"Yep." She sat motionless, staring out the window.

"I had no idea. How much time does he have left?" Rob asked.

Rachel shrugged. "No one knows."

"Doctors won't make a prediction?"

"No. What does it matter? If it's three days or three weeks?" she said, pushing to her feet and clearing the dishes from the table.

"Let me do that," Rob said, picking up a sponge.

"The great Deke Walsh washes dishes?" Rachel cocked an eyebrow.

"Cut the crap. I want to help." He turned on the water.

"You have. Just by being here. He was much more animated than I've seen him in weeks." Rachel put away the food.

"Are you prepared? For his passing?" he asked, wiping the sponge over a plate.

"Are you?"

"You know what I mean."

"If you mean do I have the funeral and burial plans worked out, yes, I do. Gramps told me what he wanted. And I'm doing it."

"Nothing too weird, I hope."

"Nope. Just Gramps being Gramps."

He turned off the water. "Thank you for doing everything."

"Somebody had to," she said, turning toward the door.

Rob grabbed her arm. "I know. I should have been here more. I'm sorry."

She patted his arm, and he released her. "It's okay. You're here now."

Rob tromped down the stairs and picked up his luggage.

"The spare room?" he asked, raising his eyebrows.

"Yeah," she said.

Chapter Fifteen

Rachel wanted to be mad he even had to ask where he was sleeping, but she couldn't muster the energy. Maybe she should be glad he still wanted to sleep with her? What did she want? She had no clue, but she knew she needed space to figure out things. Seeing him again after the big engagement to Wendy Cochran seemed like time travel. They slipped right into the roles they'd had before. Having him here lifted the burden of facing Gramps' last days alone.

He'd cheered up the old man simply by showing up. She wouldn't admit his presence had had the same effect on her. But it did. After he dumped his suitcase in the tiny room, he made the rounds of the cabinets in the kitchen.

"There's no food in this place," Rob said.

"Gramps isn't eating much, anyway."

"What about you and me? Don't we have to feed the hospice nurse too?"

"I suppose."

Rob snatched the spare keys to the old truck from the hook on the wall. "Come on. We're going food shopping."

"But Gramps?"

"How long will he be out?"

"I don't know."

"Then we'd better hurry," Rob said, taking her arm.

They roared out of the parking lot and returned an hour and a half later.

"You said something about making stew?"

"Yeah, so?"

"You cook. I'll get this place fixed up," Rob said, toting in bag after bag of food.

"Okay. Coffee?" she asked.

"When I'm done."

After checking on Gramps and seeing he was still breathing but fast asleep, Rachel put away the food. She left out the stew ingredients and put on a pot of coffee. When the brew was ready, she poured a cup and stood by the window, watching Rob.

He lugged a bag of rock salt from the barn and shoveled the walk and the parking lot, salting each, until she could see the asphalt. The front walk was clear too. The sun peeped out for a while, helping him.

When she heard the loud scraping of the shovel, she peeked out the back window and saw him tackle the back walkway. Damn, it was good to have a strong man around. Halfway through her mug, she put it down and got started on the stew.

While the meat browned, she cut up vegetables. Singing softly to herself her favorite Taylor Swift song "Invisible String," she created an exquisite meal. The scent of the bubbling stew filled the store. Rachel prayed it would inspire Gramps' appetite.

At five, the sun started its journey, lighting up the sky and splashing orange and pink across the horizon. Rachel stood at the window with her mug, watching Mother Nature's show. The tinkle of the bell at the door drew her attention. She heard the heavy footfall of Rob as he climbed the stairs.

"Is that the stew I smell?" he asked, filling the kitchen doorway with his tall frame.

"Yep."

"Smells great. I could eat a bear," he said, pulling out a chair.

"How about a cup of coffee and a scone?"

"Great. Thanks."

Rachel poured the beverage. The scone already sat on a plate on the table.

"Thanks for clearing off the snow. I know Edie will appreciate it too."

"Edie? Oh, oh. The hospice lady. Got it," he said before taking a bite of his scone.

Rachel joined him at the table. He took her hand in his briefly.

"I know this isn't a good time to talk about us, but I have to. Please believe me, I'm not engaged to Wendy. I love you and always will."

Rachel slid her hand away, then returned it. Maybe he was telling the truth or maybe he wasn't. But this might be her last, her only time to be alone with him. Her heart filled.

She offered him a second scone and took one herself. He moved his chair closer to hers. "Tell me about your new movie," she said, pushing to her feet. "More coffee?"

Rob held up his mug. "Thanks."

She eased down into the chair and got comfortable. With a smile on her face, she faced him.

"*Thunder and Patch*? It's a great adventure story..." he began.

GRAMPS WAS AWAKE WHEN Edie arrived right on time. She helped bathe him and dress him for dinner.

After Rob took a shower, he put on a fresh flannel shirt and jeans. Once in the kitchen, he hauled the big pot of stew to the table, noticing Rachel set out the good china dishes and silver. They all held hands while Gramps said grace.

Gramps stuffed two pieces of meat into his mouth and munched on a carrot and a piece of potato. He did drink a beer, though.

"Rachel, did I ever tell you the story about the dirt, the worms, and Bobby's mother?"

"No, I don't think so," she said.

"Edie. You'll like this too. Remember, Bobby?" Gramps asked.

"I don't, Gramps," Rob said.

"It's one of our fishing stories. I got a million of 'em with Bobby." Gramps went on with the tale.

"We dug in the ground, looking for worms to put on the hooks. Bobby's mom called him in to dinner. So we shoveled the dirt and worms we were working with into a box. Bobby carried it into the house. He was so excited he ran into the living room to show his mom..."

"Oh God! Now I remember! The moisture from the soil had soaked through the cardboard box. And the bottom fell out!" Rob said.

Gramps guffawed. "Dirt and worms all over his mother's nice clean carpet!"

"Mom was furious!" Rob said, laughing.

As they ate, Gramps continued to regale them with funny fishing tales. Rachel figured some of them might be tall tales, especially about the size of the fish they caught. They seemed to get bigger and bigger with each story.

Rachel wondered where the old man got the energy to be so animated. He was like the man she'd known for so many years. Even so, the telltale faint rattle coming from his chest continued, and he coughed more often—a deep in the chest cough. She wanted to be happy, but his decline continued to be obvious. After dinner, Rob and Edie cleaned up, and Rachel put Gramps to bed.

"Tell Bobby I want to see him, okay?" Gramps said.

"Sure," she said, tucking him in and adding an extra blanket as the forecast was for an especially cold night and the man was all skin and bones.

Before he went in, Rob took Rachel aside. "Will you come in with me? I don't want to be alone with him, in case anything happens. You know?"

"Of course." She patted his shoulder.

Rob entered the room. The lamp gave off dim light on the bed only, leaving the rest of the room in a shadow. Gramps appeared small and frail buried under a heap of covers.

"I'm here, Gramps. Is it okay if Rachel is here too?"

"Yep," he said, wheezing like it had taken him a lot of energy to utter his reply.

The old man inched over, and Rob sat down gingerly on a corner of the bed. Gramps took his grandson's hand. Rachel perched on a stool in the corner of the room, covered in darkness.

"You're cold," Rob said, rubbing the old man's hand.

"Nah. Just something that happens at this time of life. Listen to me," the old man said, his voice barely a whisper. Rob leaned in closer. "You're a fine lad, Bobby. You've turned out real nice. Not fooled by all that Hollywood nonsense. Just a regular guy," Gramps said, then paused to catch his breath. "Your parents would be proud you turned out so good. I sure am." He patted Rob's hand and took another breath before continuing. "Are you really engaged to some Hollywood hussy?"

"No, Gramps, I'm not. It's a lie, just publicity."

"Good. Marry Rachel, boy. She's the best there is. None finer."

"I agree."

"You two was headed that way before you left."

"She has to agree," Rob said.

The old man let out a chuckle. "Son, she's always loved you. Since she was like five. Only you never did see it."

"So you think she'll say yes?" Rob asked, without turning to face her.

"Good God, yes! She needs someone to look out for her and I won't be here to do it. Not that she isn't independent and all that crap. She takes good care of me. And that ain't easy. I can be cantankerous sometimes."

"No, you don't say?"

Rachel saw Rob cover a smile with his hand.

Gramps slapped him. "Stop makin' fun of me. You're perfect for the job. She'll listen to you. She doesn't listen to a lot of people, but she'll listen to you."

"I agree, Gramps. And if she agrees, that's what we'll do," Rob said.

The old man wheezed, then let out a sigh. His chest rattled, and he grinned. "Now I can rest easy. Everything is taken care of."

"Don't talk like that," Rob said, an edge of panic in his voice.

"Don't be a dope. We all know the truth. Can't stop Father Time, Bobby. Now scoot. I'm tired," the old man said. He lay back in the bed and closed his eyes. Soon a gentle snore accompanied the sound from his chest. Rob pulled the covers up over the old man's shoulders. He slowly rose from the bed and doused the light.

He turned full eyes to Rachel. She slipped her arm around his waist. He draped his over her shoulders and pulled her close. Together, they crept quietly out of the old man's room.

ROB CARRIED A SMALL armchair into Gramps' room for Edie. She made herself comfortable and pulled out her phone.

"Will you be okay in the dark?" he asked.

"I can read just fine on this." She sat down, pulling a throw over her legs. "Good night, Rob and Rachel. Sleep well."

As Rachel turned toward the stairs, Rob stopped her.

"It's late and dark. Let me walk you home," Rob said.

"Okay."

When they got to the cottage, Rob leaned down and kissed her good night.

"Call me if you need anything," he said.

"Look, about that stuff Gramps said. About marrying me. It's okay. You don't have to."

"Can we table this discussion until tomorrow? I'm beat."

"Oh. Okay. Sure. Of course. Jet lag on top of everything else."

"Sleep tight," he said, cupping her cheek for a moment before picking his way across the path back to the store.

Rachel undressed and climbed into bed. The cottage was cold. She didn't like to leave logs on the stove when she wasn't there. If the place burned down, she'd be out on the street. Lying in bed, the dark and quiet surrounded her. Usually, those elements soothed her, and she'd drop off to sleep quickly. Not tonight. She tossed and punched the pillows. Being alone wouldn't cut it tonight.

After forty-five minutes of wrestling with the bedcovers, she threw on sweats plus her coat and tromped across the frozen lawn to the store. She opened the door slowly so as not to make the bell ring. Then she crept toward the back of the store as silent as a mouse. She opened the door to Rob's room. Stifling a grin, she moved closer. The big man had somehow rearranged his body to fit in the small bed. She took off her coat, hanging it on a chair, then her boots.

She approached the bed and touched the covers.

He opened his eyes. "Rach?"

"You're awake?"

"Everything okay?" he asked.

"Yeah."

"You couldn't sleep either?"

"No. Cold and lonely in the cottage."

Rob threw back the covers. "Not a lot of room, but we can do it."

She crawled in next to his large, warm body. Immediately, the heat from Rob warmed her bones. He slid his arm around her waist, pulling her into a spooning position. She curled against him. God, they fit together perfectly. He threw the blanket over them and rested his chin on her head.

"Good night," he said.

"Good night," she replied.

Within minutes, the pair was fast asleep.

The sound of the door opening woke Rachel first. Looking out the window, she saw total darkness. Her nerves tightened as the door opened wider.

"Rob?" It was Edie's voice.

"He's here. I am too," Rachel replied.

"Oh good."

Rachel sat up and stroked Rob's hair, then touched his cheek. "Rob. Edie's here."

"Edie? What? What? Something happen?" Rob yawned and sat up.

"Yes, I'm afraid Gramps' time has come. He's gone."

"Gone?" Both Rob and Rachel said at the same time.

"Yes. He slipped away quietly during the night."

Stunned, the would-be lovers sat still.

"You want to see him before I call 911?"

"Yes," Rob said. Rachel nodded. They pulled themselves from the warm bed into the cold before-dawn air. Rachel donned her coat. Rob wrapped a blanket around his half-clad body. They followed Edie into Gramps' room.

"I'll leave you," Edie said.

"Thanks," Rachel said.

She touched the old man's hand. "I can't believe it."

"Me either."

Tears streamed down her face. Rob drew her into his embrace and cried against her hair. A gentle knock at the door reminded them they weren't alone. Edie entered.

"I have to make the call. I've put on water for tea, or would you prefer coffee?"

"Tea for me," Rachel said.

"I'm gonna need strong coffee," Rob said.

"Okay, I'll get on it."

"What time is it?" Rachel asked.

"Four-thirty," Edie said right before she exited the room.

"I'd better get dressed," Rob said.

"Can I come with you?"

"Sure."

They went to his room and turned on the light. Rachel looked outside to see the sun was not ready to make an appearance yet. She kept her coat on and hugged herself against the cold knowledge that death had visited the store a short time ago.

There was no need for a siren for the ambulance. They heard two car doors slam shut and knew the medics had arrived to take Gramps away. Rachel rushed downstairs to let them in, but Edie had arrived first. She explained things.

"I'm sorry to hear this, Rachel," one of the medics said. "He was a nice old guy."

"Thanks. Yeah, he was," she replied.

Rob joined her, slipping his arm across her shoulders. She leaned against him. Shock and sadness filled her heart. What she had dreaded for so long had finally happened. As she watched the medics wrap Gramps in a sheet and put him on the gurney, a chill seeped into her bones.

The medic, Edie, Rachel, and Rob followed the gurney down to the ambulance. As the medical staff went to close the door, Rob stopped them.

"Wait. I want to ride with him."

"Relative?"

"Yes. His grandson."

"Okay. Get in."

Rob took a seat in the back. Rachel's heart rose to her throat. Again, as the door was about to be shut, Rob spoke. "No. Wait." He reached out his hand to Rachel, palm up. She nodded, placed hers in his, and climbed in next to him.

"She's my fiancée," Rob said.

"Hmm. Thought you were engaged to someone else," the driver said.

"Nope."

"Everyone in?" the medic asked. When he heard silence, he closed the door. Edie waved. The driver put the ambulance in gear, turned on the siren out of respect for Gramps, and roared out of the parking lot.

ROB SCRATCHED HIS STUBBLY face. A nurse sashayed by and offered him a cup of coffee. He glanced at her, then looked away. He could hardly believe she flirted with him. Talk about inappropriate! He took the cup and handed it to Rachel.

"Thanks," he said. His mouth hungered for that java, but he'd be damned if he'd play that woman's game. She needed to know he was there with Rachel.

The nurse made a face and turned to walk down the hall. Rachel handed the cup back to him.

"You need this more than I do."

"You're right." He accepted it and took a healthy sip.

The hospital smelled like all hospitals. People moved around quietly, nurses checking with doctors, doctors carrying charts, business as usual. A woman in a suit stopped by.

"Mr. Walsh, you were George Walsh's grandson?"

"That's right."

"Why don't you come into my office? We have some forms to fill out. Miss? Are you with him?"

"She's my fiancée."

"Oh. Okay, she can come too if you want."

"I do."

Rachel smacked his arm, leaned in, and whispered, "Stop telling people I'm your fiancée."

They followed the woman into the small office and sat in the two chairs facing the desk. Rob noticed a name plate, Rosalie Woods.

"Did the ER doctor ask you some questions?"

"Yes," Rob said. "I gave him the number of the hospice nurse too."

"We still have to have the medical examiner determine the cause of death. Most probably it was natural causes, but we need to follow the rules."

"I understand."

As Ms. Woods asked questions, Rob laced his fingers with Rachel's. She sat by quietly, listening and gripping his hand.

They returned home at noon. Edie was gone, and the store felt empty, the silence solemn. The couple returned to Rob's bed and slept for several hours. When they awoke, Rob treated them to dinner at Homer's. With a table close to the robust fire in the fireplace, Rob felt his bones warm.

"I invited Drew Armstrong to the funeral."

"Drew?"

"He's a good attorney. He has Gramps' will and can read it to us after."

"There won't be anyone coming to the funeral, will there?" Rachel said, gazing at the flames.

"You might be surprised. Those who liked him will come to pay respects, and those who didn't like him will come to spit in his grave."

Rachel cracked a smile. "You may be right."

They spent the next few days taking care of all the details required for planning a funeral. Rob and Rachel worked together. On their phones or running errands, they stuck together. By mutual agreement that didn't require a discussion, they resumed sleeping together in Rachel's bed in the cottage.

Rob managed to avoid the press and go about his business undetected. Rachel and Pine Grove were his home now. A week after Gramps passed, Rob got a call from the realtor. She'd found a buyer who offered almost the asking price for his home. He gave her the green light to accept.

His next job, after the film was in the can, would be to pack up that huge house he'd never called home, sell as much as he could, and ship the rest to Pine Grove. He didn't know where he'd put it yet, but he'd figure that out when the time came.

Rachel had defrosted the leftover stew she'd stowed in the freezer for their dinner.

"So you're selling?" She picked up a piece of meat with her fork.

"Yep. Found a buyer. As soon as *Thunder and Patch* is done, I'm getting rid of everything I can and bringing the rest back here."

"Where will you put it? Where will you live?"

"I don't know," he said, spearing a carrot. "I'll know more after the will is read."

"What do you mean?"

"I have a hunch Gramps left me the store," Rob said, picking up his glass of water.

"You're not going to come back here and run the store, are you?" Rachel narrowed her eyes.

"No. I don't know shit about running the store. Let's wait and see. Don't want to count on anything yet."

"Good idea."

"But I'm coming back," he said, shoveling a piece of meat into his mouth.

"Really?" She lifted her eyebrows.

When he finished chewing and swallowed his food, he spoke. "You can count on it."

Chapter Sixteen

A *week later, 7 a.m.*
Rachel awoke bundled in Rob's arms and surrounded by the comforter. It was cold in the cottage. She leaped out of bed, grabbed her flannel robe, and shoved two logs into the stove. Then she put on slippers and padded to the kitchen. Though it was early, the sun already poked a few rays into the sky. It was the day of Gramps' funeral.

"Rob, time to get up," she said, giving his shoulder a gentle shake.

"It's fucking freezing in here," he mumbled, cracking open one eye.

"I put a couple of logs on and turned on the oven. Coffee's hot. Come into the kitchen." She breezed out of the bedroom.

As she pulled a pan from the cabinet and put it on the stove, she heard grumpy grumblings and some swear words mumbled from the bedroom. Yawning and rubbing his face, Rob stumbled into the kitchen. Although he wore a robe, it wasn't fastened across his body, hanging loose over his shoulders instead. Rachel tried not to stare, but his chest was simply too perfect to ignore. He stopped at the table.

"Good morning. I think," he said.

She sashayed over to him and rested her palms on his pecs. Gazing into his eyes, she smiled. "Good morning to you too. Hungry?"

"Coffee."

"Okay." She filled a mug, added milk, and handed it to him. He took several sips before plunking down on a chair and guzzling the hot drink.

"Yeah. Tough to wake up today," she said, refilling her mug.

She pulled a carton of eggs and some butter from the fridge and started on breakfast.

He pushed up and joined her, snaking his arms around her middle. He bent to kiss her neck.

"Now I'm feeling human," he whispered.

"We were up too late last night."

"Yeah," he said, wearing a sly grin, reaching up to rest his hand on her breast.

She giggled and smacked his hand.

"I can't help it if I get horny around you."

"Let me be or I'll burn the eggs."

He let go and returned to the table. Within minutes, the two dug into plates of perfectly scrambled eggs. Rob buttered the toast and handed a piece to Rachel.

"I feel like I should be making toast for Gramps," he said, casting his gaze to his plate.

"I know." She put a forkful of eggs in her mouth.

"I thought he was invincible. He seemed so strong, so sharp. I swear in the last ten years he didn't age at all."

"He did. You just didn't see it."

"We're not going to go there again, are we?" His voice took on a sharp edge. "I've apologized a hundred times for being off living my own life and not watching over Gramps."

She squeezed his forearm. "I'm sorry. I didn't mean that. I meant even when you were here, you didn't see how different he was." She took a bite of toast.

"He was always the same old Gramps to me."

"Yeah, well, he put that on for you. He didn't want to let you down. Didn't want you to think less of him—see his vulnerable side."

"I wouldn't have thought less of him." Rob scooped up some eggs with his fork.

"He thought he always had to be your hero. That you counted on him. He couldn't show weakness. Even when he was weak."

"He sure showed it at the end. It's like it all came crashing in on him at once. I swear, I thought he'd be here forever," Rob said, putting down his fork. He covered his eyes with his hand.

Rachel leaned over and kissed his head. "I know. So did I."

They finished eating and cleaned up the kitchen in silence. They showered, giving each other a wide latitude. There was no time for loving. Rachel checked the clock.

"It's almost nine. Service starts at ten."

Rob stood at the mirror, tying his tie. Rachel slipped a dark red dress over her head.

"What's the temperature?" she asked. Rob checked his phone. "A balmy thirty degrees."

"Not too bad for the first of February," she remarked, fishing a scarf and hat from a drawer.

"Ready?" He turned.

She took a breath. God, in his black suit, white shirt, and sky-blue tie, he looked gorgeous. She'd never get over gazing at him and remembering anew how handsome he was.

"You look great. Gramps would approve," she said.

His gaze roamed over her. "You too." The sound of a car honking drew his attention. "Let's go."

They took their time down the steep stairs, grabbed their coats, and got into the waiting limousine provided by the funeral home. According to Gramps' wishes, the funeral would be graveside.

IT WAS ABOUT A FIFTEEN-minute drive to the graveyard. When the car pulled up to the Catskill Cemetery, Rachel spied the casket and the open grave. Her heart sped up for a few moments.

A few people milled around, looking uncomfortable. The gray clouds parted to let in some sunlight.

"Gramps always loved a sunny winter's day," she murmured.

Rob got out of the car and offered her his hand. She stood up and wobbled a bit. He caught her and drew her close.

"I don't remember the last time I wore these heels."

"I can see that." He grinned. "Don't worry, I've got you."

Arm-in-arm, they walked slowly up the path. The funeral director and Drew Armstrong raised their hands in greeting. A small crowd gathered. People meandered up from the parking lot. Rachel and Rob had put up notices around town and there was a mention in the local paper.

Laura and Barney were there as was Rachel's friend, Winnie, the waitress at Java the Hut. Derek Larch from the hardware store, who did odd jobs for Gramps, stood looking cold and uncomfortable in a suit. Flint McKay represented the fire department. Grey Andrews, the town supervisor, arrived with his wife, Carrie.

"I didn't expect this many people," Rachel said.

"He knew everyone in town," Rob said. The couple greeted people, shook hands, and thanked them for coming. The size of the crowd warmed Rachel's heart. Seems as if Gramps had touched many people in Pine Grove.

Laura approached them. "We're inviting everyone back to The Cozy Café for coffee and pie after the funeral," Laura said.

"You shouldn't have," Rachel said.

"Gramps was a fixture in this town. An institution. It's the least we can do. People took up a collection to pay for it. So, no worries," she said, patting Rachel's arm.

"Thank you."

The funeral director approached. "Ready, Rob?"

"Yep." He drew a folded paper from his pocket.

"Folks, could you gather around, please? We're ready to start," the director said, gesturing.

Rob opened the paper and read a few lines from a famous poem...

"'And I, I took the road less traveled by. And it has made all the difference,'" Rob said. He pulled a handkerchief out of his back pocket and wiped his eyes. "I don't think anyone here today would disagree that Gramps, George Lawrence Walsh, took the road less traveled. He was unique. One of a kind. Never met a man or woman he didn't like. Worked hard all his life. And loved that crazy old general store.

"He was my rock, my family, when my family was gone. He believed in me and always supported me. I take much with me from his example and his instruction. He taught me to have compassion and how to split a log, how to balance a checkbook, and how to make a campfire. Thank you all for coming to say a final goodbye to Gramps. He was a wonderful man and will be sorely missed." Rob sniffed, blew his nose, wiped his eyes, and stepped back.

The funeral director came forward. "Rachel, do you want to say a few words?"

She stepped forward. "Gramps was my father, my grandfather, and my friend—all rolled into one. He corrected my mistakes and applauded my victories. Taught me how to stock shelves and when to reorder inventory. He taught me to laugh when life got tough. And to be grateful when it got good. He was a beacon of positive life and energy. I'll miss him every day." She drew a tissue from her pocket and wiped her eyes.

The funeral director pressed a button, and the casket was lowered into the grave. While Rob and Rachel stood aside, people came by and tossed in small remembrances or flowers. When the gravediggers started filling in the grave with dirt, Drew Armstrong approached the couple.

"Are you going to The Cozy?" he asked.

Rob looked at Rachel. "Sure. Yeah. Why?"

"Why don't you come by my office tomorrow morning, and we'll read the updated will."

"Okay. Good, Rob?" she asked.

"Yeah. Fine. Thanks, Drew."

Rob and Rachel piled into the limousine, which took them to The Cozy Café. There was a sign outside that said: "Closed for Private Party". Rachel smiled. She knew they'd let in anyone from Pine Grove for free coffee and pie.

After hanging up their coats, Rob and Rachel took a seat. Laura and the staff brought them beverages and slices from four different kinds of pie—apple, coconut custard, pecan, and lemon chiffon. As they sat and ate, people came over and related stories about Gramps.

Some Rachel knew, but others were new. When she finished eating, she took Rob's hand under the table.

"So when are you two gonna get married? Or are you just gonna live in sin?" one woman asked.

Rachel sucked in air.

"I don't think Gramps would've liked that," the woman went on.

Rachel simply stared.

"We haven't set the date yet. But I'm sure you'll hear about it when we do," Rob said, patting Rachel's hand.

Rachel widened her eyes and shifted her gaze to him. He wore a sheepish grin. Satisfied, the woman smiled, nodded, and walked over to the pie table.

Rob leaned over and whispered in her ear, "Got rid of her, didn't I?"

Did he say that to get rid of the busybody, or did he mean it? And how could they set a date if he hadn't even proposed and was still engaged to someone else?

AFTER THE PIE RECEPTION was over, Rob and Rachel went to Homer's for some real food and drink. They shared a bottle of wine and burgers. Homer offered to drive them home, and he dropped them off with a wave.

Since they'd been gone all day, the front lights on the store weren't lit. It was dark, cold, and forbidding. A frigid wind howled through the trees behind the building. Rachel shivered. Without Gramps there, the store had an eerie, strange feel.

"I hope he didn't leave the store to me," she said, hurrying up the path.

"Why?" Rob asked.

"Because I don't want it. It's creepy without Gramps here. No fire lit, no warm smells from the kitchen. No one to ask me how I am. No thank you." Her frozen fingers fumbled with the keys.

"You wouldn't have to be here all alone," Rob said, waiting for Rachel to unlock the door.

She managed to turn the key, and the door swung open. They stepped inside. It wasn't much warmer in the store than outside. Rachel stomped her feet to get her blood running. The store was pitch black. It was so dark she couldn't see her hand in front of her face. Reaching out to where she thought the light switch was, she felt around the wall until she found it.

Even with the lights on, the store seemed cold and unwelcoming. It was too quiet, the air still, the shelves stuffed with boxes and cans. Loneliness penetrated her coat and seeped right into her bones. Soon Rob would return to the West Coast, and she'd be alone.

Rob put his hand on her shoulder. "Let's stay in the cottage tonight."

"Good idea," she said.

Happy to leave the spooky store, she locked the door behind them. The idea of being alone in the store terrified her. She pushed it out of her head. No, she'd not stay here after he left. She'd go back to her cottage if it was still hers. Or she'd leave. Get a job somewhere. Teaching maybe? She knew her days in the store were numbered. It simply was not the same familiar place she'd grown to love.

They hurried down the path to get out of the cold. She opened the door, and they scooted inside. Even the cottage was dark and cold.

"I'll get a fire started in the stove," Rob said, disappearing into the bedroom.

"I'll get the kettle on," she said.

As she gathered tea, sugar, and milk and took down teacups from the cupboard, she contemplated her future. For a planner, an organizer like Rachel, she'd completely forgotten to have a plan for her life after Gramps passed on. She'd always pushed that gruesome thought out of her head rather than dwell on it. So it had happened, and she didn't know what she'd do. She'd saved up some money, but not enough to last more than a year or two.

Where would she live? Certainly not in the store. She chewed her lip as she raised the flame under the kettle. Mentally, she chastised herself for not having a plan and for not making arrangements for herself. Nope, always too busy taking care of Gramps and the store, which was like a toddler and needed constant tending.

Now she'd have to deal with the consequences of refusing to face reality. Having a plan would have brought comfort. How good it would be to simply slip into a tailor-made new life, a new place to live, a new career. It would have made facing this day easier. But she hadn't done it and now she'd be in crisis mode. The reading of the will would happen the next day. Drew said it was an updated will. Did Gramps leave her the cottage, like he said he would? If everything went to Rob, would he let her stay on until she had somewhere to go? Insecurity shook her.

Before she set up the tea, Rob appeared in the doorway.

"Stop," he said.

She turned to face him and raised her eyebrows.

"It's nine already. I'm done. The day is over. I've got the stove started. Let's go to bed."

Rachel turned off the kettle and followed him into the bedroom. They undressed in silence. The only sound was the howl of the wind. Some icy air crept inside through minute cracks, and places where windows no longer had a tight fit.

Rob ripped down the covers, and the lovers slid into bed. He pulled up the blankets and drew Rachel close. Before they could make love, both were fast asleep.

The next morning, they awoke with the sun. Rachel dressed quickly and headed for the kitchen. Rob called out from the bedroom.

"Let's go out to breakfast."

She turned. "All this eating out is getting expensive."

"Don't worry. I can afford it. Come on. Let's make it easy. Then we can head over to Drew's."

"Okay. But coffee here first?"

"Sounds good."

As she stood measuring coffee grounds into the machine, Rob came up behind her. He folded his fingers over her shoulders, bent to kiss her neck, and whispered, "Don't worry about anything. I'll take care of you. You won't be alone."

Rachel closed her eyes and wished she believed him.

ROB HELD THE DOOR TO Drew's office open for Rachel. He hoped to get answers from Drew. The bank had transferred ten thousand bucks a month from Rob's account to Gramps' for years. What happened to that money? Why were they living like paupers? That should have been enough money to pay for the essentials, like wood for the stove and food and property taxes, with plenty left over.

Gramps had bought the store from Cassie McKay. Two years ago, Rob had paid that loan off. So what happened to all that money? Gramps was a believer in blood being thicker than water, so Rob had no doubt he'd left his store to his grandson. But what about Rachel? Did he cut her out of his estate? Anxiety grew in his chest and sweat broke out on his forehead, even though it was cold outside.

Drew's office wasn't exactly chilly, but it wasn't toasty either. Like many Pine Grove residents, the room was heated by a wood stove. A kettle rested on top of the stove. Drew rose from his chair when the couple entered.

"Tea?" he asked.

"No thanks. Just finished breakfast," Rob said.

"Me too," Rachel said.

"Sit down, sit down. First, I want you to know I'm so sorry for your loss. Your grandfather was a fixture in this town. He will be greatly missed."

Drew indicated two chairs across from his impressive desk, and Rob and Rachel each took a seat. The lawyer rummaged through a small stack of papers on his desk before he pulled out Gramps' will. He sat forward, leaving the will on the desk and reading the contents.

"I leave the general store, its contents, the barn, the outbuildings, and all twenty acres to my grandson, Bobby. A fine young man."

Rob let out a breath. He wanted the store and now it was his. His pulse jumped as Drew turned the page. Was there something for Rachel?

"As I promised many times, I leave the little cottage on the property to Rachel Cohen."

Just as Rob was about to ask about the money, Drew held up his hand and cleared his throat. "That's not all."

Rob sat back, his eyes on the lawyer.

"Through the generosity of my grandson, I've been able to put aside a little money. He's a famous actor and a rich man, so I know he doesn't need it. I leave all my bank accounts and the cash under the floorboards in the kitchen to Rachel Cohen."

"Cash? Gramps didn't have any money. We lived hand-to-mouth," Rachel said.

"Not true. You may have thought you were living hand-to-mouth, but George put away a tidy sum. He had an investment account through Pine Grove National Bank."

"He did?" Rachel raised her eyebrows. "Really?"

"Yes, really," Drew said. "And if you'll wait a minute, I have the latest statement here."

Rachel faced Rob and grinned. "Crafty old guy," she said.

Rob nodded. So that's what the old man did with the money. Rob chided himself for not figuring it out. Since he'd never had much, Gramps had always been frugal. A leopard doesn't change his spots, does he?

"Ah yes. Here it is. Let's see. Hmm. As of yesterday, the account has three hundred fifty thousand dollars in it," Drew said, reading from the statement. Then he looked up. "And it's all yours, Rachel."

Rachel sucked in air. "What?!"

"Three hundred fifty-two thousand, twenty-three dollars, to be exact," Drew said. "What are you going to do with all that money?"

"Don't forget the cash under the floorboards in the kitchen," Rob added.

Rachel's eyes welled. She covered her face with her hands and sobbed. Rob moved closer and slipped his arm across her shoulders.

She buried her face in his shoulder. When she contained herself, she fished a tissue from her purse and straightened up.

"Why that old so-and-so! All the times we scrimped, and he'd been socking away a fortune."

"Do you have plans for the money?" Drew asked.

"Plans? I had no idea there was any money. Or that it would come to me. I'm shocked."

Rob smiled. "Glad to know he did the smart thing with that money. Now you have options, Rachel."

Her face brightened. "Yes. I do."

"I'll prepare the paperwork and get in touch with the bank. I'll call you when everything is ready. I'll need your signatures and I have the deed for the property. George made sure everything was legal and in one place. Bless him for making this easier for me," Drew said.

"Okay," Rachel said.

"In the meantime, I took the liberty of cashing three thousand dollars, so you'd have some money to live on until the papers are ready. I have no idea how much is under the floorboards." Drew opened a drawer and took out a fat envelope. He handed it to Rachel. She took it, stared at it, then stuffed it in her bag.

"I can't believe it. Crafty old guy." She faced Rob. "What are you going to do with the store?"

"Not sure yet. But I have some ideas."

Drew stood up. "Let me get to work on transferring everything." He offered his hand. "Good luck to you both."

They shook his hand, then headed outside and got in Rachel's rust bucket of a car.

"I'm sure you have your own ideas about the money, but please tell me the first thing you're going to do is buy a new car!" Rob said.

"A new car? Great idea. Let's get a big one. An SUV," she said, grinning.

"How about we head to Ray's dealership right now and pick one out?" Rob said.

"Perfect! Let's go. Do you think they'll give me anything on a trade-in for this one?" she asked.

"I think they'll charge you to dispose of it," Rob said, laughing as he closed the door and turned the key in the ignition.

Chapter Seventeen

After choosing her new car and watching Rob negotiate a good deal, Rachel got back in her jalopy.

"Come on. I'm going to take you to lunch—for a change," she said.

"That cash burning a hole in your pocket already?"

"I'm going to deposit some on the way. Let's go to Java the Hut. I want to tell Winnie."

"Works for me," he said, leaning back against the worn springs in the cracked seat. "I'll be glad when you can pick up your new wheels. This thing feels like it's going to fall apart while I'm sitting in it."

"This baby has been through a lot. Give her some respect."

"I'd like to give her a spot at the car graveyard."

Rachel laughed. Thrilled at the beautiful new car she'd be picking up the following week, Rachel's heart swelled.

"You know I had no idea Gramps had squirreled away all that money."

"I know. When you told me how you were scraping by, I couldn't figure out what he'd done with it."

"I guess he figured we could get along okay and he wanted to leave me something."

"Did he actually pay you a salary?"

"Not really. He'd slip me fifty or a hundred bucks when he could. I did substitute teaching when I could get it. I didn't have rent and Gramps paid for food, so my expenses were low, and I was careful."

Rob frowned. "When was the last time you bought a new dress?"

She shrugged. "Don't remember. I don't wear dresses much. Jeans are more like it. And you'd be surprised how long you can make those last."

Rachel pulled into the parking lot. The temperature had dropped to a frosty twenty degrees. She tied her scarf around her neck for the mad dash from the car to the front door. Since it was only eleven, between the breakfast and lunch crowds, the restaurant was fairly empty. Only one other customer sipped coffee at the counter.

"Take any table you want," Winnie called out, grabbing two menus.

They took a booth by the window. A chickadee snatched a seed from the bird feeder and flew by.

"God, it's cold. I forgot how bone-chilling it gets in Pine Grove," Rob said, rubbing his hands together.

"Don't you have gloves?" Rachel asked.

"Nope. Don't need 'em in Southern California."

Winnie hurried over. "How are you doin', Rachel?" The waitress drew her eyebrows together.

"I'm okay. I mean, he couldn't last forever, could he?"

"No, honey. Still. It's not easy."

"No, it isn't."

"Whatcha havin'?" She placed menus in front of the couple.'

"What's your soup today?" Rob asked.

"Homemade chicken and rice. Darn good too. Burgers are on special too."

"I'll have a bowl of chicken soup and a side salad," Rachel said.

"Aw, rabbit food. It's cold outside," Rob said. "I'll have a bowl of soup and a cheeseburger with fries."

"Changed my mind. That sounds good. I'll have the same," Rachel said.

"Coming right up." Winnie hustled away to the kitchen to place their orders.

"So, what are you gonna do with the money?" Rob asked.

"I don't know. Need time to think about it."

"It's a lot of money."

"Maybe not for you, but it is for me."

"It's a lot for anybody," Rob said.

Winnie strolled over with a coffeepot. "Coffee?"

As he sipped his coffee, Rob suggested things she could do with the money. "You could blow this hick town and move to California."

"I like it here. I have friends."

"Okay. Then buy yourself an apartment in the city."

"It's not that much money," she replied.

The food arrived, and they dug in. Conversation stopped. Rachel stared out the window. The sun came out, glistening on the snow. With the trees bare, she could see Marsh Street in the distance. With a blanket of snow on everything, the old Victorian house painted yellow and white stood out and caught Rachel's eye.

It was huge, empty, and rumored to be haunted. Maybe, like her, the old place simply needed some TLC to become a star, like it must have been in its day.

"So what are you gonna do?" he asked.

"I've gotta think about it for a while." She couldn't stop staring at that house.

WHEN THEY WERE DOWN to the last few fries, Rob's phone rang. It was Barbara.

Rob excused himself and took the call.

"When are you coming back?" Barbara asked.

"We just buried him a couple of days ago." He picked up two fries.

"That's done. Why are you staying?"

"There are a few things to clear up."

"One more day. The studio is down my neck. You're holding up the whole production."

"I know, but..."

"But nothing. Finish up tomorrow and get your ass back here. It wouldn't be impossible to replace you, you know."

"Really?"

"Yeah. If you didn't have Wendy doing a ton of publicity, I'm not sure the studio would have given you this much time."

"Is she still shooting off her mouth?" He drained the last of his coffee.

"Yeah, and the media is eating it up."

"Ask yourself this, Barb. If she's my fiancée, why isn't she here in Pine Grove? Why didn't she go to the funeral?"

Silence.

"Yeah, I thought so. No reason. Because she's *not* my fiancée."

"Whatever. Just get back here. I've made plane reservations for tomorrow and ordered the limo. Be ready." The phone went dead.

Rob raised his eyes to Rachel's. "You heard?"

She nodded.

"I do have to go."

"If you have to sign anything else, I'll send it to you." She dipped the last of her fries in the ketchup on her plate.

Rob took her hand in his across the table. "It's just for three months."

"Then what?" She ate the last bite of her burger.

"Then I'm coming back."

"Oh? What about Wendy?"

"I'm coming back to marry the woman I love. *You.* And settle right here." Rob finished his last four fries.

"I wish I could believe you." She wiped her mouth with a napkin.

"I'm telling the truth."

"Once they get their hooks into you, you'll be finished. There's always something. Some reason to stay, isn't there?"

"Not this time. This time there's a huge reason to come home. Back here. To you. If you'll have me." Rob balled up his napkin and put it on his empty plate.

"Ask me again in three months." Rachel picked up the check.

"You won't find someone else while I'm gone, will you?"

She laughed. "In this sleepy little town? Who?" She fished some bills from her purse and left them on the table.

"Just don't. Promise?"

"I promise. Now you promise not to marry Wendy."

Rob laughed. "That's easy. I promise."

The couple bundled up, then hurried out to the car, and drove back to the store.

"The store is yours now," Rachel said, getting out of the car. "What do you want me to do with it?"

"Sell everything. Keep the money."

"And reorder?"

"No. Just sell off the stuff. Let me know when the shelves are empty. I have plans for the store."

"You're not going to tear it down, are you?" she asked, fitting the key in the lock.

"Nope."

He followed her inside.

"Then what?" she asked, taking off her coat and hanging it on a hook by the door.

"It'll be a surprise."

She laughed and shook her head. "Just when I think I've got you figured out..."

Rob took off his coat and then backed Rachel up against the wall. He lowered his mouth to hers for a hungry kiss.

"We've only got until tomorrow. Let's not waste time talking about the future," he said, sliding his hands up her chest to cup her breasts.

She wound her arms around his neck. "Let's not talk at all," she said.

Rob lifted her up as if she weighed nothing and carried her to his small bed. Rachel turned on the space heater while Rob ripped off his clothes.

"Now you," he said, helping her undress.

Heat from their bodies made the space heater unnecessary. He put Rachel flat on the bed and got on top. He squeezed her breast as he drew his leg up between hers, pressing against her sex. She ravaged his mouth. He pinched her nipple gently, sending a zing straight to her core.

She reached down and closed her fingers around his erection. He was rock-hard.

"Damn," she murmured.

"You do that to me," he breathed.

Rolling on his side, he replaced his knee with his hand. After pressing against her clit with his palm, he rotated it. When she started to moan, he slid his fingers down and entered her.

"You're wet."

"Yeah. You do that to me."

He chuckled, then pumped his fingers in and out.

"I can't wait," he said, mounting her.

She raised her legs, hooking one on his shoulder. He groaned when he entered her.

"So damn good," he said.

He moved quickly, building up incredible heat. Rachel tried to hang on, but his steady rhythm brought her to orgasm quickly. She cried out, clutching his back, burying her face in his neck.

"Oh, baby. Yeah. Come for me," he muttered.

He lowered his lips to her head, thrust hard and fast, then stopped, moaning. They lay in each other's arms. She stroked his back, then ran her nails over his skin.

"Damn. That feels good," he said, closing his eyes.

Rob pulled the covers up over them, and within minutes, they were fast asleep.

Chapter Eighteen

After making love two more times during the night, the lovers were woken up by the insistent, repeated honking of a car horn. Luckily, Rob had already packed his suitcase. They leaped out of bed, and Rob threw on a robe and ran out the front door to the parking lot.

The driver of the limousine rolled down the window.

"I'm gonna be a little late," Rob said.

"I'm a little early. You've got twenty minutes to get ready. Then we have to roll or you'll miss your plane," the driver said.

Rob gave a tight smile, then ran back inside. Rachel was in the kitchen fussing with the coffeemaker.

"I've got to get dressed and leave," he said, ripping off his robe and racing into the bedroom.

Before he could button his shirt, the aroma of freshly brewed coffee tantalized his nose. He joined Rachel in the kitchen.

"Here," she said, handing him a mug of Joe doctored the way he liked it.

"Did I ever tell you you're indispensable?" he asked, bringing the steaming mug to his lips.

Together, they sipped in silence. Rob glanced at the clock. He had five minutes left. Rachel poured more coffee into a travel mug and sealed it.

"Take this with you," she said.

"There's so much I want to say, but there's no time."

"Yeah. I know." She brought her gaze up to meet his.

"I love you. We will make this happen," he said, emptying his mug. "I will be back."

"Yeah. Sure," she said, casting her gaze to her hands.

He grabbed her chin and eased it up until their eyes met. "You can make book on it."

"What about Wendy what's-her-name?"

"Forget her. You're still going to be here when I get back, aren't you?"

"Where would I go?"

"Now that you have some money, you could go anywhere. Bangkok, Paris, Iceland..."

"Iceland? You're kidding."

"I am," he said, grinning. "But you could. You'll have the money to start over anywhere."

"Yeah, but I won't have you."

The honking of the horn interrupted them.

Rob grabbed her and held her tight up against him. "I'll miss you."

"I love you," she said, then whispered, "come back to me," before their lips met in a passionate kiss.

When they broke apart, Rob grabbed the travel mug and his suitcase and hurried toward the door. Rachel ran after him. The limo driver stood. He stashed Rob's bag and shut the trunk. Rob stopped to wave one time to Rachel, who stood in the doorway, her arms wrapped around herself. Then he slid into the back seat and the driver closed the door.

As the driver took command of the car, Rob opened the window and waved. Then they sped out of the parking lot and onto the road leading to the highway. Facing back, Rob watched Rachel waving until they turned a corner to enter the expressway. He sighed and blinked rapidly. He couldn't remember a happier time in his life than the past few weeks. Even though he'd had to say goodbye to Gramps,

Rachel's love surrounded him, keeping sadness at bay. Now he had nothing, and the chill of loneliness permeated his bones, making him shiver.

"Should I turn up the heat, sir?" the driver asked.

"Sure," Rob replied, even though he knew no amount of heat could chase the cold from him. As the car sped along, he made a mental note of things he needed to do. Then his phone rang. It was Barbara.

"Tell me, please, you're on your way to the airport?"

"I am."

He heard her sigh. "Oh, thank God."

"Did you think I'd actually run out on this film?"

"You've been acting crazy ever since you went back to Pine Grove. I didn't know what to expect."

"I'm okay. Stop worrying."

"Good. Great. And Wendy?"

"Wendy is a producer's pipedream. Not happening. I will call her when I get home." He stopped. But L.A. wasn't home anymore, was it? Pine Grove was home now. "Back to L.A."

"And tell her what?"

"I don't know."

"Remember that guy I told you about?"

"Andrew something?"

"Yeah. I think he's a better way to go. Sit back and listen. I've got an idea," she said.

Rob opened the travel mug and sipped coffee while Barbara laid out her plan.

RACHEL GLANCED AT THE outdoor thermometer. It was an icy twenty-two degrees. Feeling the cold penetrate her flimsy robe, she scampered back into the store. She closed and locked the door and hurried up the stairs. After pouring herself another cup of hot coffee, she put on a flannel-lined fleece she kept in the store.

"Cash under the floorboards?" Rachel said aloud to herself. Drew had said the money was in the kitchen. Curiosity tempted her. She had to find that money, figuring it would probably be grocery money for a week or two, like maybe two hundred bucks. But she'd never have guessed Gramps had saved so much to leave to her. So...she started poking around, knocking on any board that looked loose until she found the right one.

Using a sturdy serving fork, Rachel pried up the suspicious board. Sure enough, there was a jar there with a wad of cash rolled up inside. She pulled it out and replaced the board. After refreshing her coffee, she opened the jar and pulled out the bills. She laid them out and counted.

Twenty-five hundred dollars, mostly in hundred-dollar bills! After she finished counting, she counted again. Her mouth hung open. "You sure surprised me, old man," she said to the walls. "I'll put this to good use." She added the bills to her purse and sat back.

The quiet in the store was deafening. No more Gramps and no more Rob. She rustled up some scrambled eggs and sausage. Sitting by the window, she watched the chickadees at the feeder. Rob had started an idea in her head. In a day or two, she'd have a whole lot of money. He was correct that she'd have the means to go anywhere and set up a new home.

Dreams about international travel when she'd been a teen returned. Curious about all sorts of places, she'd looked up the most exotic ones and wondered what they were like. But now that the opportunity to find out had arrived, she didn't want to go. What fun would exploring be alone? What she wanted was a stable, warm place to live—preferably with real heat instead of a wood stove.

She wanted to own something. To have a little business of her own. Obviously, Rob intended to do something with the store, and she'd not be a part of it. At least he hadn't asked her to participate. Checking her watch, she realized she'd be expected at Drew's office to pick up a check made out to the dealership. Today was the day she'd get her new car. And damn, it had better have a good heating system!

She cleaned up the kitchen, donned her down jacket, cranked up the old rust bucket, and left. Drew was the executor of Gramps' estate and had the power to turn over money to her before the estate finished probate. She picked up the check and thanked him, then drove over to the dealership.

She signed the paperwork for her brand-new white RAV 4 and turned over the check. When she got into her new vehicle, she fiddled with the heat until the inside grew toasty, then drove the vehicle away. The car seduced her. She didn't want to stop and drove all around town, trying it out on back roads and the highway, ending up on Marsh Road. She parked the car in front of the old, beat-up yellow-and-white Victorian and got out.

As she stared at the building, her eyes played tricks on her. She ceased to see the flaws, the peeling paint, and the broken windows. Instead she saw how beautiful it would be with fresh paint, new windows, and some TLC.

She walked up the old flagstone path overgrown with weeds poking through between the stones and tried the front door. The knob turned, and the door opened.

"It's not locked?" she said aloud to herself as she stepped over the threshold. A musty, empty-house smell greeted her. She heard the sounds of tiny mouse-like feet scurrying away. Although what met her eye had deteriorated to a sorry state due to neglect, she saw past that.

"Good bones," she said to herself. Rachel walked slowly through the entryway and into the large living room. Charming molding proudly hugged the tall windows. The wood floor needed refinishing but looked hearty. She continued to the kitchen, which took her back to the 1950s with its ancient appliances and loud colors.

"Maybe even three hundred thousand isn't enough?" she asked herself. Approaching the old, steep staircase, she stopped. Glancing up into the darkness at the top, she got chills. The house was cold and the staircase spooky and forbidding.

"If there are ghosts living here, they're up there," she said aloud. She approached the stairs slowly. The first step creaked. Rachel jumped back.

"Maybe doing this alone is dumb," she said. Backing away from the stairs, she left the house and stopped on the path. She took out her phone and took a picture of the weathered real estate sign stuck firmly in the ground.

Raising the collar on her coat against the winterish wind blowing off the lake, she sped up her pace and headed home. Once inside the store, she loaded logs into the stove, put up the kettle for tea, and took down the "closed" sign.

Perched on the window seat in the front of the store, she sipped tea and stared out at the day that had turned overcast. The grayness seeped into her bones.

"Winter," she muttered.

Before she could finish her beverage, two customers came in.

"Are you having a sale?" one woman asked.

"A sale?" Rachel asked.

"Yeah. I mean now that Gramps is gone. Are you gonna reduce prices to get rid of stuff?"

Rachel's eyes widened. People sure didn't wait long to zoom in like vultures and pick at the bones of the dearly departed, did they?

"No, actually I was thinking of raising prices," Rachel remarked, putting down her cup.

"Raising prices?" The woman's eyebrows shot up.

"Gotta pay for the funeral."

"Oh. I see," the woman said and turned toward the door.

The lady in the back came forward. "Is this all you got in flour?"

"Whatever's there," Rachel replied.

"You gonna get in more?"

Rachel shook her head. "Nope. This is it."

"Oh. Okay. Sorry about Gramps, Rachel," the woman said.

"Thanks. Do you want the flour?"

"Yep."

Rachel rang up the purchase and put the sack of flour in a bag. Gramps never would have approved of a sale because he passed. She'd stick to her guns. She had three months to get rid of everything. No reason to rush into a sale, was there?

She picked up her phone and dialed.

"Larch Realty," a woman said.

"I'm calling about that big yellow Victorian on Marsh Street," Rachel said.

"Oh, yes. I'm handling the sale. Do you want to see the house?"

"How much is it?" Rachel asked, her fingers crossed.

"Well, it's quite an old house. Though it needs repair, it's an antique," the woman went on.

"How much?"

"You are direct, aren't you?"

"How much?"

"Seventy-five thousand."

Rachel sucked in air.

"You interested? What's your name?"

"Rachel Cohen."

"Interested?"

"I don't know. I'll get back to you," Rachel said and ended the conversation. Next, she called Will Lennox.

"Hi, Will. Rachel Cohen. Say, do you have time to take on a new project?" she asked, fingers still crossed.

ROB'S HOUSEKEEPER HAD been at his house during his absence. He opened the fridge to find it full. She had left some of her specialties in the freezer. Plastic containers of lamb stew, chili, and chicken casserole were stacked neatly. He licked his lips in anticipation of a great meal to come.

His doorbell rang. It was Barbara. He opened the door, and she stepped inside.

"Welcome home! Here," she said, thrusting a small shopping bag at him.

He pulled out a bottle of champagne.

"Thanks. Say, you got a couple of hours to kill?"

"For you, sure. Why not?"

"Good, come with me," he said, taking her arm and leading her to his car.

Four hours later, they returned. He invited her to stay for some lamb stew, but she declined.

"I have a husband expecting me home for dinner."

"Thanks for all your help today."

"I hope you know what you're doing," she said.

"I do. And once we put your plan in place, things will be fixed, and it will be smooth sailing."

"Really? Isn't that a lot to expect?" Barbara asked.

"Not when you have a woman like I do. And no, not Wendy. Rachel. How about a quick toast?" He opened the split of champagne.

"Sure. What are we toasting to?"

"To happiness. Love and happiness," he said.

"And fat movie contracts?" she added.

Rob laughed and poured the wine.

They sat in his spacious living room.

"Are you just going to spring it on her?"

"Wendy? No. I'm going to give her a chance to end things peacefully. To keep her dignity."

"And if she doesn't agree?"

"Then all bets are off. It's every man for himself. And we put your plan in play."

"Do you think she'll be mad?" Barbara asked, taking a sip.

"Furious."

Barbara raised her eyebrows.

"I don't care. She's fucked over my life. I want it back. I'm taking it back. She'll have one chance to slip out gracefully. If she turns that down, that's it."

"She's done your career some good," Barbara said.

"Maybe. Maybe not. She did it for her career. And I'm sure she's boosted that beyond her wildest dreams. But it's over or going to be. Real soon."

"Good luck," Barbara said, putting her empty glass on the coffee table. "Andrew Somers. Write it down," she said, pushing to her feet.

Rob saw her to the door. Then he retrieved a sack of birdseed from the kitchen and walked outside. He refilled the feeders, grabbed his champagne flute, and sat on the glider. Small birds flocked to the feeder. Chickadees, juncos, house sparrows, and goldfinches claimed their perches and chowed down.

He thought about the plan but knew he needed to give Wendy an out first. He sorted out the points he wanted to make, finished the champagne, and picked up his phone.

"Deke! Wow. What a surprise. Great to hear from you. Have you seen how much publicity we've gotten? The production company has even offered to pay for the wedding."

"Wendy, there is no engagement. You turned me down. I accepted your refusal—months ago."

"I know, but I changed my mind."

"You don't intend to go through with this, do you?"

"Oh yes, I do. It's absolute gold! We're getting a ton of free publicity."

"We're not engaged."

"Everyone thinks we are."

Rob rose to his feet and paced in his garden. "But you and I know we're not. There's not going to be a wedding."

"Aw, come on. You can get it annulled a week later."

"No. No wedding. In fact, I want you to call off the engagement. Now!"

"I can't do that."

"Yes, you can. And you will."

"Or?"

"Or you're in for the biggest embarrassment of your life."

"What?"

"I can't tell you. But I'm giving you fair warning. Call it off. Make up any excuse you want. Make me out to be the bad guy. Go on and on about your broken heart. Just do it. And do it now!"

"I'm all booked up for modeling gigs for the next nine months. You want me to flush that down the toilet?"

"I want you to tell the truth. No engagement. Pretend we broke it off. I'll play along. But you have to do that now."

"No."

"Wendy."

"No. I'm not going to destroy my career because you don't love me."

"It's not just that I don't love you. I never should have proposed. And yes, I don't love you."

"No!"

"You'll regret it, Wendy."

"Oh really? What can you do to me? You'll just make yourself look bad. Worse!"

"I don't care. You have one week to call it off."

"Or?"

"You'll find out. Remember. One week." He put down his phone. Anger boiled through his blood. How could he ever have proposed to such a selfish, vain, spiteful woman in the first place? Oh yes. He was looking for a family. He set his jaw and clamped his teeth together.

Damn, he'd be getting the family he wanted. She'd better be prepared for the consequences if she didn't change her mind. Fury whipped through him. He desperately wanted to talk to Rachel, but he'd be damned if he'd drag her into this. It would be best if she knew nothing about his plan. He needed to keep her name out of this mess and out of the papers.

He took out a frozen meal and popped it in the microwave. Then he sat down at his laptop and looked up Andrew Somers.

Chapter Nineteen

P *ine Grove, two weeks later.*
There was a big brown UPS truck parked in the store's parking lot and Rachel could have sworn she didn't re-order any merchandise. Must be a mistake. She threw on her jacket and trudged out to the lot.

"You must be mistaken. I didn't order anything," Rachel called out to the driver.

"You Miss Rachel Cohen?"

"Yes, but..."

"Then I have some packages for you." He got out of the cab and went around to the back of the truck.

"But I didn't order anything."

"Look, miss. I just deliver. If you got this stuff by mistake, it's not my fault. You can make arrangements to send it back and I'll come pick it up."

"That's stupid. Let's just send it back now. Where is it from?" She poked her nose into the truck bed.

The driver pulled out five packages and looked at the labels.

"It's from California. Says here *Mademoiselle* on Rodeo Drive. I'm not great at geography, but it seems to me you don't want to send back nothing from Rodeo Drive." He piled the packages on the dolly and wheeled it as best he could around the snow to the front door.

"Rodeo Drive? I never ordered anything from that place. This must be a mistake," Rachel said, increasing her pace to keep up with the driver.

"Miss, I don't know who sent this stuff, but it's my job to deliver it and that's what I'm gonna do." He wheeled up the ramp to the front door. "Can you get the door, please?"

She opened the door.

"Where do you want this stuff?"

She shook her head. "I don't know. There. Over there. On the table." She pointed to an empty table by the window.

"You got it." He unloaded the packages. "You have a nice day, miss. Somebody must love you a lot to be sendin' stuff from Rodeo Drive." He grinned, grabbed his dolly, and hurried out to his van. Rachel looked at the pile of bundles and then glanced outside and watched the van drive away.

"Rodeo Drive?" she said. "Rob? Rob bought this?"

She picked up the largest package first and opened the box. There was a card. It read:

Date clothes for my girl. Love, Rob

Her eyes grew as big as saucers as she unwrapped outfit after outfit. The feel of the silks and satins on her work-roughened hands was gentle and sexy. Black satin pants, silver top, gold top, black silk top. Some with sequins, some plain. A dress in red silk, a skirt in forest green soft wool, and a white cashmere sweater.

After opening the last box, Rachel plunked down in a chair, put her head in her hands, and cried. Was this a farewell gift? It didn't seem like that. But there were thousands and thousands of dollars of the finest women's clothing on her table. Either he intended to return or this was the world's most expensive goodbye gift.

After calming down, she washed her hands and face and gently carted the clothing out to the cottage. She shoved aside her worn work clothes to make room for the elegant garments. As the sun set, Rachel threw together a quick dinner, then spent the evening trying on each piece. Damn, the man had gotten all the sizes correct.

When the last piece was safely back in the closet, she picked up the phone.

"Why did you do it? You spent a fortune."

"Rach? Don't you like the clothes?"

"I love them, but…"

"They're for you. You need something to wear when we go out," he said.

"Out where?"

"To the inn. To New York City. We can go there for a weekend and see shows. Okay?"

"Okay, okay. Yeah."

"Great."

"Are you okay?" she asked.

"Yep. Shooting started. I've been busy."

"And Wendy?"

"That'll be over soon. Watch the news."

"I will. I love you," she said.

"I love you too, honey. Just two more months."

"Seems like a lifetime." She sighed and hung up.

Two seconds later, it rang. It was Will Lennox.

"I have the estimates ready. I'll text 'em to you. Let me know when you want to begin," he said.

"Okay."

Rachel looked over the estimates to fix the old house and texted. *I close Monday. Let's start on Tuesday.*

She checked to make sure the door was locked, climbed into bed, and doused the light. She lay there wide awake. Her life had been so defined, so simple, yet so hard. And now everything had been tossed like a salad. Nothing remained the same. Soon she'd be moving into that cavernous, haunted old house and selling off everything in the store. She'd have to sell the cottage to live since most of her money would go toward the renovation.

Was the shake-up good or bad? How would she make a living? She had no idea, but she waited anxiously for the next curve on the roller coaster that was her life.

ROB STOOD AT THE MIRROR in his bathroom, shaving and going over his lines in his head. As soon as he finished, he recited the day's dialogue out loud as he washed and dressed. It didn't matter what he wore since wardrobe had clothes for him.

After pulling on jeans, he whistled as he finished and strode toward the door. Grinning, he counted the days left until they could put Barbara's plan into action. It would depend on Wendy and the availability of everyone involved. It was six in the morning when he slid into his car and turned on the motor.

Traffic hadn't choked into the usual snarl yet. His phone rang. He propped it up on the dashboard. It was Barbara.

"Did you call him?" Rob asked.

"I did."

"And?" He steered his car down a side street heading to the highway.

"And what?"

"Did he buy it?" Rob asked.

"He bought it hook, line, and sinker," Barbara said, laughing. "Now you have to call Wendy."

"Got it." Rob took a deep breath, then exhaled.

"Give me the exact day and time and we'll be ready to roll," Barbara said.

Rob hit cruise control. "You're the best, Barb. This is genius. Definitely a win/win."

"That's what I thought. Call me when you have the loose ends tied up."

"Okay."

They ended the call, and he tossed around word choices in his head. What could he say to get her to come down to the studio? An idea struck him. He grinned. This would be foolproof. He dialed.

"Deke?"

"Yeah, Wendy. Hi."

"What do you want? If you're calling to try to talk me out of the engagement, don't bother. I'm not budging."

"No, no. Just the opposite. I have been offered a bonus if I redo the proposal and give you a ring in front of the cameras," he lied, wincing.

"Really? How much?"

"I can't tell. It's part of the deal." Lie number two.

"When and where do you want to do this?"

He let out a breath. "Next week. At the studio. How's your schedule?"

"I can squeeze it in. Are you really giving me a diamond ring?"

"Just for the cameras. Then you have to give it back." Lie number three.

"If we actually get married, I'm keeping the ring," she said.

He gritted his teeth. Anything just to get her to go along. "Fine. When can you be there?"

They firmed up plans, then. Rob eased off the highway. He drove the remaining two miles to the studio, focusing on his lines for the day. Speaking his part aloud in his car, he turned into the studio parking lot. He hated the subterfuge, but he had to shake Wendy loose, and she'd left him no choice. Feeling grumpy, he hit makeup and wardrobe.

"Aren't we a cloudy day today?" the makeup woman said.

"Yeah, yeah. Sorry."

When she finished, Rob picked up his phone. On the way to the set, he dialed Barbara and gave her the day and time.

"Okay. I'll finalize things at my end," she said.

"Call me to confirm, will ya? This has to go off like clockwork. No mess ups."

"Got it. Will do. Good job," she said.

"Sometimes it pays to be an actor in more ways than one," he said and then ended the call.

RACHEL EXPECTED THE truck that pulled into the parking lot to belong to Will Lennox. The sign on the van read "Larch Hardware." She hadn't ordered any hardware. In fact, she'd sold most of the store's goods. The shelves were practically empty. Just an occasional lonely box of spaghetti, a can of baked beans, and some mousetraps remained. She'd bit the bullet and advertised a sale. After all, she had to get rid of everything by a certain date. So she reduced the prices on all items, finally settling on fifty cents for anything. The shelves cleaned out fast.

Will had promised to load up her dresser in his van and drive it over to the old Victorian. He'd finished the floor in the bedroom and had painted the room. It was ready for her to move in.

With a small crew, Will had fixed all the broken windows. Now there was one man scraping the outside in preparation for painting when the weather warmed up. Another ran a huge sanding machine over the floors on the first floor while another one skim-coated the walls.

Rachel selected a sunny room on the second floor for her bedroom. The first floor had a spacious entryway, a grand living room, a large dining room, a den, and a huge kitchen. Will had promised to finish the kitchen as soon as she moved into the bedroom, so she could actually live there and not be carting food over from the cottage.

Rachel returned her attention to the Larch Hardware truck. What was it doing in the store's parking lot? She wrapped herself in a shawl and traipsed across the snowy lot to find out.

"Miss Cohen? Miss Rachel Cohen?" the tall man with silver hair asked.

"Yes. That's me. Who are you?" she asked.

"Bill Larch, ma'am," he said, extending his hand.

She took it. "And you're here, why?"

"I've been hired by Mr. Rob Walsh to do some work on the store."

"Oh, I see," Rachel said, nodding. But she didn't see at all. "And what work would that be?"

"I'm afraid I can't say. Mr. Walsh asked me not to discuss it with anyone. He told me you'd be here, asking a lot of questions," Bill said, grinning.

Rachel laughed. "He was right about that."

"I'll have to ask you to vacate the store, ma'am, if you don't mind. I need to get started."

"Vacate the store?"

"Yes, ma'am."

A tall young man stepped out of the passenger seat of the truck.

"This is my son, Derek," Bill said.

The young man shook Rachel's hand. He was blond and good-looking. Rachel could feel herself blushing. Dressed in old sweats, she sure wasn't prepared for company.

"Nice to meet you," Derek said.

Rachel swallowed and then nodded.

"He'll be doing most of the work," Bill said.

"Okay." She padded down the path to the cottage. After all, the store didn't belong to her. It was Rob's store, and he was free to do whatever he wanted with it. So many changes...too many. Before she reached the front door to the cottage, Will Lennox pulled up.

He rolled down the window and called out, "Hey, Rachel. You got your dresser emptied out so we can move it?"

"Yes. I'll be right out," Rachel said, scurrying inside.

She carried out the drawers while Will wrestled with the body of the dresser. Then she packed several bags and boxes into the back of her new car. Once everything was loaded up, she stopped to watch Larch and his son carry equipment and supplies into the store.

"Hey, Rachel, what about the bed?" Will asked.

"What? Oh yeah. We need to drop that off at the dump. I've ordered a new one."

"When's it coming?" Will asked, getting behind the wheel.

"I don't know. Let me check," Rachel fiddled with her phone, "ugh. Not until tomorrow."

"One more night in the cottage won't kill you," he said.

"Be careful with the dresser. It's an antique," she said, returning her gaze to the store.

"Just a fancy name for old junk, if you ask me," Will muttered, putting the van in gear and stepping on the gas. "You coming?"

"Sure, sure. In a minute," she said.

Will drove off and Rachel approached Derek. "Here," she said, pulling a key off her key ring. "You'll need to lock the place up every night when you're done."

"Yeah. Thanks," Derek said.

"You have everything of yours from the store?" Bill asked.

"Almost."

"Please get it now. Once we start, we're not allowed to let anyone in until we get the okay from Mr. Walsh."

"Okay." Rachel entered the store and climbed the steps. She spent the next hour gathering the few belongings that were hers and carting them to the cottage. Derek and his father helped. Once she'd tucked the kettle under her arm, she descended the stairs for the last time.

She put the kettle in her car. Might as well settle it in the new house now. She got behind the wheel, waved to Derek and Bill, and pulled out of the parking lot.

Tears stung at the backs of her eyes. While the workers tore away her past, she'd be getting used to her future in the new house. She had no clue how to turn this grand place into a bed-and-breakfast. She made a mental note to call Drew Armstrong. She figured he'd probably know what to do.

Even with all the money she'd inherited, buying and renovating the house would use up the lion's share of it. Without a job, she had no way to earn more to live on. She sighed. There was always teaching. Could she go back? At least to substitute teaching? She doubted it would pay enough to heat her new home. She sighed. Perhaps she'd bitten off more than she could chew? Sure would help if she could count on Rob coming back. She shuddered, then sighed. Uncertainty was the only thing she could count on now.

Chapter Twenty

The next morning.

As Rob got behind the wheel of his car, the phone rang. It was Rachel.

"Hey, this guy, Bill Larch, and his son are working on the store. They won't tell me what they are doing. So how about you telling me?" she said.

"Good morning to you too," Rob said, smiling.

"Cut the crap. Why won't you tell me?"

"What good is a surprise if you already know?"

"Why does it have to be a surprise?"

Rob turned on the vehicle. "I have to get to the studio."

"Okay, okay. You're not going to tell me?"

"Nope. How are you?"

"I'm fine and dandy. Moving into my new house."

"New house?" He steered the car into the street.

"Didn't I tell you?"

"No, you did not!"

"Hmm. I see. Let it be a surprise. Have a good day." The phone went dead.

Rob laughed. Rachel was a real pisser. She gave as good as she got. Okay, it was fair for her to keep her life a secret, wasn't it?

His nerves kicked into high gear. The "Barbara Plan," as he'd come to call it, was about to go live. There were quite a few moving parts, and he prayed nothing would go wrong. He didn't have to be on the set until ten, so he drove to the jewelry store to pick up the diamond ring.

He pulled up in front of the store and parked.

"Yes, Mr. Walsh, your ring is ready," the clerk said, handing Rob a tiny shopping bag. The man beamed the biggest smile. "And may I say congratulations. You're a lucky man!"

"Oh, you have no idea. Yes, I am the luckiest man in the world."

In the car, he dialed Barbara.

"Is everything ready?"

"Yes."

"There can be no glitches. This has to be perfectly timed," Rob said, pulling back on the highway.

"It's going to go like a secret CIA mission, Deke. Trust me."

"You've double checked everything? The press? Andrew Somers?"

"Yep. I'm bringing him myself. And the press was all over me. We'll have at least three major magazines and about a dozen broadcast teams there...not to mention podcast people."

If he hadn't been driving, Rob would have rubbed his hands together. "Excellent."

Barbara laughed. "I have to admit, I'm enjoying this."

"Me too. See you later."

"Synchronize watches?" she said with a giggle.

"Let's not go overboard."

He hung up. His pulse raced. His whole life was on the line today. Everything had to work as planned. Nice and civilized. A quick misunderstanding cleared up and dissolution of their "engagement."

He dialed again. Rachel picked up.

"Can't go into detail. Watch the news tonight."

"Okay."

"Have a great day. I love you," he said and ended the conversation.

He pulled into the parking lot and strode quickly to makeup. Restless and anxious to get the scheme moving, he begged the makeup lady to take him first.

"But you're not on until after Betty."

"Please. Trust me."

She shrugged. "Okay. You're the star. Get in the chair."

So nervous, he could feel himself sweat. "Is it hot in here?"

"No. And I'm not upping the AC," she said, applying makeup to his skin.

"I know why he's so nervous," Betty, a supporting player, said.

"Oh? Why?" the makeup woman said.

"He's giving Wendy an engagement ring today. On the set! It's gonna be a big event," Betty said.

"How do you know?" Rob asked, his heart rate bumping up. If she knew, how many other people knew? Would this destroy the plan? How could it? No, no. Everything was going to be fine, he reassured himself.

"Everybody knows," Betty said.

As soon as he finished, he'd lope over to the set. They'd be shooting a hotel lobby scene. The director came over to him.

"As soon as the scene wraps, we'll have the proposal and ring presentation, okay?"

Rob nodded. "Is Wendy here?"

"Yep. Right over there. In the corner," the director pointed. Rob glanced over and saw her wave. Good. Perfect.

"Great. Let's go."

"You got the ring?"

Rob patted his pants pocket. "Right here."

"This is gonna be great. Amazing publicity for this film. Thanks for doing this, Deke."

Guilt added to Rob's stress. Would this ruin the movie? Would it ruin his career? Maybe. At this point, he didn't give a damn. Tired of being Deke Walsh, movie star, phony, shallow man with no family, no life, he didn't care what happened.

Of course, he didn't want to ruin anyone else's career, but he doubted what would transpire would wreck anyone else's career. Only his. It was time to blow his image to smithereens. He took some deep breaths, downed a bottle of water, and got into character.

AS SOON AS THE SCENE wrapped, the security guard opened the door, admitting a swarm of media people, reporters, and photographers with flashes ready to pop.

"Don't go! We have a special presentation," the director called.

The cast and crew stopped. Wendy dashed out from the darkness. She wore a slinky dress, showing a ton of cleavage. Rob wondered if her boobs would pop out if she bent over. He grinned. Wouldn't a wardrobe "malfunction" add so beautifully to the chaos about to take place?

Wendy came forward, reaching out for Rob. He pulled the box out of his pocket and got down on one knee. Flashbulbs lit the place up like a dozen spotlights. Then he heard it.

There was a commotion off-set. A whistle blew. Deke heard "You can't go in there!" He smiled. It was about to begin.

"Wait! Wait! You can't go in there!!"

It was the security guard. Rob could barely contain his laughter. He placed his hand over his mouth. A man raced onto the set, followed by a group of five security guards.

"Here we go," Rob murmured to himself.

All heads turned toward the strange man racing toward the set.

Wendy gasped. "Andrew! What are you doing here?"

"You Jezebel!" he hollered, then turned to Rob. "Who the fuck do you think you are?" Andrew grabbed Rob by the lapels and yanked him to his feet, then squared around and punched him right in the jaw. Wendy screamed.

Rob fell backward. Wait a minute. It wasn't supposed to happen like this! He rubbed his jaw and rolled away as Andrew flew through the air aimed at Rob. Security surrounded Rob and one man tried to corral Andrew.

Rob saw Barbara in the crowd mouthing, "I'm sorry."

"Call the police," one security guard said.

Rob picked up the box with the ring in it.

"Is there a ring in there?" Andrew asked.

"Yes."

"Were you really proposing to her?" Somers asked.

"Yes," Rob lied.

Wendy gasped. "No!"

Andrew turned and hissed at Wendy, who had stopped screaming. "You told me this was fake. Just for publicity! You said it wasn't real." Then he faced Rob. "She's engaged to me! Not you. She's not going to marry you!"

Lightbulbs flashed again and again. Rob kept rubbing his jaw. He looked around and spotted it. A huge cake. It said, "Congratulations Wendy and Deke." He didn't notice that Andrew spied the cake at the same time.

He broke away from the guard and raced to the cake. He grabbed two handfuls of cake and threw it at Rob. Then he took more cake and smeared it all over Wendy. She screamed, hitting him with tiny fists.

The security guards were too old to do much, but Rob got into the act.

"You can't do that to the woman I love!" Rob hollered, playing his part to the hilt, and jumped on Andrew, smearing some cake from the glob on his chest onto Andrew's face. The men fell on the floor, rolling around in the spilled cake and frosting, punching each other.

The only young security guard grabbed Rob's arm. "Break it up, break it up."

Rob pushed to his feet, wiping the cake from his face. Andrew stood up just as Wendy dumped some cake on him. He smeared it on her chest.

"You can't do that to her," a director said.

"Oh, can't I? I can and I can do it to you too!" Andrew said, shoving cake in the director's face. A free-for-all ensued. Cake flew everywhere. Whistles sounded. Sirens cut through the screaming. Police entered. They cuffed Andrew and Rob. As they led him away, Rob stopped to grin at the cameras. He caught a glimpse of Barbara off in the corner. She'd doubled over with laughter. She waved, then looked away.

Reporters shoved mics in Andrew's face, then Wendy's. Finally Rob's.

"Wendy, it's over. Andrew, you can have her." Rob couldn't contain his laughter when he spied Wendy, cake frosting dripping from her breasts and her nose, her hair matted with cake, and her hands covered in frosting.

"Was this a fake engagement, Deke?" a reporter asked him.

"Ask Wendy."

"Are you breaking it off?" another one asked.

"Of course. Andrew proposed first. I wish them good luck," Rob said, struggling to keep a straight face.

"Okay, okay. That's enough. Let's go down to the station and sort this out," a policeman said.

Rob followed along. Barbara ran up to him. "It wasn't supposed to happen like this. It was supposed to be civilized," she said quietly.

"I guess no one told Andrew. This was much better than our plan," Rob said, walking along with the officer. "Meet me at the station and bail me out."

"Of course, of course," she said, still laughing.

Before he put him in the patrol car, the cop removed Rob's handcuffs. Sitting in the back seat, Rob texted Rachel.

I'll be on the news tonight. Please watch.

RACHEL DIDN'T KNOW what to make of Rob's message. At five-thirty, she drove to Java the Hut because she didn't want to watch the news by herself. Her friend, Winnie, greeted her.

"Hey, lady. How are you? Heard from Bobby lately?"

"He's going to be on the news. Could you turn on the TV? Can I get a cheeseburger with fries and a coke?" she said, planting her butt on a stool at the counter. "I think I'm going to need food."

"Sure thing, hon." Winnie placed the order with the cook, delivered Rachel's drink, and flipped on the TV.

"True love for the most popular couple in the country hit the skids today...in a big way," the reporter said. Footage of a brawl with cake flying everywhere came on the screen.

Rachel spit out coke when she saw Andrew Somers hit Rob. "Oh my God!" She covered her mouth with her hand.

Winnie hustled out from behind the counter and plopped down next to Rachel.

"Holy hell! What's going on?"

"Listen," Rachel said.

The news program continued. "Today's public wedding proposal by Deke Walsh to Wendy Cochran came crashing down when it was interrupted by what appears to be her real fiancé, Andrew Somers, star relief pitcher for the New York Nighthawks," the news anchor said.

Rachel and Winnie watched quietly, except for the occasional gasp. The newscaster went into detail while the camera followed the brawling men as they slipped and slid on the mountain of cake and frosting all over the floor. Members of the crew got into the act, throwing cake at reporters and cameramen. The fight grew so large it had to be broken up by four cars of police.

Rachel's eyes grew big, but as the shock wore off, she laughed. Winnie joined her and the two women laughed so hard they cried.

After the brawl was over, the police cuffed Rob. Wendy approached, spitting fire, her eyes aimed at Rob like the barrels of two guns. "This was your idea, wasn't it?"

"You wouldn't listen, so I..."

"You arranged it, didn't you?"

"I gave you a chance..."

Wendy hauled off and slapped Rob across the face so hard, he fell into the policeman.

Rachel gasped and pushed to her feet.

"Lady, that's assault," the cop said, righting Rob, then grabbing Wendy's arm. "Now you gotta come along too." Before she could speak, the policeman clicked the cuffs closed on her wrists. The officer hustled the two would-be lovers over to police cars, placing them each in a different car.

The newscaster could barely keep from laughing. After two more minutes, she finished up. "And it looks like that's the unhappily ever after ending to the most popular love story so far this year."

"OMG, did that woman hit Rob?"

"Hell yes!" Rachel slumped down on the stool. "All because of me."

"Really?"

"Yeah. He kept telling me he wasn't really engaged to that lunatic. That it was all fake, only for publicity, but I didn't believe him."

"I bet you do now."

"Damn right I do." She picked up her phone and dialed him, but it went right to voicemail.

"I'm not sure they're allowed to have cell phones in jail," Winnie said.

Rachel left a message.

Rob, I'm so sorry I didn't believe you. Are you hurt? Are you okay? I believe you now.

Winnie poured herself a cup of coffee and joined Rachel. "Do you think he planned it like that Wendy person said?"

Rachel picked up a French fry. "Oh yeah. I think he did. In fact, I know he did. And I think his agent, Barbara, was in on it too." She ate the fry and then took a big bite out of her burger.

"I guess that's love, eh?" Winnie said.

Chapter Twenty-One

*S*ame day, early evening.

    While he followed Barbara out to her car, Rob rubbed his wrists.

"We didn't plan on anyone getting hurt," Barbara said, stopping to face him. "Are you sure you're all right?"

"I'll probably have a black eye or a bruise on my face the size of a fist tomorrow morning, and I'm a little sore. But I'll live."

"Well, it worked, didn't it?" she asked, unlocking her car and opening the door.

"Yep." He moved his jaw back and forth, gingerly and winced. "I guess." Rob got in the passenger seat of Barbara's Mercedes.

"You guess? It's all over the press that your engagement is off. And Wendy is taking the blame. That was the idea, wasn't it?"

"It was." He plugged his phone into the outlet on her dashboard. She turned on the car and put it in gear. His phone sprang to life. Rob said a short prayer to himself as he checked for messages. He spotted the one from Rachel. He attempted a grin.

"Ow!"

"What?" Barbara looked over.

"I guess smiling is not going to happen for a while."

"And what were you smiling about?"

"My real girlfriend saw it all on the news. She believes me, that I'm not engaged or wasn't engaged. Either way."

"That's what this was all about? I really didn't get why you cared if Wendy pretended to be engaged."

"I didn't so much as Rachel did. And she didn't believe me when I said I wasn't. I had to prove it."

"And my plan was the perfect solution?" Barbara asked, steering the car onto the highway.

"It was."

"Did you eat anything?" she asked.

"No. I'm starving. Stop at The Middle Child. I want to buy you the best dinner in town."

"Lobster?" she asked.

"Lobster. And filet mignon. Whatever you want."

Barbara glanced briefly at his phone. "Must be good news."

"The best news ever," he said, attempting to smile. "Ouch."

"Save the smiles," she said, laughing.

Rob texted Rachel.

I'm a little banged up, but okay. I'll call you tomorrow. Love you.

Barbara turned into the restaurant parking lot. When they entered, the owner greeted them at the door.

"Hey, everybody! It's Deke Walsh!" Tony called out to his customers. A cheer went up from the crowd. "Son-of-a-gun!! Are you okay? I saw you on the news."

Rob raised his palm. "I'm fine. Do you have a good table for me, Tony?"

"For you? The best. Always the best." He called over the maître d' and selected a choice spot for Rob and Barbara.

"What a liar that Wendy Cochran was! Geez." Tony shook his head and then a wide grin appeared. "So you're free now, eh? A bachelor loose in the land of beautiful women," Tony said, wiggling his eyebrows.

"I've got a girl back home."

"You movie stars. Always a lady in your back pocket."

"This one is for real."

"That's a reason to celebrate! Drinks are on the house," Tony said to the waiter.

When Barbara's Coke and Rob's whiskey arrived, they placed their food order and sat back, tackling their drinks.

"One question. How did you get Andrew Somers to show up on the set?" Rob said.

"Funny you should ask. It wasn't easy. When I first approached him, telling him about your engagement, he laughed."

Rob's eyebrows shot up. "Laughed?"

"He said he knew all about it and that it was just a publicity stunt."

"What did you do?" Rob asked, raising his glass to his lips.

Barbara grinned. "I told him you were going to propose in public."

"Did that convince him?"

Barbara shook her head.

"So? What did you do?"

"I told him you had a ring. A real ring. And I'd seen it, and it was a whopper."

"You said that?"

Barbara shrugged. "I had to say something. You were expecting him. And if he didn't show, then you'd be engaged for real, splashed all over the papers, and sunk for good."

"Oh my God. I came that close?" Rob said.

"That close," Barbara confirmed.

"So what did he say?" Rob picked up his glass.

"He threw a complete fit, went totally ballistic! For a minute I thought he was going to hit me."

"What did he do?"

"He grabbed me and demanded to know where she was. I told him and offered to drive."

Rob laughed.

"And he fell for it. We jumped into my car and sped to the set. Of course, on my way over, I embellished a little. I went on and on about how much you loved her, and that you had plans to start a family right away. And that you put your house on the market so you could move in with her. Needed to keep him revved up. Couldn't let him calm down and think about talking things over rationally with Wendy. That would never work."

"Barbara, you're a genius."

"By the time we got there, he was like a raging madman, like a huge can of gasoline, and seeing you down on one knee was the only match needed to set him off!" She burst into laughter.

"You can laugh. You're not black and blue from that asshole."

"You wanted it, Deke."

"True. You did a great job. Thank you."

"You're welcome. I'm thinking of giving up Hollywood and applying for a job at the CIA."

They raised their glasses in a toast to true love.

Rob reached into his pocket and pulled out the small velvet box. He tossed it on the table.

"What's this?" Barbara asked, picking it up.

"The ring."

She opened the box and took out a dazzling, gigantic diamond ring.

"Wow!"

"Don't get carried away. It's fake. Just glass." He grabbed the ring and crushed it with his drink.

"Could've fooled me," Barbara said, staring at the glittering shards littering the table.

"That was the idea."

Just then, their food arrived. Barbara and Rob had ordered shrimp cocktails, full, steamed lobsters, and tiramisu for dessert.

When the meal was over, he was stuffed so full he could barely stand up and walk out of the restaurant. His legs were stiff, and his back was sore. He figured there were probably bruises all over his body. He needed a hot bath. As he made his way through the crowded room, following Barbara, strangers stopped him.

"Good riddance to that phony woman."

"Glad you dumped the two-timer."

"She had a lotta nerve."

He smiled as best he could with a sore face, happy to see people didn't realize he'd engineered the breakup. When they got in the car, he turned to Barbara.

"I can't believe it. No one picked up on the fact that I was behind Somers coming to the studio."

"Your fans love you, Deke."

"Yeah. Or they're more willing to believe the woman is the bad guy."

"But she *was* the bad guy. It was her idea. And yes, it looked like she was two-timing Andrew. So she deserved the hit."

"Somers will forgive her when he hears the truth. She can marry the rich ball player and not have to worry about her career anymore."

"She can stay home and have babies."

Despite his injuries, Rob laughed. "If she'd been willing to stay home and have babies, we wouldn't be here, and this would never have happened, and I'd be engaged to her for real right now."

Barbara stared at him for a moment before turning her attention back to the road. "No foolin'?"

"No foolin'," he said. "And I would have missed out on the greatest woman in the world."

EVEN AFTER SOAKING for an hour in a hot bath and a good night's sleep, Rob awoke the next morning sore and bruised. He checked out his swollen face.

"Makeup will handle it," he muttered to himself, staring in the bathroom mirror.

He called a limousine service, then dressed slowly. No way could he spend an hour behind the wheel. Once he was ready, he sat on the front porch and dialed Rachel.

"How are you?" she asked, her voice heavy with concern.

"A little sore, but I'll be okay. How are you?"

"I'm fine, but I didn't get punched in the face by a major league baseball player."

Rob laughed. "Yeah. I didn't realize the guy was so big." He moved his jaw until pain shot up through his skull.

"Was it necessary to be so rough?"

"I had no idea what the guy was gonna do. I thought he was just gonna yell. Anyway, it's over. I'll be back to work today."

"When are you coming home?"

"Film is due to wrap in two months. Can you wait for me?" He pushed to his feet to relieve his backache.

"Yes."

"You're not seeing anyone else, are you?"

"Who would I be seeing?"

"I don't know. Who's doing the reno on your house?" He paced slowly.

"Oh, you mean Will Lennox and Derek Larch?"

"Is Larch doing the house too?"

"No, just the store. By the way, what, exactly, are you doing with the store?"

"It's a surprise." The honk of a horn interrupted his conversation. "Limo's here. Gotta go. Love you."

"Love you too," she said.

He stepped gingerly down the few steps to his driveway. As he looked out the window on the drive to the studio, he thought about his life. He wondered what Gramps would say. He grinned. The old man probably would have been mad that Rob didn't slug Somers. He loved a good fight and taught his grandson to punch back, not run away. Still, Somers was a formidable opponent, tall and strong.

Rob wiggled his jaw again, remembering. Would he be happy with the new direction of his life? Could he count on Rachel? Gramps' words returned to him.

"Ain't no guarantees in life, Bobby. You're smart. You'll figure it out."

Would the old man approve of Rob leaving his old life behind to forge something new in Pine Grove with Rachel? He didn't know. But right or wrong, the wheels were set in motion, and it was too late to stop now.

He called Derek to check on the progress of the store and made a mental note to send him a check for the next part of the project.

"This old place needs a lot of work," Derek said. "I don't know why you want to save it."

"It's landmarked. We have no choice. Besides, I like it."

"Okay. It's your money."

The limo pulled into the studio. As Rob made his way across the set, he received a standing ovation from the cast and crew. After taking a little bow, he hustled over to the makeup tent.

"Wow! This is gonna take some time," the makeup woman said, staring at his face, then opening her kit. "You get hit by a truck?" the woman asked.

"Weren't you here for yesterday's brawl?"

"Oh yeah. But I didn't stay. That was you?"

"It was. So, please be gentle," Rob said.

"I'll do my best."

At the break, Rob called Barbara and hired her to help him relocate. There's always so much to do but moving cross country would require more time than he had.

"I want to be ready the moment the movie wraps to hop on a plane and head for Pine Grove. I don't want to spend any more time here than necessary. Can you help me?" he asked.

"I don't come cheap, but I'll get you ready to leave. Kind of nice to be working on the side of true love for a change."

"Thanks, Barb. You're the best."

After a grueling day on the set, Rob eased his sore body into the back seat of a limousine and headed home. While eating dinner, he checked his email. Damn! There was a list of a dozen tasks from Barbara. He read down the list, making mental notes of which to tackle first.

There would be no rest until he was settled safely in the arms of Rachel and the peaceful countryside of Pine Grove.

TWO MONTHS LATER.

"You sure you want my furniture?" Rob asked on a Zoom call with Rachel. They ate dinner and chatted.

"The house is so empty, it's like an echo chamber. Send me everything you've got."

"Okay. You asked for it. What are you eating?" Rob took a bite of his takeout hamburger.

"I made spaghetti and meatballs. When are you closing on the house?" she asked, twirling pasta on her fork.

"Right after we wrap. Then I'm getting on a plane and heading straight to you."

"I can't wait," Rachel said.

Rob eyed her food. "That looks good."

"I put some in the freezer for when you get back."

"It seems like years since we've been together," Rob said, popping a fry into his mouth.

"I know."

"I can't wait to see the house," he said.

"And you can see my plans for running a B & B." She put a forkful of spaghetti into her mouth.

"Whatever you want to do, honey. It's all gonna be good."

When they finished eating, they hung up. Immediately after, he got a call from Drew Armstrong.

"I found the papers deeding the general store to your grandfather."

"I didn't know they were missing."

"His files were kind of messed up. You probably shouldn't have started work there until I found the deed."

"I doubt Cassie would have complained."

"Probably not. But if she did and we couldn't find the deed, you might have lost the store."

"Thanks for digging into this."

"Don't worry about thanking me. I'll send you a bill. On another subject, the house Rachel is turning into a B & B?"

"Yeah? What about it?"

"Where will you live when there are paying guests staying there?" Drew asked.

"I don't know. I haven't seen the house," Rob said.

"You know which one it is. The old yellow Victorian on Marsh Street."

"I've never been inside."

"Oh. Okay. Yeah, well, there aren't any bedrooms on the first floor. So, your bedroom will be on the same floor as a guest room or even two guest rooms," Drew said.

"You've been over there?"

"I have. I don't think it works as a B & B unless you have another place to live."

Sweat started under Rob's arms. "So we're going to live in this gigantic house just the two of us? Rachel wants this."

"I know she does. But the house isn't set for it. It's old, built back in the day when people had six kids."

"Hell, we're not going to have six kids."

"I figured. Thought you should know before you come back," Drew said.

Rob paced. "What can I do?"

"Well, I have an idea."

"You do?"

"Yep. But it'll cost you something," Drew said, slowly.

"I don't care. I don't want Rachel to be disappointed. She's been so happy setting this up."

"Okay, well, it might work if..."

Rob found a comfortable chair and settled in to listen to Drew. When the lawyer was finished, Rob spoke. "It's the perfect plan. You really are a lifesaver."

"You want to go ahead with it?" Drew asked.

"Full speed ahead. It's got to be a done deal before I come home."

"I'll get right on it."

Rob ended the conversation and ambled out to his back porch. He stood watching the birds at the feeder. The film was due to wrap in a week to ten days. He'd miss watching the birds. But they had birds in Pine Grove too. He made a mental note to buy a bird feeder—no, wait, two bird feeders. He hoped the house would have a back porch or a deck or something.

After his conversation with Drew, Rob grew restless. He wandered through his house, making sure all the things going to Rachel had the proper tags. He needed to start his new life. His patience had run out, and he wanted to be with her, looking toward new challenges and leaving the shallow life he'd led behind.

He poured the remaining birdseed into the feeder. "One more thing done and off my list," he said with a sigh. Then he sat quietly, watching the birds and dreaming of days in Pine Grove.

Chapter Twenty-Two

R achel sat at her small kitchen table at the cottage and made a
new list.

"So, I'll just put this list in the pile with all the other lists, shall
I?" She chuckled as she talked to herself. Although it was still too
chilly in the mornings to eat on her small back deck, she planned to
have an early dinner outside.

Renovation progress on the new house sped up when the weather warmed up. The first floor was almost finished. The kitchen needed major work, electrical and plumbing, new cabinets, and counter-
tops. Will and his helpers had worked night and day to finish it fast
so Rachel could move in. Will and his men still had to refinished
floors and paint the walls of a handful of rooms.

Since she wasn't allowed in the general store via Rob's orders, she
didn't know if any of Gramps' furniture had been saved. Not that she
wanted it. Lord, that stuff had passed decrepit about five years ago.
Still, it would be nice to have a chair or two and a small table in the
new house so she could enjoy meals there.

It had been a mistake to have her new bed delivered so soon.
Now she had to sleep in the unfinished chilly house by herself. Sleeping alone in the big house felt creepy. The creaking of the old wood
when the temperature changed, or the wind howled scared her.

She started sleeping on the sofa in the cottage, deciding to wait
until the new place was almost finished and Rob had returned before
officially moving in. Rachel sorted out her stuff, making a pile for a
garage sale and boxing up what she wanted to take with her. At night,

she'd have a glass of wine and wonder what she'd do with the cottage. Maybe rent it out? She'd grown attached to it The place was the only thing in her life that had been hers—even though, technically, it hadn't been. The idea of strangers living there, maybe painting the walls barf green or taking down her curtains upset her stomach.

Any day soon it would be warm enough to paint the outside of the house. She'd decided on a soft shade of yellow with white trim and black shutters—exactly like the original. It gave the house history and character. Perhaps her nerves also involved the other changes in her life, like living full time with Rob, moving out of the cottage for good, and starting a business she knew nothing about. She had been treading water, floating in place for so long, change, while welcome on one level, terrified her on another. What if she couldn't make a go of the business? What if things with Rob didn't work out? Where would she go? What would she do?

She decided to bag eating leftovers and headed to Java the Hut for an early dinner. Winnie set her up at a nice table for two by a window. Rachel ordered their homemade pea soup and a salad. When she brought the food, Winnie slid into the seat opposite Rachel.

"Got some good gossip?" Rachel asked.

Winnie had her ear to the ground and between her and Laura Dailey at The Cozy Café, the two women knew everything that went on in Pine Grove.

"I heard that little brown house behind your Victorian was sold," Winnie said.

"Damn! I was gonna ask Rob to buy it and tear it down. It's ruining the view. Who bought it?"

Winnie shook her head. "I don't know. Can't be too smart. That place has been empty for years."

"Probably full of cobwebs," Rachel said.

Winnie shivered. "Gross."

"It's in the way of my view. I wish it was gone."

"I doubt someone bought it to tear it down."

"You never know," Rachel said.

"You think they're gonna tear it down and put up a high rise?" Winnie laughed. "Imagine that. A big apartment building in Pine Grove."

"They'd have to put in another grocery store," Rachel said.

"And a gas station," Winnie added.

The women laughed. Still, when Rachel got in her car to drive home, aggravation at this new development tugged at her. She changed into her flannel nightgown, wrapped herself in her down quilt, and settled down on the sofa with a book. She was asleep within minutes.

"YOU'RE NOT GOING TO the wrap party?" the director asked.

"No. I've got commitments back east. Sorry. It was a great experience working with you." Rob gave the man a hug.

"Good luck. Maybe we'll meet again on your next picture?"

"Maybe," Rob said, slowly making his way to the exit. The next picture? Nope. There would be no next picture. Rob would put Deke Walsh in cold storage and start a new life. On his way out, he checked his phone. There was a text from Barbara.

I'm in the parking lot.

He waved, and she pulled up.

"Okay. Bringing you up-to-date first to the lawyers to sign some papers and turn over keys. Then go over the checklist of what's shipped."

"Is the house empty?"

She nodded.

"When will the furniture arrive in Pine Grove?" he asked.

"About ten days."

"Ten days!"

"Deke, it's cross-country, thousands of miles by truck."

"Okay, okay. You're right," he said.

"Then the airport. You're on the red-eye tonight."

"Good. Excellent." His nerves kicked up. So many changes in the past three months brought him up short. Had he considered all angles? Could he do this? Giving up a lucrative career...was it wise? As if she read his mind, Barbara put the car in park and faced him.

"Are you sure you want to do this? It's not too late to change your mind," she said.

"Gramps always asked me how much money did I really need. I never had an answer for him. I think I do now. Whatever I have now, that's enough."

"I should hope so. You're not exactly broke."

"I might be by Hollywood standards. But it will be much more than enough for Rachel and me to live in Pine Grove."

"So it's final. Your last word?"

"It's final. Time to have a real life like other people." His nerves kicked up.

"Okay then. That's all I wanted to know," Barbara said, putting the car in gear.

Rob reached out and closed his fingers over her forearm. "Do you think I'm making a mistake?"

"I have no idea. I don't think so. But you're the only one who needs to believe in what you're doing."

"Okay. Yeah. Right. Let's go." Rob withdrew his hand and sat back. His breathing returned to normal. He looked out the window at the scenery he wouldn't be seeing again for a long time, maybe never. Visions of spring days in Pine Grove, of birds, lush greenery, meadows, cornfields, and cows flitted through his mind. He smiled. Those would be his scenery from now on. Perfect.

The day flew by in a blur of tasks, car rides, quick meals, and checklists. Barbara joined him for a late supper at a restaurant a stone's throw from the airport.

"I don't know when we'll see each other again," she said, sipping a glass of chardonnay.

"You'll have to come out to Pine Grove."

"What the hell would I do in Pine Grove?"

"Slow down a little. Enjoy fresh country air and home cooking," Rob said.

"Are you really killing off Deke Walsh?"

"I wouldn't say killing him. Maybe retiring him is a better word."

"How can you walk away from your career?"

Rob laughed. "Oh, it's sooo very easy. I'm not walking away from it as much as I'm walking toward something else."

"Are you gonna marry this chickie?"

"I hope so. If she'll have me."

"And have kids?"

"I hope so."

"Wow. Mr. Mom. You're gonna make some househusband."

"I'll find stuff to do. Believe me. There's always stuff to do in the country."

"I wish you luck. Here's to your new life," Barbara said, raising her glass.

Rob clinked his with hers and they drank. When they finished, Barbara pulled up to the entry for departing flights and got out of her car. She hugged Rob.

"May all your dreams come true," she said, then kissed his cheek.

"I meant it about coming out to visit," he repeated, handing his bags off to a porter to be checked.

She got in the car and pulled away from the curb. Wondering if he'd made the right decision, he watched Barbara drive away. A sharp pain shot through his system.

"You're all checked in, Mr. Walsh. Can I have your autograph?" the baggage clerk asked.

Rob snapped back to the present. "Sure." He signed the paper and walked inside. After making it through security, he boarded and settled into his first-class seat. As the plane took off, he watched out the window and said a mental farewell to the glitter and glitz of Hollywood.

He settled back and closed his eyes. Soon he will be in the arms of the only person who really cared if he lived or died—Rachel. Images of her floated through his brain until sleep took over.

BOUNDING OUT OF BED at six, Rachel busied herself with cleaning and straightening the cottage, then the Victorian. Her heartbeat double-time as she waited for Rob's arrival. Pacing on the front porch of the cottage, she chewed a nail, her gaze glued to the road. Finally, a black limo rounded the bend and came into view. She had to fight to keep from running toward the car.

When it stopped and Rob got out, her control evaporated. She ran to him and threw herself into his arms. He swung her around and bent to kiss her. When his bags were unloaded, Rob slipped the driver a twenty and scooped Rachel into his embrace again.

"I can't believe you're actually here," she said.

"Me either. It feels great."

"Come inside. I'll make breakfast."

While she cooked, Rachel brought him up to date on the progress of the Victorian.

They downed scrambled eggs, toast, coffee, and juice.

"I want to see the new house," Rob said.

"Okay. Let's go."

They piled into Rachel's car and added his luggage. Will's men were putting the finishing touches on the paint job on the outside of the house. It looked refreshed and sturdy.

"It's amazing! Rachel! What you've done with this place?" Rob stared as she opened the front door. He dropped his bags in the foyer. Rachel took his hand and led him through all the rooms on the first floor. As she gushed on and on about each detail of the renovation, he simply strolled along with her and nodded.

"The kitchen isn't finished yet but will be by the end of the week. Let me take you into the library or den or whatever you want to call it," she said.

As he walked through, he understood what Drew had meant when he said Rachel had not planned a bedroom for them on the first floor.

"The house is beautiful," Rob said.

"Wait until it has furniture!"

"My stuff is due to arrive in ten days. I have to buy a new car. I sold my old one."

"In the meantime, we can bring over a few things from the cottage. Let's go upstairs," she said, taking his hand.

"This is our bedroom. Look, it has a terrace," she said, opening the French doors to the cool April breeze. "There would be a much better view if that ugly ole house wasn't blocking the way," she said, pointing.

"Wait a minute, hon," s said. He took her hand and stepped out onto the terrace. After reaching into his pocket, he dropped down onto one knee. Rachel's eyes grew as wide as saucers, and she covered her mouth with her hand.

"Rachel. You are the light of my life. I love you with all my heart. Will you marry me and start a new life together?" He popped open the small velvet box to reveal a five-carat diamond solitaire.

Rachel gasped. The dream she'd had from childhood that she'd abandoned years ago had come true. Her eyes filled, and her breath caught in her chest. She couldn't breathe or talk, just gawk and let the tears stream down her cheeks.

"What? What's the matter? Don't say you don't want to marry me?" Rob sprang to his feet, panic evident on his face.

"I do. I do," she managed to choke out.

"Thank God! You scared the shit out of me," he said, hugging her to his chest.

With trembling fingers, he tried to steady her hand enough to slip the ring on. After several tries, he was successful.

"This ring is for you and you alone," he said.

She tilted up her chin, and he lowered his mouth to hers. When they broke apart, he leaned over to whisper in her ear, "Since we're in the bedroom," he said, unbuttoning her blouse, "we might as well..." but her mouth covered his before he could utter another word.

AFTER MAKING LOVE, they laid in bed and watched an eagle circle and then head for Cedar Lake to find his lunch. Rob tucked Rachel into him. He drew lazy circles on her bare shoulder with his fingertips.

"I forgot to ask you. Do you want to have children?" he said.

"Yes."

"How many?"

"Let's start with one," she replied.

"Okay. Then maybe a second one?"

"If we can handle the first one, a second would be ideal," she said.

"Works for me."

Contentment flowed through his body. It had been too long since they had made love. Desire between them appeared to grow even stronger since they had been apart. He drew the covers up as he contemplated a second round.

"See? That ugly little house is in the way," she said, pointing.

He sat up straighter. "No, it's not. I don't think it's ugly. I think it's cute."

"Cute?" She snorted.

"Yeah. And kind of the perfect size for two people, even a small family of four."

She sat up and stared at him. "Wait a minute. What do you know about that house?"

Rob cleared his throat. "Well, I know this. If you run this as a B & B, there will be no private place for us in this big, beautiful house."

"No private place?"

"No privacy. You've assigned all the rooms on the first floor. Besides, I want to live in a house where I can walk around naked, and my wife can too. Gee, my wife, that sounds so great." He grinned.

"So you don't want to live here? What does the brown house have to do with anything?"

"Well..." he paused, "I bought it. So, it's now our house too."

"You bought it?"

"Yep. Since you've become such an expert at renovating—I thought you wouldn't mind supervising another one. I want that little house to be our private playground. Just the way we want it. Every room."

"And how many rooms does it have?"

"Seven. And two baths."

"Seven?" She raised her eyebrows.

"Yeah. Two regular bedrooms, one smaller bedroom—perfect for a nursery. A den on the first floor. Fireplaces in the living room and den and the master bedroom upstairs."

"But no terrace like this," Rachel said, pointing.

"Nope. We'll have to create one. And you can paint it any color you want."

"So, we'll have the beautiful view from that house?"

"Yep. From that house. Is it okay?"

"Might have been a good idea if you'd discussed it with me first. But you're right about this house. If it has guests staying here, we won't have privacy."

"And the little brown house is right there. The front and back doors are almost touching. We could easily get over here to take care of anything and wait on guests, whatever you need to do with a bed-and-breakfast. You wouldn't even need to put on a coat."

"Me? What about you?"

"I'll do whatever you need me to do to make this a success."

"When did you buy the little brown house?"

"Oh, let's see, maybe a week ago."

Rachel snuggled down, slipping her arm around Rob's waist. She kissed his chest. "You're something else," she said, softly.

He stroked her hair. "You're not mad?"

"No, no. You're right. I like the idea of us having our own private place."

"You'll supervise the renovation?"

"Will you help?" she asked.

"I'll do anything, anything you want."

She cocked an eyebrow. "Anything?"

He blushed. "Anything."

She reached up and pulled his neck down so she could kiss him. Pressing her breasts against his chest, she moaned softly.

"Make love to me."

He grinned and slid his palm down her back to cup her behind. Reaching under her thigh, he raised it and slipped his leg between her, easing it up against her sex. She groaned.

"Honey, whatever you want," he breathed into her ear. He pulled her hips closer, positioned himself at her entrance, and pushed in. She gasped.

"You okay?" he asked.

"Oh yeah. More than okay. Don't stop."

He thrust in and out until she arched against him in orgasm. Eyes closed, she thought she'd touched a little bit of heaven.

Snuggled together, Rob stroked her hair. "When do you want to get married?"

"I don't know. Does tomorrow work?"

"Tomorrow? Are you kidding?"

"No. Why not tomorrow?" She sat up.

"Isn't there a waiting period?" Rob asked.

"I don't know. Is there?"

"Might be."

"If there is, we'll tell the judge we can't wait. We've waited twenty years. Isn't that long enough?" She snickered.

Rob laughed. "Yeah. We've waited long enough. Tomorrow it is."

EPILOGUE

T he next day.

Rachel didn't want a big wedding. She pulled out the fancy clothes Rob had bought her from the Rodeo Drive store and selected the outfit she liked best. He dressed in his best and they headed to Oak Bend Jewelers to pick out wedding bands. Then they went to the justice of the peace in the town hall. He waived the waiting period.

"Being a movie star moves mountains," Rachel whispered.

With Rob at the wheel, Rachel could stare at her rings all the way home.

"Now that we're married, can you please tell me what you've done to the store?"

"Even better. I can show you. The sign is up, so let's go."

"Sign?" Rachel drew her brows together. "What sign? The store has a new sign."

"We'll be there soon enough, and you can see for yourself."

They rode in silence for half an hour, then Rob pulled into the store's parking lot.

He put the car in park and turned off the engine. After exiting the vehicle, he took Rachel's hand.

"Come on. I haven't seen the sign yet, either."

They stopped in front of the building, now painted a spanking new bright white with blue shutters. Rachel looked up and read out loud.

"The George Walsh Youth Center!" She covered her mouth with her hands. Tears poured down her cheeks.

Rob's eyes welled too. Finally, Rob found his voice. "Come on. Let's go inside." He unlocked the combination lock and pushed through the brand-new shiny door.

Inside the aisle-dividers had been taken down to make one enormous room. Shelves remained on one wall. They were partially filled with books and magazines.

"I haven't bought all the books yet. I thought I'd get some help from the Oak Bend Library on what to buy," Rob said, pointing, and then he pulled her further into the room.

"A pool table. A ping pong table. Three computer stations. Benches, easy chairs. And look in the back yard." He pulled her along to the back of the building. "A basketball court and goals for soccer."

"This is amazing."

In a separate walled-off space upstairs that had once been Gramps' bedroom, there was a study table and reference books.

"Now you'll have a place to help the kids who need extra help. And the kids who have no supervision at home and no place to go can come here."

"Gramps would have loved this," Rachel said.

"You like it?"

"It's awesome! The kids are going to love it."

"I hope so." He took her hand. "And you?"

"I love it too. Now I know what to do with the cottage. We can turn it into an office where we can keep all the records for the B & B and the youth center."

"You're not mad that I kept it a secret?"

"No. It's a brilliant idea, Rob."

They spent three hours talking over plans for the youth center, what to buy, and what kind of activities to schedule. They ate dinner at Homer's, drawing diagrams and making notes. When it was time for dessert, Homer wheeled out a wedding cake.

"Surprise!!" hollered their friends.

Homer made a toast to the couple. Then he leaned over and whispered, "Welcome home, Rob." He cut the cake Laura had made and opened several bottles of champagne.

Under the table, Rob squeezed Rachel's hand. "It feels good to be home."

THE END

Pine Grove Series Books

All Pine Grove books are complete and stand alone, no cliffhangers.

1. Unpredictable Love
2. Break My Heart
3. Renovating the Billionaire
4. You Belong to Me
5. Just One Kiss
6. Rewrite the Stars
7. Some Kind of Wonderful
8. Too Late for Goodbye
9. For You and You Alone
10. A Pine Grove Christmas (coming soon)

Find these novels where fine books are sold.

MORE BOOKS BY JEAN C. JOACHIM

FIRST & TEN SERIES
Griff Montgomery, Quarterback
Buddy Carruthers, Wide Receiver
Pete Sebastian, Coach
Devon Drake, Cornerback
Sly "Bullhorn" Brodsky, Offensive Line
Al "Trunk" Mahoney, Defensive Line
Harley Brennan, Running Back
Overtime
A Kings' Christmas

HOLLYWOOD HEARTS
His Leading Lady (prequel)
If I Loved You
Red Carpet Romance
Memories of Love
Movie Lovers
Love's Last Chance
Lovers & Liars

BOTTOM OF THE NINTH
Dan Alexander, Pitcher
Matt Jackson, Catcher
Jake Lawrence, Third Base
Nat Owen, First Base
Bobby Hernandez, Second Base

Skip Quincy, Short Stop
Will Grant, Center Field
Extra Innings (to come)
THE MANHATTAN DINNER CLUB
Rescue My Heart
Seducing His Heart
Shine Your Love on Me
To Love, or Not to Love
LOVE LOST & FOUND
Love Lost & Found
Dangerous Love, Lost & Found
NOW AND FOREVER SERIES
Now and Forever 1, a Love Story
Now and Forever 2, The Book of Danny
Now and Forever 3, Blind Love
Now and Forever 4, The Renovated Heart
Now and Forever 5, Love's Journey
Callie's Story
The Beginning
NEW YORK NIGHT'S NOVELS
The Marriage List
The Dating List
ECHOES OF THE HEART
Heather & Mike
Sandy & Rafe
Liz & Nick
Paige & Bill
THE CATSKILL SAGA
Abigail's Journey
Sarah's Dilemma
Sam's Decision (coming in 2023)
MOONLIGHT SERIES

Sunny Days/Moonlit Nights
April's Kiss in the Moonlight
Under the Midnight Moon
Moonlight & Roses (prequel)

HOLIDAY & OTHER STAND-ALONE BOOKS

Christmas Duet
Hanukkah Hearts
The House-Sitter's Christmas
Champagne for Christmas
Santa's Surprise (short story)
The Christmas Party (short story)
The Final Slapshot
Unforgettable
Tuffer's Christmas Wish (short story)
Midnight in Central Park (dark urban fantasy)
The Adventures of Amanda & Emily
in The Secret of the Hidden Road
Sweet Love Remembered (novella)

www.ingramcontent.com/pod-product-compliance
Lightning Source LLC
Chambersburg PA
CBHW070855250626
47159CB00003B/1076

*9 7 8 1 9 4 5 3 6 0 8 8 6 *